MANEATER

MANEATER

Mary B.
Morrison

Noire

KENSINGTON PUBLISHING CORP.
www.kensingtonbooks.com

DAFINA BOOKS are published by

Kensington Publishing Corp.
119 West 40th Street
New York, New York 10018

All Kensington titles, imprints, and distributed lines are available at special quantity discounts for bulk purchases for sales promotions, premiums, fundraising, and educational or institutional use. Special book excerpts or customized printings can also be created to fit specific needs. For details, write or phone the office of the Kensington special sales manager: Kensington Publishing Corp., 119 West 40th Street, New York, NY 10018. attn: Special Sales Department. Phone: 1-800-221-2647.

Dafina and the Dafina logo Reg. U.S. Pat. & TM Off.

ISBN-13: 978-0-7582-1321-1
ISBN-10: 0-7582-1321-2

First hardcover printing: June 2009
First trade paperback printing: June 2010

10 9 8 7 6 5 4 3

Printed in the United States of America

CONTENTS

CHARACTER OF A MAN

Mary B. Morrison

For Eve Lynne Robinson

5 Things I Love about Your Character

Date:

Given To:

Given By:

Personal Message:

Have His Dick Your Way

I want my tasty ladies to listen up.

A change in how women respond to men is here . . . with or without your consent or awareness. Most men are faithful, yet those same men are not monogamous. There is a difference. If you're not already on board, I want you to join men and get on the sexual liberation train right now. Cost: free. Well, that's not completely true. It takes time to perfect being a maneater. First, you'll have to invest time in honing in on your pussy prowess skills. Pussy rules. Believe that. Hopefully, you are establishing the pace and not allowing men to eat you at their discretion.

Here's one of my maneater tips. Buy a dildo—cyber, realistic, ultra—of your liking. Buy a set of BenWa balls and/or Pleasure Pearls. I prefer the pearls because they are plastic coated. These are your pussy aerobic tools. Insert both pearls into your vagina. Then use your dildo to push the pearls into your pussy cul-de-sac. Sit on the edge of a chair, squat, or lie on your back with your knees bent. Tug on the dildo. At the same time squeeze the dildo for resistance. Do three sets, ten repetitions. Next, hands free, push the dildo out using your vaginal muscles. Do the same number of sets and reps. Finally, without using your hands, use your vagina muscles to pull the dildo all the way up inside your pussy or as deep inside of you as you can. Whew! I did say this was pussy aerobics. Don't be afraid to work up a sweat. You'll experi-

ence the benefits when you can fuck your man or husband by working his dick without moving your ass.

Maneaters do not attempt to figure men out. Maneaters are well
educated about men, hygiene, sex, and how to get what they want—
emotionally, physically, and sexually—from a man in and out of bed.
First, you must realize dick is succulent, pretty, plentiful, and *free*. Like
selecting beef at the grocery, picking the right piece of meat can be
tricky, and if you're not careful, disastrous. Any man who brags about
how good he is in bed is generally a bad fuck who's trying to talk himself up on your good pussy. My advice is to listen to his lies over a
meal. Let him take you out. Enjoy the moment. If the waiter is a sexy
guy that you're attracted to, ask his name, introduce yourself, and
then leave your card on the table. If he's interested, trust me, he'll
call you. At the end of your date, you've had a good meal and possibly
a better prospect for your next date.

I don't care how much money a man spends on you, he is not entitled to your good pussy. You and only you can make that determination. Not him. A good way to tell if a man is passionate about you is to
have him start by sucking your freshly washed toes or your fingers. A
professional will go for the crevices, the arch, or the palm. Do not
take off any of your clothes until you're 100 percent sure you want
him inside of you. If he doesn't know how to please you with your
clothes on, he's not a good lover.

Next, safe sex is mandatory. Ladies, always keep a few condoms in
your purse. One size fits most, not all. I like lubricated, non-spermicidal
Magnum, Lifestyle, and Trojan condoms. Spermicidal condoms report-
edly make women more susceptible to urinary-tract infections and
sexually transmitted diseases, including HIV. For more information,
visit http://www.fda.gov/oashi/aids/condom.html.

Never have sex with a man who layers his genitals with talcum pow-
der/baby powder. The chemicals in talcum powder may cause uterine
cancer. For more information, visit http://www.preventcancer.com/
consumers/cosmetics/talc.htm. Every woman must take the time to
acquire knowledge, then take control of what goes into her vagina
and her mouth.

Your pussy. Your responsibility.

If you want to keep a man, treat a man like a man. You've got to know when to dog him and know when to do him. When to love him and when to kick him. Not literally, but, honey, they all need a strong push once in a while, some more than others. Know when to be nice and when to be naughty. Know when to fuck him and know whether you should feed him. Never cook for a man before he takes you out to eat. The primary dessert a man should lick is your pussy. Don't be shy. Stroke your pussy with his favorite dessert.

Oh, ladies . . . never serve what you wouldn't eat, okay?

Never let a man play you twice. Yep, everybody plays the fool sometimes. I've ridden that train before, with a one-way ticket to his world, and the return trip was to my destination, not back to his bullshit. Only a foolish woman gets dogged out all the time, and I pray you're not that type of woman.

No matter how pissed off you get, you've got to maintain your cool. Some men love when a woman gets jealous—when she curses, cries, screams, threatens the other woman. Those types of men do not love you. If they did, they wouldn't relish watching you suffer. Men with shallow egos thrive on attention. Don't hate on him, and never chase him, especially if you catch him with another woman. Fuck whether or not he has a big dick; he's not the only big-dick man hangin' around. All men are trainable. Trust me, I know. Your goal is to reform, not conform.

A real maneater never cheats, creeps, or sleeps on her man. She doesn't have to. She's in complete control, and she keeps her options open. Cheating is a state of mind, not a state of doing. A maneater has got a dick at home and a dick on the side. A dick at work and a dick buried in the dirt in case she needs to be boned. Maneaters are never desperate to have a man.

Men think that they're in high demand, and therefore that women should cater to them. Not true. There may be a shortage of men, but there is no shortage of sex. Whether he likes it or not, you call the shots . . . and sometimes that means walking away from a man who believes he's better than you.

Ladies, be crazy in love with your pussy, and he will be, too. You are in charge. But you don't have to wear the pants to exhibit your pussy power. All you need is knowledge of the man/men you're interested in.

The top three requirements for being a maneater are:

- Knowledge
- Confidence
- Passion

That's it.

These are the key elements to an overall happy and successful life. It doesn't matter if you're a size 2 or 22; knowledge, confidence, and passion are sexy and often intimidating. Intimidation utilized properly is a benefit to women. A self-assured woman who loves herself, loves her body, and can talk openly about sex commands a man's attention. Even if he acts like he's not interested, trust me, he is. Don't be shy. Controlling men adore shy women. If any man has the desire to dominate you, tell him to get a dog. Seriously.

Ladies, have his dick *your* way . . . 24/7.

Are You a Maneater?

Take the Test

(Score yourself later. The answer key is at the end of the book.)

1. Do you suck dick / give head / perform oral copulation on the first date?　　○ yes　○ no
2. Do you feel obligated to pay the bill on any of your dates?　　○ yes　○ no
3. Are you uncomfortable approaching a man that you like?　　○ yes　○ no
4. Do you have clitoral, vaginal, and anal orgasms?　　○ yes　○ no
5. Can you make him cum without touching him?　　○ yes　○ no
6. Can you fuck a man and not care about talking with him ever again?　　○ yes　○ no
7. Do you know how to establish dominance over a man without being aggressive?　　○ yes　○ no
8. Can you fuck for your pleasure, not caring if a man cums?　　○ yes　○ no
9. Do you have at least five potential booty-call numbers in your cell phone?　　○ yes　○ no
10. Would you strap on and fuck a man in the ass if he asked you to?　　○ yes　○ no
11. Can you ejaculate like a man?　　○ yes　○ no

Chapter 1

Seven

"Lose the weight, or the wedding is off."

What the hell did he just say to me? The air in my lungs caught in my throat, struggling to escape. Where did his unwarranted demand come from? His words echoed like ping-pong balls, slamming against my temples fast and furious. I took a deep breath, restraining from screaming in his face. *Forget that.* Why should I be the sensible one?

"You didn't say that last night, when I was sucking your dick!"

Casually, he said, "Timing would've been off. Agree?"

I was in shock, a quiescent mime unable to respond.

Ping-pong! Round after round. *Somebody please stop the ricochets!*

Sitting in silence, I prayed, *Give me a sign that this is an April Fool's joke in the middle of October. Someone please drop a coin in the invisible metal bucket perched at my feet, triggering him to say,* "Baby, I was kidding. I love you just the way you are." Motionless, breath trapped inside my throat, I waited and waited and waited. He didn't speak a word.

Mama used to tell me, "Don't be an angry woman. Be a thinking woman. If you feel pressured, silence yourself, take a few deep breaths, and think about what is best for you."

As silence filled the air, we emotionally drifted apart.

Swallowing the despair clawing at me, I mustered myself and said,

"I can't breathe." Claustrophobia overwhelmed me, causing me to lose my composure and slump into the sofa beside my callous fiancé.

All I'd done since he'd proposed was joyfully plan our perfect wedding. Two years living together, the last year engaged, and this was his way of calling off the wedding? Sweat seeped between and underneath my thighs, soaking my black Chicago Bears panties. I'd understand his behavior if we'd argued, fought.

Was his love a façade?

I loved this man with all my heart, my being, my soul. But that's my fault, not his.

"Who?" I dreaded asking what I had to know. "Is she prettier? Smaller? Smarter? Is she better than me in bed? I can please you more. Do some other things if you'd like. Anything. I'll do anything to make this . . . work." The words strangled me with desperation. Fear of losing the man I loved to another woman consumed me. "Who is she? Please tell me."

No woman was a bigger freak than me. My big, delicious caramel titties with bubble-gum-sized nipples had easily sandwiched many dicks when I was in high school and in college. I'd done things to make grown men cry like babies. A few women, too. I could prove it to him. Right here. Right now. I called myself being safe. Careful not to scare him away, I'd reserved my best bedroom skills to blow his mind on our honeymoon in St. Barts.

He remained stoic, gazing out of the living-room window, beyond Highway 41, to the blue waters of Lake Michigan. Flatly, Maverick said, "There is no she. All you need to know is you mean the world to me."

I scratched the brow above my twitching left eye. Maverick hadn't witnessed the best or worst of what I could offer him. *Think, Seven. Think.* "You can't be serious," I said faintly, lightly strumming my numb jaw. "Something or someone changed you overnight. You don't love me like you used to. Last night, the sex, my updating you on our wedding plans, then our watching the presidential debate, I had no idea. No clue you felt this way. What's wrong with my body?"

I sat up straight, rubbed my stomach, swallowed air while forcing back tears. I nervously tugged a fistful of my long, curly hair. "I thought you liked my body. You've never complained before. There has to be someone else. Is she younger? Older? Or are you tripping off of your father again? He's dead, honey. Stop letting him ruin your life from his grave."

His parents and mine were deceased. I couldn't imagine any parent being as cruel as Maverick said his dad was to him. We were both only children. I had one best friend, Zena, and he had two close friends from high school. At times Maverick acted more like a child than a grown man. Nothing was ever his fault. I had to think my way out of what was bothering him.

Last night, Obama made me believe change was good and that all things were possible. McCain made me fear four more years of a Republican administration, declining property values, vanishing stocks, bank failures, homes foreclosing, more major companies and small businesses filing for bankruptcy, and diminishing 401Ks forcing retirees back to work.

At this moment, Maverick made me think I'd slept in the same bed for two years with a complete stranger. While the economy was unpredictable, my relationship was supposed to be recession-proof. So I'd thought. *Foolish me.* I wasn't giving up on him.

"Ouch." I touched my bottom lip, glanced at my finger, and rubbed the speck of blood on my white Devin Hester jersey. Disappointment layered my sadness with disgust. The slits of my lids narrowed, shrinking his six-foot frame to the three inches he made me feel. Scooting to the opposite end of the apricot-tinted Italian leather sofa, I stared at my fiancé. My palms ached to slap him upside his shiny bald head.

His rejection overwhelmed me. For the first time in my life, I felt fat. Miserable. Dirty. Sticky.

Don't slap his selfish ass. Calm down. You are not a violent person. You're just upset. Maybe this is some sort of last-minute pass or fail test from him. The kind that reassures him he's not about to marry a woman who is violent or vindictive.

Finally, he answered, "I'm dead serious." He pulled from his pocket a pair of my yellow Lycra boy-cut underwear with SWEETER THAN HONEY embroidered in gold across the pubic area.

Sideswiped by premeditated premarital sabotage, I tried my best not to look at him. I might go off.

Why'd he have to pick the yellow ones? Any other color would've appeared smaller. Black. Red. Snatching the drawers from him, I threw them in his beautiful brown-sugar face, then watched them fall to his lap. A well-trimmed shadow beard trailed a thin line from his ears to his chin, framing his succulent lips with a perfectly aligned goatee, a replica of G. Garvin's. I shouldn't have prepared so many of Gerry's mouthwatering recipes. Too late to regurgitate any of the carbs from my hips. Fat cells had already doubled, tripled, inviting cellulite to the sides and backs of my thighs.

Maverick's stern demeanor hadn't wavered.

A bottle of tequila would help me through a liposuction procedure, a few hCG injections, laser cellulite treatments, and a series of body wraps. A quick fix might salvage our relationship or keep me from . . .

Quietly I stood, went upstairs to his library, removed the shoe box from the top shelf. I held Maverick's prized possession in my hand. Cold, heavy like my heart. I placed the gun in my laptop bag, closed and locked the safe, then returned to the living room. Here I was, not married yet, already fighting to hang on to my man. I sat beside him. He was not leaving me. Not alive.

I hate you . . . Kiss me. Hold me. Please tell me you're not serious. I love you so much. It hurts.

Magnificent crystal gray eyes, dilated black coal pupils sparkled like carbonado diamonds. Maverick was perfection personified. A self-made multimillionaire. The wealthiest, most eligible bachelor in Illinois, according to the tabloids. He'd given me more than any of those housewives of Atlanta and Orange County had combined.

"That's cool," he said, twirling my drawers on one finger. "But getting upset isn't going to help your case. I spent a half mil on an engagement ring, which is in the jewelry box because it doesn't fit!" Calmly, he continued, "That means the wedding band won't fit, either. You need to get real about your fat ass or get up out of my house. It's just that simple."

Ooh wee, Seven, don't go back upstairs for the gun. Tears streamed down my cheeks. Breathing heavily, I thought, *Mama, what should I say to this man?*

"I'm not a damn Barbie doll! I'm a woman. I have feelings. For God's sake, can't you see how much I love you?" I didn't know what to do or say next. I struggled to rationalize his behavior but couldn't.

Maverick replied, "True. Barbie is white," adding no comment about his love for me.

I sat there on the verge of a nervous breakdown. This man was my everything. My friend. My lover. My fiancé. I had to marry him.

Chapter 2

Maverick

Had a lotta shit on my dick.

Seven didn't know me. No one knew the real Maverick Maxamillion. I was a motherless child, knew I wanted to be loved, and was not so sure I was capable of loving. I was money hungry, and money masked my insecurities and promiscuity. I was certain that Seven loved me, and I loved Seven the best I knew how. How could I keep a secret from her?

Best to let her go now, spare her the shock of discovering what I'd taken from her without her permission. The choice to decide if she wanted to marry a bisexual man. Shit was complicated. My reputation was at stake if I came out. Couldn't give my father another reason to disown me. My business partners would force me out. Clearly, I needed Seven more than she needed me.

Seven sat there, searching my eyes for answers I'd never share. She was so damn gorgeous. Large, brown, dreamy eyes. Thick, full, pouting lips, which men craved to have on their dicks. Flawless skin, softer than a baby's. Long, silky jet-black hair, which nicely framed her grapefruit-sized natural breasts. Sexy, shapely legs. She'd put on more weight than I desired. Wouldn't hurt her to get it off before the wedding, but her weight gain wasn't the reason I had to have space.

"Think about how we can work this out. I've got to go to my office for a few hours," I lied, then said, "We can finish this discussion when I get back." I stood, kissed her on the cheek. I looked over my shoulder as I walked away. She hadn't moved or stopped crying.

I retrieved my cell phone off the coffee table, got on the elevator, strolled past the doorman at the front desk, walked outside, then strode to my town car.

"You sure you want to go there?" Danté asked, holding my door open.

"Yeah, I'm sure, man. Drive," I said, closing my eyes before he'd shut my door. Leaning my neck against the leather headrest, I felt tears escape as I visualized Seven crying.

In many ways, I was perfect and fucked up. Parental rejection had ruined my childhood. Truth was, I wished my father were dead. Better to lie to Seven about my parents than to have her deal with the bullshit I'd been confronted with all my life—death threats, rejection.

"I hate that motherfucker," I said, struggling to suppress my sniffles. Hated him for emotionally breaking me down.

Stomp! The sole of my leather shoe landed against the back of the driver's seat. Adjusting my black slacks, I spread my thighs, held my dick.

"Don't know why you put yourself through this every week," Danté said from the driver's seat. His deep voice excited me. "Just whup your old man's ass, get your mother out of his house, and let her live with us."

I wasn't going to argue with him. I'd told him the house I was building based on Seven's architectural plans was for Seven, not for him. Initially I'd asked Seven to leave so I could keep our new home, the home she'd fantasized about, a surprise. I was tired of Danté's insecure ass being in competition with my fiancée.

My immediate concern was my mom. I had to find a way to free her. She was miserable, but refused to leave my trifling father. They'd probably die together. The same way Jesse Jackson had offered no genuine apology to Obama for saying, "I wanna cut his nuts off." Right or wrong, I would not apologize to my dad for disrespecting him.

The closer Danté got to my parents' home on the South Side of

Chicago, the slower he drove. We bypassed Soldier Field, where I'd be Monday night watching the game from my owner's suite. A few days after that, I'd be at the United Center, in the suite I owned.

Danté parked in front of my father's house. The lawns adjacent to his one-story, three-bedroom, two-bath, two-thousand-square-foot home had grass up to my knees, with FOR SALE signs on them. I should purchase both homes so no one would hear him scream when I beat his ass to death.

I walked up five wide cement steps to the front door, glanced over my shoulder, saw Danté sitting with his car door open, feet planted on the sidewalk, watching my back.

Knock. Knock. Knock. The side of my fist banged on the screen.

Quickly, my dad appeared. Unshaven. Grumpy. Shirt wrinkled. Hair woolly. Halitosis slapped me in the nose.

Stepping back, I said, "I came to see my mother."

"Where's your damn respect, boy?" he grumbled, coughing through the screen. "You ain't stepping foot in my house until you learn to respect me."

"You sorry-ass motherfucker!" I shouted, then spat in his face. "That's my mother."

"Got it twisted. She was my woman before you came along," he said, wiping my spit from his eyes. "Wait right there. I got your motherfucker for you." He disappeared into the house.

Peeping into the living room, I saw my mom rocking in her favorite chair. When my dad came into view, she jumped from the cherry-wood rocker, grabbed his arms, and screamed, "Leave my baby alone! No, Frank, don't kill him!"

"Let me go, woman," he said, pushing my mother to the floor.

Pow!

A bullet ripped through the screen, barely missing my shoulder.

Seconds later, Danté was on the porch, dragging me away, when *pow,* another bullet darted between our faces.

Jabbing my fists in the air toward him, I yelled, "You're not the only one with a gun. Be a real man. Put the gun down. Confront me to my face. This ain't over. I'll be back for your sorry ass." Danté dragged me down the steps, forced me into the back of the car, slammed my door, then sped off.

"You got a death wish? You're not going to be satisfied until he kills you. This is our last time coming over here," Danté commanded.

Danté made me realize that by showing up at Frank's doorstep every week, I was more afraid to live than to die.

Chapter 3

Seven

You know the saying "The way to a man's heart is through his stomach." What was that all about? I thought Maverick was happy with my cooking. Was I not supposed to eat the food I'd cooked for him? During our twelve-month engagement, I'd admittedly gained a few pounds. Hips fuller. Waist thicker. Face slightly rounder. I honestly loved my man so much, I'd do anything to please him. I stood over the stove to prepare his breakfast and dinner seven days a week and served him lunch when we were home lounging on the weekends.

For the first time in our two years together, I slept alone last night, not knowing where Maverick was. Worrying if he was safe. He hadn't answered or returned my phone calls. Came in this morning, five o'clock, no conversation, then crashed with his clothes on. I'd given him three hours to rest.

"Maverick, why? Why bring this up eight weeks before the wedding?" I said, nudging him in his side. Forcing back tears, I sat on the edge of the bed, staring at him. "You could've said something two, four, six, eight, even ten months ago if you didn't want me gaining weight."

Eyelids closed, eyebrows raised, he mumbled, "Are you serious? I shouldn't have had to say anything at all. You don't have to work. You're home all day or out shopping with Zena. Zena hasn't gained weight. You're the one who chose not to exercise. You're not a kid. You're an adult. Common sense should've made you realize your ass was spreading. I shouldn't have to tell you what to do."

"Oh, you mean like when you told me, 'I don't want my wife working. Stay home. Seven, stop hanging out late at night with Zena. She's a single woman. Find some married friends. Stop going to happy hour with your college friends, because you're about to be a married woman. I'm an icon in Chicago. I will not have my wife-to-be giving me a bad reputation by being seen with the wrong kind.' You mean you shouldn't have told me what to do the day after you proposed?" I waited for his answer to that.

Rolling over twice, then getting out on the opposite side of the bed, he said, "That was pathetic. I don't care what you do with your life, but don't change the subject. You can't even fit into the fifty-thousand-dollar wedding dress I bought you. I'm not wasting money on another one. Nor am I altering the one you have. That's final, sweetheart. I hope, for your sake, whatever you decide to do works for me. I can arrange for you to go to a weight-loss camp for the next six weeks," he said, heading to the bathroom.

I followed him, talking to his back. "Fuck you, Maverick," I finally said. Staring in the mirror, I allowed my gaze to scroll to his stomach. He'd put on a few pounds, too; his gut was bulging farther than his dick.

"Seven, don't go there," he said, removing his clothes, pressing his hand against his abs. "I can lose these few pounds in one week. All my shit still fits, including my ring. Stay focused. This isn't about me. I love you, baby, but there's no way I can walk down the aisle with you looking like you're five months pregnant when you're not having a baby. What's going to happen when you do get pregnant and put on twenty-five more pounds on top of the twenty-five you've already gained?"

Five months pregnant? More like a week late with my period. Maybe my rhythm was off due to my excitement at becoming Mrs. Maxamillion. I wanted us to be pregnant, to surprise him with our child. After the wedding, not before.

"Where were you last night?" I asked, watching him aim his dick, hands free, over the toilet.

"Looking for your replacement," he said. "A woman who's not fat. Find a fat farm today, and I don't mean p-h-a-t."

"What the hell is wrong with you?" I asked.

Forcing back stinging tears, I thought of all the foods I'd eliminated from my diet after leaving my parents' house in Mississippi to attend college in Chicago. Ham hocks, collard greens, sweet potatoes and mashed potatoes loaded with real butter, fried chicken, smothered pork chops with gravy, pound cake from scratch, red beans with pickled rib tips, cheese grits, pancakes, bacon, sausage, eggs, bagels with cream cheese and preserves. When I met Maverick, I started cooking those foods to impress him with my beauty, brains, and domestic skills.

"I can't leave. I have too many wedding details to finalize . . . the rehearsal dinner, the cake, the champagne, the reception catering—"

Shaking his dick, Maverick flushed the toilet, then abruptly interrupted. "See, all you think about is food. Zena has helped you with all those things. She's your maid of honor. She'll take over the planning until you get back."

"What! Zena? Ms. Pisces, control freak, 'shove her ideas down everyone's throat, then force them to swallow' Zena? Are you serious? Baby, this is our wedding, not hers. I know I can get the weight off without going away. Hire me a nutritionist, a personal trainer, or somebody to assist me," I pleaded, tears streaming down my cheeks.

Zena was an amazingly attractive workaholic who Maverick couldn't stand having in our house for more than an hour. Whenever she came over, he wouldn't ask her to leave; he'd leave. As long as I was at home with Zena, he didn't complain. But my going out with my best friend after dark had become a discussion not worth having.

Zena and I had shopped around for my wedding gown and reception dress. I'd let her select her dress, along with the style for my two bridesmaids. She'd helped me select my shoes and veil. Our personalities were opposite, yet our taste in clothes, men, and cars was the same. Expensive. Elegant. Sexy. Our sizes had once been the same, too.

Soulful soul food, the same food that had hooked Maverick, now made him sick. Not from the food. From me. I should've stuck with calisthenics and low-carbohydrate meals. Lean Cuisine, Weight Watchers, Slim-Fast meal replacement shakes a few times a week, and my anti-aging fresh green smoothies—spinach, cucumber, celery, apple, ginger, lemon, lime—which Dr. Oz had Oprah drinking and had more than sufficed for maintaining my curvaceous physique before I said, "Yes, Maverick. I will marry you."

When I met Maverick, I was a grad student at the University of Illinois at Chicago, finishing up my master's in architecture. School was a full-time job that left me with no desire to cook. A sexy hourglass torso had once complemented my hips, my ass.

Breaking the silence, he said, "I'm not going to sit in the owner's box suite at the games with you sitting by my side like a blimp. Hell, you might as well be on the field, helping out the defense." To demonstrate his point, he bent over and spread his fingers on the white marble tile.

My lips tightened. That was mean, malicious, and unnecessary. "I got your defensive player," I said, eyeing the plunger.

"I don't want to see *my* wife looking the way you do. All the men and women in the suite used to lust over you. Now all they do is make jokes behind your back. What if you continue to put on weight, instead of losing it? Then what? I'm not going to be the brunt of your fat jokes anymore," Maverick said, looking at me upside down, between his legs.

I gripped the plunger.

He gave me a cold, penetrating stare. "That would be the biggest mistake of your life," he said, standing up and stepping into the shower.

In denial of all Maverick had said, I truly believed our honeymoon and a baby would reverse our love lives, make him happy again.

"Fine. I'll find a place to go," I said, returning to the bedroom. I sat on the foot of the bed, gazing toward the 104-inch projector screen embedded in the wall-to-wall mirror in our bedroom. The morning news was under way. I pressed the power button on the remote. The news reporter's image disappeared, revealing my naked figure in the mirror. Maverick walked into the bedroom. "But you're paying for it," I told him.

Patting the towel all over his body, Maverick went to the closet, put on a pink tailor-made shirt, a purple tie with pink stripes, purple boxer briefs, and a gray suit with vertical pink pinstripes.

"I already have. You're doing the right thing. I'll be back tomorrow. Ms. Stephens, be gone before I return," Maverick said, kissing my cheek. "It's tough love, baby. You'll thank me later."

"Wait, don't leave me like this. There's something else I need to say," I cried.

Walking out the door, Maverick never looked back at me as he replied, "Seven, I've heard enough."

Chapter 4

Seven

"**D**amn you, Maverick!"

The sunshine beamed through the window. I sat on the bed, in front of the mirror, scared to start over. Had no desire to search for a new man worth getting to know. A man who appreciated my mind, respected my body. A gentleman I could live with. How soon would I find another one worth marrying?

My cell phone distracted me. Sniffling, praying it was Maverick calling to apologize, I hurried to the dresser, removed my PDA from the charger.

It was Danté.

Flatly, I answered, "What?"

"Hey, Seven. Maverick asked me to call. I'm out front whenever you're ready to leave," he said, his voice professional, yet more compassionate than Maverick's.

"Thanks, but I don't need you to do anything for me," I said, almost ending the call. "Wait. Danté?"

"What?"

"How well do you know Maverick?" I asked.

He paused, then said, "Not very."

"But you're his best man. You must know why he's sending me away."

"Seven, I'm Maverick's friend, not yours. All you need to know is . . . I'll never betray him."

Ending the call with Danté before I cursed his ass out, I headed upstairs to the office. I carried my laptop bag to my favorite room, the library. The heaviness of the gun in the bottom of my bag weighed me down. I scanned the built-in shelves; fiction books were my escape from reality. Textbooks were my source of knowledge. I missed my mother, missed my college days. Studying. Socializing. Constantly in transit to an exciting destination, occasionally unknown. I removed my laptop, powered it on, sat gazing out the window. Exhaling, I logged on, tapped a few keys; the Web site appeared.

Punany Paradise.

A blend of cello, harp, and the sultry voice of a man moaning, "Umm," barely above a whisper, relaxed me, sweeping away the tension that tightened my shoulders, my neck.

Seductively, he groaned, "Hey there, sexy."

I admired his long, lean naked body, his muscles in the right places, his chest, abs. His dick reclined on his stomach.

"Yes, yes," he said, nodding. "It's real."

My tongue slid along my bottom lip, paused in the middle. I read the site aloud, "Exotic. Private. For women only. All-inclusive nude resort," then softly smiled.

I circled the tip of my finger around my areola. Slid my hand over my stomach, lightly teased my clit with tiny circular motions. Opened my thighs.

Mama used to say, "Baby, when a man hands you lemons, he's not a real man. Real men, like your father, care about the women in their lives. If a man hurts you, he's trying to burden you with his psychological garbage. He's intentionally putting you down to lift his spirits or cover up a lie. Seven, don't ever let a man get or keep you down, baby."

Waterfall sounds resonated from my speakers, from my vagina. Staring at my laptop, I sat quietly in Maverick's library, realizing I was in his, not our, house. The tropical island I'd dreamed of visiting was before my eyes, underneath my fingertips. A getaway I'd imagined traveling to two summers ago, right before I'd met Maverick. Before I'd gained twenty-five pounds. Before I'd gotten engaged. Before he'd changed the way I viewed myself inside and out.

The banner beckoned, "Come be my lady." Eyes were fixed on me. Hands behind his head. His dick rose slowly, stood there, midair, as he said, "I'll teach you how to release your inhibitions. I'll stroke your mind with every part of my anatomy. Have me your way. Your satisfaction is our guarantee."

Our? More than one?

Deliciously sculpted naked men, one after another, faded in and out of the photo slide. As I scanned them from their lips to their dicks, my pussy dripped with delight. Day before yesterday, none of these men would've tempted me. Today Maverick couldn't physically measure up to these men. He granted them space in his sanctuary. Maverick's lemons were sour but exactly what I needed. A new perspective on *my* life.

Thanks, Maverick, for reminding me how beautiful I am, I thought, recalling the men I'd dated in college. *There's nothing wrong with me.*

Thanks to my fiancé, I was ready to unleash the woman in me, fornicate, and pursue my fantasies in a safe environment before becoming his wife. Closing my eyes, I envisioned running barefoot in the sand, diving naked into the ocean, inhaling fresh, salty sea air, having handsome men cater to my desires.

"Do it, Seven. Fuck that fat farm. Go to the island of sexual seduction," I said aloud, drooling over the fine-ass men licking their lips at me as though they were tasting my punany.

Punany Paradise was a place where no one would judge me, where men from all over the world would adore me. I'd get back that time in my life when I was happily single. When I proudly dated men, expertly flipping the script . . . a time when I boldly exhibited the character of a man. A time in my prime, before I'd met Maverick.

Call a man after a date? Why bother? That was solely his responsibility. If he was interested, he'd call. A seventy-two hour delay in his calling meant his number was deleted from my phone. Next. I'd usually been out with a few other guys since my date with a man who hadn't called in three days. Foolish men—some educated, others not—thought there was some sort of shortage of men, as though they were the hottest commodity in the highest demand.

"Damn, these guys look good enough to eat. All of them," I said, licking my fingers like they'd been dipped in chocolate.

I clicked on the video of Jagger, and my pussy puckered when he smiled at me. I took a deep breath, ready to dive into the screen.

The money I'd inherited from my mother earned interest daily. I'd let Maverick believe I was a struggling college student. That was his assumption.

My mother had constantly told me, "Seven, listen to me. No man will ever treat you worse than you treat yourself, and no man should treat you better. No matter how much money he has, always be great to yourself, baby."

I missed my mom. She'd outlived my dad, but I hated that now they were both gone. I felt abandoned. Nothing had filled the void in my heart until Maverick came along. Maybe going away by myself would give me time to find myself, the true Seven Stephens.

Exhaling, I wiped my tears, then dried my hand on my I AM WORTHY T-shirt. The vacation I craved teetered under my finger hovering over the mouse. My eyes were fixated on the words: "Ground transportation to and from the resort. Daily massages. Fantasies. Liberation. Libations. Unforgettable pleasurable encounters guaranteed or your money back." The money back part didn't matter to me. I refused to spend my money to meet Maverick's egotistical demands. There was no way I was going to a boring-ass weight-loss camp to run myself insane until I passed out from exhaustion with a group of overweight people I didn't want to know.

The next scrolling banner of naked men read, "All we want is you. Leave your luggage. Your clothes. Your suntan oil. And your man . . . Ladies, we've got you covered."

Damn, when was the last time my pussy had twitched from thinking about sex with a stranger? The fantasy intrigued me. I sat in Maverick's library, contemplating whether or not to click on the thirty-five-thousand-dollar MAKE PAYMENT button.

Glancing next to the laptop, at a picture of us dining outdoors at Mercat a la Planxa, a sidewalk restaurant, smiling, laughing, sharing a small serving of garlic shrimp, listening to the live band playing in

Grant Park, reminded me of how we used to eat for quality, not quantity, until I started cooking from Gerry's *Dining In* cookbook. I didn't count calories or grams of fat or sugar. I didn't monitor the ingredients based on how healthy I was cooking. I measured my dishes for taste: a pound of butter, two cups of sugar, salt before and after tasting. Never again would I unconsciously cook or eat anything.

"Ooh, wee," I yelled. Twenty-six dicks and thirty-five days should give me enough opportunity and time to lose twenty-five pounds, if I worked out with each man, limited my intake of calories, fat, and processed foods, and faithfully consumed eighty-eight ounces—half my weight, but in ounces—in water each day. Drinking that much water would be hard, but I could do it. I tried hard to convince myself that leaving Maverick for six weeks right before our wedding would make our relationship stronger. Plus, I'd be in great shape to push hard in the delivery room.

Nine months seemed so far away. The thought of having my first baby made me scared. Would I be a good mother, like my mom was? Would I end up a single parent? An unhappy wife?

"Girl, what are you thinking? You don't even know if you're pregnant," I said aloud. "A week late is nothing. Probably stress."

Picking up the phone, I called my best friend, professing, "Zena, I need you."

"Girl, what's wrong with you? Why do you sound so sad?" Zena whispered.

"I'm sorry. I didn't mean to bother you at work. It's just that . . . it's just," I said. I sniffled in Zena's ear like a baby.

"Where are you?" Zena asked.

"Home. At Maverick's house," I answered, massaging the lump in my throat, regretting I'd given up my apartment to move in with him.

"I'm ending a business call on the other line, and then I'm on my way, girl. I'll be there in twenty minutes or less," Zena said.

"Thanks," I said, ending the call. Then I closed my eyes and clicked the button. Within seconds the charges were billed to Maverick's business credit card. My trip to Punany Paradise was confirmed.

Mama used to say, "Never kiss and tell. It's not worth it. Better to ask the Lord for forgiveness than to ask your man."

Chapter 5

Zena

A woman without at least one secret hadn't experienced much. Pussy was powerful, but I didn't spread my legs for Deuce Callahan until after we'd gotten married.

"Zena, you proper? You need anything, honey?" Deuce asked, sitting on the edge of my desk.

"I'm making do. Business is a little slow but—"

Deuce reached into his jacket pocket, retrieved his checkbook, scribbled, then handed me a check for ten thousand dollars. "Here. Pay your mortgage, go to the spa, and take care of yourself."

I placed the check on my desk, shook my head, looked into his eyes. I wouldn't give him what he wanted most.

"I know. You don't have to say it," he said. "I have someone who's willing to have my baby. As soon as my citizenship is final, we will divorce. I will marry her, bring her to America, and she will have my kids."

Deuce's mother was Nigerian. His father, European. Marrying me had allowed him to become American, too.

Six years ago he'd said, "Man should be free to roam the world freely. Once I am an American, I can go wherever I please. Marry me, Zena, and I promise to take care of you always."

I touched his thigh, which felt hard like steel, then asked, already knowing the answer, "Deuce, can't we just be in love, make love, and not have kids?"

He stood, kissed my lips, then said, "A woman's body is her temple. I want to worship the woman I make love to. I want to hold her in my arms, put my dick in her, and fill her with love while we make love to create our baby. I cannot disrespect you. If you need anything, except this," he said, touching his huge dick, "I'm here for you."

Why me?

That six-nine, 250-pound, beautiful African man with the whitest teeth had made love to me one time. I'd been shocked. He'd eaten my pussy so good, made love to me until I passed out from satisfaction, then cooked me breakfast the next morning. That was the same day we got married.

Should've kept my mouth shut and my legs open. No, I had to tell him, "I don't ever want kids." Well, that was the truth. I refused to ruin my figure or my life. My mother was a single parent by the time I was two, my brother was four, and my sister was six. Three kids, and my daddy left her, married some other woman with three kids, took care of them, and forgot about all of us. I vowed that would never be me. Marriage had no guarantees.

"I'll walk out with you," I said. "Gotta go check on my girl Seven."

Walking down the stairs, Deuce said, "You tell her not to marry that man. He is gay."

I flashed him a look, nodded in the direction of my secretary. "Donna, I'll be back in two hours."

"Okay, Ms. Belvedere," she said, trying to pretend she hadn't heard what Deuce had said.

Once outside, I said, "Maverick is not gay. You think all Americans are gay. Besides, you've never met him. You've only seen pictures of him."

He shook his head in protest. "Not all Americans are gay. Most. The others are either fornicators, molesters, rapists, or perverts. That one, that Maverick is no maverick. I looked in his eyes. His eyes are glossy, like marbles. Once a man has been penetrated in the rectum by another man, he loses his armor."

We stood outside my office building on North Michigan Avenue.

"Look deep into my eyes, Zena. Tell me, what do you see?"

I stared at Deuce. My heart softened as I said, "Love. I see love."

"The eyes do not lie, baby. Problem with most Americans, they look but do not see others, only themselves. If you change your mind about having my babies, let me know before it is too late. I'll stop by again soon."

Babies? More than one? What he really wanted was his own basketball team.

Just like that, Deuce Callahan disappeared into the crowd of tourists strolling along the Magnificent Mile. He'd be back. No one knew he existed, not even my best friend, Seven.

Chapter 6

Seven

Foolishly, I believed Maverick would love me the way I loved him, unconditionally. I'd never leave him over a few pounds. Irrespective of age, weight, or physical features, a body was a shell encasing the spirit, sheltering what mattered the most, the heart.

Mama had told me, "Peel away the skin, strip away the fat, and we all look the same."

I'd forsaken my last year of grad school, fourteen units shy of getting my master's degree, to design state-of-the-art real estate in exchange for becoming Maverick's trophy.

A voice chimed in my ear. *Write yourself a check for a half million dollars, sign his name on it, cash it for relationship restitution in case Maverick kicks you out.*

"I can't do that," I responded aloud.

He'll never miss the money, my inner voice replied.

I countered, "Stealing is bad karma."

The devil on my shoulder poked me with a pitchfork. *You have my permission. It's not stealing.*

I sighed, "His accountant will definitely notice."

My subconscious jumped in. *It's compensation.*

My forehead wrinkled. "For what?"

The devil clarified. *Postponing your career. Possibly carrying his baby.*

Still not convinced, I said aloud, "My rhythm was off. Whose fault was that?"

Confidently, my subconscious replied, *His.*

I removed a personal checkbook from Maverick's desk, picked up his favorite Montblanc Starwalker Cool Blue pen. *Stop it, Seven!* My mother's voice resounded in my head. Embarrassed, I tossed the pen and checks into the drawer. Racing downstairs to the spacious bedroom walk-in closet, I snatched my suitcase, then tossed it onto the bed. I had a better idea. If Maverick truly loved me, I'd know for sure by the end of my trip.

Just lose the weight, and everything will be all right, I thought, with an upside-down smile.

He'd asked for my hand in marriage, and I'd given him my life. How could he throw me away with the same mind-set as putting out the trash?

Thankfully, the doorbell chimed, interrupting the monologue in my head.

Abandoning the overstuffed suitcase in the middle of his bed, I trotted to the first floor of Maverick's condo, located on the third floor of the building, then opened the double glass doors. Zena spread her arms wide. Collapsing into my friend's embrace, I clung to Zena, with streaming tears. I needed her to hold me.

Zena gently reassured me. "It's okay, honey. Whatever it is, it's okay. I'm here for you no matter what." She dangled her keys. "See? I was prepared to let myself in if you hadn't answered."

I smiled a little, glad I'd given her a spare set of keys to everything I owned—my car, my house in Mississippi—and to Maverick's home. I'd added Zena's name to the list of guests with authorized entry to the condo so she wouldn't have to check in with the doorman. Maverick would deny her access and demand his keys back if he knew. I had keys to Zena's home, too. We shared almost everything.

Closing the front doors, I headed upstairs to the kitchen, reached for the cold pitcher of sweetened iced tea, then shifted my hand, retrieving two bottles of flavored water. "Here," I said, handing a crystal glass to Zena, along with the passion fruit-flavored water.

"Girl, I don't need a glass. I'm listening," Zena said, unscrewing her bottle top as she followed me into the dining room.

Exhaling, I swallowed a sip of my passion fruit water, then said, "I'm leaving in the morning."

Zena shoulders rose to her ears, then fell back into place. "And?"

"I'm going away for five, I mean, six weeks. If I don't lose every single pound I've gained since my engagement by the time I get back, twenty-five pounds to be exact, Maverick is calling off the wedding."

"Shut up. Girl, you are lying. Please tell me you're lying," Zena said, then bit her bottom lip.

"I wish I were." I sighed, unable to tell Zena that Maverick wanted her to take over planning our wedding. I knew she'd do it for me. I just couldn't ask.

"Fuck Maverick. You can live with me. You don't need to leave for no five damn weeks. We've all put on a few pounds, but on our worst day, we are two of the sexiest divas in Chicago. What about his ass? Is he going to lose weight, too?" Zena asked.

Zena was more upset than I'd imagined. She never cursed or got the details wrong. It was six weeks, not five.

"You know how men are. They figure they are always the prize, no matter what," I said, thinking about how my mother had taught me never to tell my girlfriends too much about the men in my life. Zena knew me well, but she knew very little about how well Maverick treated me. Well, used to.

"Thanks for the support. Girl, you're working so hard. Haven't you noticed you've actually lost weight?" I paused, then exhaled heavily. Maybe she had noticed and didn't want to hurt my feelings. "I'ma go, but I'm not going for Maverick. I'm going for me." I wanted to add, "And for my baby," but didn't.

"Where are you going? You want me to go with you for moral support?" Zena asked.

"And lose what? Your mind?" Firmly, I said, "I'm not telling anyone where I'm going. I need to do this alone."

Zena snapped, "You can't just go to some strange place without telling me."

"Can and will," I countered. "I'll be careful, I promise. I'll be back two weeks before the wedding."

Zena leaped from her seat at the dining table. "The what! Wedding? You're still going to marry that asshole? I don't care how much money he has, I wouldn't marry him."

Okay, Seven. Don't get overly sensitive. I'm sure Zena isn't jealous.

Maverick wasn't an asshole. Up until now, our lives and love for one another had been perfect. Maybe the economy had impacted his investments. Maybe he was going through a tough merger or selling his interest in one of his teams and didn't want to discuss it. Men were like that, believing they could resolve every challenge on their own. Guess I wasn't much better, not telling my best friend I might be pregnant.

"He's entitled to his opinion. I don't want to make any irrational decisions I'll regret. He might be sorry later, but for now I'm good," I said, trying to reassure myself we'd be fine.

Zena studied my face as though she could decode what I'd said. Sitting across from me, she said, "Aw, hell no. The old Seven said that crap. You're up to something, good girlfriend. I can smell it. I'm going with you."

Slowly, I shook my head, concealing my smile on the inside.

Zena gulped the last of her water. "I couldn't take that much time off from running my business if I wanted to, anyway. Things would fall apart. Can't trust my employees to do the right thing for more than a few days at a time."

"That's because you're married to your business," I reminded her.

"That's because my best friend isn't allowed to hang out with me after"—Zena glanced at her watch, then continued—"six o'clock, or whenever the streetlights come on."

I had to laugh. "That's changing. If Maverick and I get married, he'll be cooking for himself, and I'll be going out whenever I want to. When I get back, we can hang out as much as you'd like. Give me a minute," I said, leaving the dining room.

Entering the library, I circled my finger on the mouse, clicked on the DELETE COOKIES button, powered off, then grabbed my laptop. I placed Maverick's credit card in the side pocket of my laptop bag. By the time his accountant received the next statement, I might have charged another thirty grand to stay six more weeks at Punany Paradise. Heading to the bedroom, I picked up my cell phone, stuffed my yellow Lycra panties in my purse, then double-checked to make certain I had my passport.

I approached Zena with open arms, giving her a big hug. "Thanks for being my true friend."

Zena whispered in my ear, "You'd better text me every day. Morning, noon, and night, to let me know you're okay. Got that?"

"I hear you," I said. "As a matter of fact, let's go hang out all day and all night. I can sleep on the plane tomorrow."

Holding the laptop bag on one shoulder, my purse on the other, I left the suitcase and his bed. My baby and I didn't have to take clothes where we were going, and we wouldn't need them when I returned. We'd start fresh. Closing the front doors behind Zena, I left my candy-apple red Lexus convertible with a white leather interior in the garage.

Cruising out the long driveway in her own candy-apple red Lexus convertible, Zena said, "I wouldn't walk down the aisle with him if I were you. If a man loves you, he loves you from the inside out, honey. Trust me, I know. Dump Maverick, and find yourself another man. I'll help you."

"You don't have time to find a man of your own," I said, fastening my seat belt.

The matching cars were our graduation presents to one another. I loved Zena like the sister I'd never had. I clung to her for friendship and female companionship. Didn't know what I'd do without her. That was, until Maverick came along. Then I depended on him for everything.

"Where to?" Zena asked.

We laughed aloud, then replied in unison, "The House of Blues." Somehow our listening to the melancholy lyrics of the blues always made us appreciate life.

Taking a deep breath, I confessed, "Zena, I might be pregnant."

Chapter 7

Maverick

Women. Emotional. Lovable. Irrational. Huggable. Gullible. Not suitable for much outside the bedroom and kitchen. Her spending too much time in either could yield a negative return on her non-monetary investment.

That was Danté's perspective.

"You need to change how you view women," I told him as he drove me to my condo, then parked at the meter in front of my building. I could've come home this morning but decided to wait until one o'clock this afternoon.

"We need to make sure she is gone," he said, opening my door, following me.

"Wait here," I told him.

"Why the fuck am I the one who always has to wait? It's time you tell her and yourself the truth. You want me more than you want her," Danté said, standing on the sidewalk, in front of the doorman.

Calmly walking over to Danté, I said in a low voice, "Make this your last time outing me in public."

"Or what?" he said, staring in my eyes.

He had no idea who he was fucking with. I could beat his ass to death right on this sidewalk. "Don't let him up," I told the doorman, then entered the building, leaving Danté outside. I picked up a copy of *USA Today* from the counter. Maybe I'd have time to read it later.

I loved Danté, but lately, he irritated the fuck out of me. Like now. I took the elevator to the third floor, unlocked my front door. Danté had become too demanding of me. Had me contemplating how to get rid of his ass. Permanently.

Nobody had ever given me a thing. Not my father. Not my mother. Not Danté or Seven. And no one should expect shit from me. Every dime I'd earned, I'd busted my ass for. Every debt I had, I'd repaid. What made Danté believe he could make demands of me? What made Seven think she could waste my money, my time? She didn't know my childhood struggles, fighting with my old man to survive in his house. Frank had taught me a few things, mainly how to take no prisoners.

In college and while starting my business, I'd capitalized on weak-minded fools who were chasing a dollar with their dreams. That shit never made sense to me. I downed my liquor like I closed business deals. Straight. No chaser. Same time. Give me my money or my property when I execute the contract.

My heart softened, a lot, when I met Seven.

Her smile, warm, friendly. Her voice, soothing, calming. Her laughter, healing therapy. The kind my mother used to have before she married my father. Once he moved in, everything changed for us. What I missed most was my mother's infectious smile. That, and the fact that she had always believed in me. Always. I was sure she still did but . . .

A lump of hatred for my father clogged my throat.

Soft men finished last. I'd learned that when my father told me, "Yo' mother ain't yo' mother no mo', boy. She's my wife. And if you ever step between us while I'm disciplinin' her, callin' yo'self tryna be da man in my house, I'll kill ya li'l five-year-old punk ass. Man the fuck up in yo' damn house when you get one. Ya hear me? Not mine. This here is Frank's house."

The day I turned eighteen, I kissed my mother's cheek, told her, "Ma, I love you," then walked out, kind of how I'd done with Seven, except under different circumstances. With a month left to go before leaving for college, I got a job, lived with my friend Chad Langston and his parents until Chad and I moved into our dorm room.

"Boy, don't you ever let yo' woman get big, fat, and nasty on ya," my father had once said. "Next thang ya know, she'll get lazy. If yo' mama don't get that weight off, I'ma beat it off of her. Every day."

I stood in my foyer. What the hell was life all about? I could buy anything and practically anyone, but I couldn't make my old man accept me. Racing to the bathroom off the foyer, I heaved the contents of my late breakfast/early lunch inside the toilet. Wiped my mouth with the back of my hand.

When I looked at Seven yesterday, I had to leave the house. All I heard then and now was my father's raging disgust toward my mother because she'd gained a few pounds. Seven was right. I should've said something sooner. I should've shared my horrible childhood with her, instead of suppressing my anger. I feared one day waking up like him. Putting my hands on Seven in a way she didn't deserve frightened me.

Rinsing my mouth, I prayed Seven was gone. I had to be harsh on her to ensure she'd taken me seriously.

I raced to the second floor, yelling, "Seven! Seven! Come here right now!" sounding just like him when he'd yelled at my mother.

Only my echo resounded.

Marching to the bedroom, I spotted the pile of clothes spilling over the sides of Seven's suitcase. "Where are you, Seven?" I called out.

No answer.

"Fuck!" When I threw her suitcase to the floor, a picture slid along the white carpet. I picked it up. Stared. It was a photo of us on our first date. Her smile made me smile. What had happened to me, to us? I loved this woman. I dialed Seven's cell. The call went straight to voice mail.

I speed dialed Zena, tapping my foot until she answered. "Yes, Maverick. What is it?"

Calmly, I asked, "Uh, do you know where Seven is?"

Zena snapped, "No. Don't you? You're the one who kicked my friend out. If I were her, I wouldn't marry your ass."

"Zena, I never kicked Seven out. She was feeling anxious about not fitting into her wedding dress. We discussed it. She decided going away to a weight-loss camp was what she wanted to do. I simply supported her," I lied.

"That's not how she explained it to me. Besides, nothing justifies kicking her out while she's carrying your child," Zena countered.

Carrying what? As in pregnant? Bullshit. "Of course not. I'd never do such a thing. Seven isn't pregnant. She's feeling embarrassed and self-conscious about her weight gain. And since you've lost weight, Seven is . . . well, she's admitted to me she's slightly jealous," I replied, then asked, "Where'd she go without any clothes? Is she with you?"

Was Seven really pregnant? Zena was lying. Seven would never leave without telling me we were having a child . . . unless she was pregnant by some other man.

"No. She's gone. She'll be back in five weeks, she said."

"Six weeks," I corrected her, asking again, "Where'd she go?"

"She didn't say. All I know is my best friend is hurting, and it's all your damn fault. You could've convinced her to stay. She could've worked out with me or a personal trainer."

I wasn't surprised Seven had shared with Zena the true story. I was stunned about the pregnant part. Seven was either a liar or a cheater. Either way, she'd made my decision to pursue other options easier.

"Changing the subject, I want to retain your PR firm to promote my new ventures. Are you available for dinner tomorrow night? My yacht. I'll have my driver pick you up at six."

A pregnant pause. I felt Zena smiling through the phone when she replied, "I wanted to represent your empire before you met Seven. You won't regret hiring my firm."

"Perfect. Hopefully, neither of us will have any regrets," I said, ending the call.

Women weren't loyal to one another when it came to having the opportunity to snatch one of society's most eligible bachelors. That was how my mom had snatched my dad, except his ass was broke. She'd pulled him right off the arm of his fiancée. I had six weeks to prove my theory right, starting tomorrow night.

After all the money I'd spent on my wedding, I was getting married with or without Seven standing beside me at the altar. The newspapers had highlighted my engagement for an entire month. I refused to suffer public embarrassment. I wouldn't give my father the satisfaction. As much as I'd demanded that Seven stop hanging with Zena, I had to admit, Zena was supermodel and trophy wife material. Slightly too independent for my liking but surely, she could fit into Seven's wedding gown, and my lifestyle, after I took her down a few notches.

Honk! Honk! Honk! Honk!

Looking out my window, I saw Danté standing on the sidewalk, with his arm inside the car.

Honkkkkkkkkkkk!

I knew what I had to do. I'd warned him. Danté had left me no choice.

Chapter 8

Seven

I'd spent the night at Zena's after we'd shut down the House of Blues. Didn't hear from Maverick last night. No messages from him when I powered on my cell phone as the plane landed on the island.

Zena had dropped me off at the airport, then headed to work, still trying to convince me to tell her where I was going. I'd refused. I'd intentionally left my laptop bag, my laptop, Maverick's gun, credit card included, in her bedroom this morning. I'd boarded my flight at O'Hare, slept all the way to my destination.

The first thing I did when I arrived at Punany Paradise this morning was stroll in the sand along the shore. Warm crystals sunk beneath my soles, filling the gaps between my toes. Warm water splashed against my legs, soaking the bottom of my emerald ankle-length halter dress.

"Ahhhh," I exhaled in relief.

Twirling in the wind, I felt free and happy. It had been a long time since I'd seen turquoise water drifting into cerulean, blending with dark blue waters, kissing the tangerine sky. Flinging my arms, I cast my problems out to sea, imagined them sinking to the ocean floor like an anchor. Some of my ancestors were probably buried in the Atlantic Ocean. Their sacrifices bolstered my determination to achieve happiness

"When I get back, I'm returning to college to get my master's," I declared aloud. The million dollars my mom had left me was safely invested, earning interest. Our home and the twenty acres I'd inherited in Webster County, Mississippi, after my dad died would remain unsold. Not that I'd move back to Mississippi after having lived in Chicago, but I'd have a quiet place to spend summers, teaching my heritage to my child. Enough of dwelling on others. The present was all about me.

I wanted to sunbathe nude on a yacht, swim naked in the ocean, snorkel, deep-sea dive, parasail, skydive, hike in a tropical rain forest, cry under a waterfall, washing away my fears, and rejoice in loving me some Seven. The next six weeks, I'd proclaim Seven's heaven.

Lake Michigan was beautiful; Punany Paradise was surreal.

Removing my cell phone from my purse, I captured the sun's diamonds sparkling on the ocean in a photo, then texted the picture to Zena with the message, I arrived safely, inviting my friend to share in my joy. Each day I'd send Zena a tiny glimpse into my world. She was the only person in the world that truly cared about me.

Instantly, Zena texted back. OMG . . . This place is unreal. Where r u? I have great news!

Keying in, Tell me your great news, but don't tell Maverick I might be pregnant. Not sure I want to have his baby, if I am, I headed toward the group of women gathering for our orientation. I stood a few feet back from the other women, who had been on the shuttle bus with me earlier. Each of them had arrived the same. A purse, no luggage, no man. I hadn't expected that some would be slim, some plus sized—and that all would be ethnically diverse.

Zena texted, I'm having dinner with Maverick 2moro nite. He wants my company to represent his. Isn't that great! Work off that w8 gf so I can convince him 2 put u in our ads.

Ping-pong.

Instantly, my head was messed up again. My heart thumped against my breast. *What the fuck?* The fading sunlight eclipsed my sight. In an instant, my joy vanished.

"You okay?" a chestnut-toned woman, with long auburn locks and a proper English accent, politely asked.

Okay? Hell, no, I'm not okay. Seven, chill out. "I'm good. Thanks for asking," I replied, a contrived smile barely spreading my lips.

I'd been gone less than twenty-four hours, and my best friend was already having dinner with my fiancé. Powering off my cell phone, I tossed it into my purse, where it would remain for the next six weeks.

"Welcome, ladies," a tall, nude, voluptuous woman said, strolling the perimeter of the infinity pool.

A tall, sexy, Greek god–looking man carefully laid white beach towels atop fourteen cushioned lounge chairs perfectly lined up alongside the pool. Waves crashing from the ocean spilled over into the deeper end of the pool. As quickly as he had appeared, he disappeared, so as not to interrupt the orientation with his dick damn near hanging down to his knees.

I wanted to slap his beautiful oiled ass. Run and jump into his arms cheerleader style. All sorts of naughty thoughts raced through my mind.

"Take a few deep breaths, and then have a seat and relax," the tall woman instructed as she sat naked at the foot of the lounge chair closest to the deep end of the pool. "My name is Serenity. I promise I didn't make the name up. My mother gave me that name. I'm glad she did. Believe it or not, birth names mean a lot."

Eyeing her beautiful body made me want to keep my clothes on the entire stay. The god of a guy emerged, carrying a tray with glasses. After handing seven women a cool yellowish drink, he left quickly, returning with seven more until each of us held a drink, including Serenity.

After scooping ice into my hand, I pressed my chilled glass against my throbbing temple, wondering why Maverick would have dinner with Zena one day after I'd left, knowing he didn't like her. *Crunch. Crunch.* I chomped on the cubes. Obviously, he'd planned this. I prayed Zena wasn't part of Maverick's scheme to get rid of me. Whatever it was, it was.

Serenity stood, held her glass in the air, then said, "A toast. To your beauty within, which shines throughout. By the time you leave Punany Paradise, every cell in your body will smile without your having to move your lips."

Beautiful was not the adjective I would've used to describe the way I felt. I sipped the pineapple, ginger nonalcoholic beverage, craving a double shot of rum. "Um, yes," I moaned. "This is good."

Serenity continued, "Ladies, you are here for one reason only. Pleasure. The only rule is if it doesn't feel good to you, do something that does feel good."

Nodding, I said, "Yep, from now on that's my philosophy."

"I know each of you is here for different reasons," said Serenity. "Some to relax. Others are starting over after a divorce. Some of you are battling depression. Addictions or a-dick-shuns. Others are here to lose weight. Some of you will be here for one week. Others for up to two months. Stay as long or as short as you'd like. The only thing we ask is, if you're unhappy being here, leave."

Who would want to leave a place like this? I'd better learn to fake being happy so I don't get kicked out.

"The unused portion of your payment is fully refundable, no questions asked. I don't do introductions. Your privacy is fully respected here at Punany Paradise. If you want to meet someone, we have a written introduction process, where you write them a note, seal it in an envelope, then drop it in the mailbox at the front desk. Your photo is on your in-box."

Dang. The pictures they took of us an hour ago were already posted?

Serenity went on. "There are several community areas on the island where you can go to socialize. You will receive a tour of the island whenever you're ready. Right now you will meet . . ."

When she paused, a long line of heart-throbbing, make-your-pussy-quiver, drop-dead-then-resuscitate-yourself, gorgeous men in vibrant-colored exotic swimwear circled the pool. My chin fell toward my collarbone. "Yes!" I desperately wanted to yell. All the men were handsome, masculine, with fantastic chiseled bodies. Twenty-six. I'd counted them all, twice.

"Oh, my, gosh. That's him. That's Jagger. The one on the Web site," I whispered.

Our eyes met. *Breathe, Seven. Breathe.* Struggling to find my breath, I looked away.

Serenity continued, "All the men here are for your pleasure. There's at least twenty-six men here at all times, sometimes more, never less, to serve and service you any way you'd like."

In sync, they removed their swimwear.

"Oh, my God," I cried, admiring each one.

Serenity nodded at me, then said, "They're all highly skilled in every area imaginable. In your private beachfront homes, your computer has a profile of each guy. All you have to do is send an instant message, and your desired guy is all yours. You can book ahead or last minute. It doesn't matter."

I inquired, "What if, say, four of us want the same guy at the same time?"

"As in an orgy?" Serenity asked, seeking clarification.

My face flushed with embarrassment. "Oh no. I'm sorry."

"We never use that word here. I don't want to hear it again. No woman is ever sorry." Serenity said, smiling. "Your question is valid. So if there are conflicts, you're assigned a number by the requested guy. If you want another woman or a group of women to join you, you have to leave a note for the woman, inviting her to your place, and you must let the guy or guys know as well. Life here is simple. Zero guilt. Take advantage of exploring your wildest fantasies. Enjoy as many men as you'd like."

Finishing my drink, I admired the last glimpse of sunset shimmering off the tight, perfectly shaped asses, wondering if I could honestly have carefree sexual encounters with strange men while not knowing whether I was pregnant. Maverick was the only man I'd made love to in the past two years.

"Gentlemen, escort your lady to her beachfront home," Serenity said, waving good-bye.

Two men escorted each of us. I joyfully interlocked my arms with each of my guys, pretending they were both mine. I lowered my head, looking side to side. Damn, they had the prettiest dicks I'd ever seen. My entire body smiled.

I was ready to indulge in pure, unadulterated pleasure.

Chapter 9

Zena

A black stretch Lincoln Navigator with room to comfortably accommodate twelve people parked in front of my office building. Mesmerized, I stood at the window, peeping out from the second floor, as the tall, chocolate, bald-headed driver, with tinted sunglasses darker than the car windows, approached the glass door marked The Zena Belvedere Agency. As I released the fold in the mini-blinds, my heart throbbed; my breath quickened. I stepped back, smoothing out my A-line skirt.

"Ms. Belvedere," my receptionist announced, "your driver is here."

Pressing the intercom button, I replied, "Thanks, Donna. Don't forget to lock up before you leave."

Nervously, I glided downstairs. *He's the limo driver, Zena,* I told myself. Yeah, but he was awakening things inside of me that no man had since Deuce. I shivered, hoping he hadn't noticed.

Donna stared at the driver, who was holding open the office door. "Have a good time, Ms. Belvedere."

There was no way I couldn't have a good time tonight.

"My name is Danté," he said, opening the back door of the limo.

Wish he'd open my front and back doors, I thought, sinking into the smooth leather seat. "Thanks," I said. Was I grinning at this tall purple-blackalicious man with glistening white teeth? Or at the view of his dick imprint, which was at eye level, until he closed my door?

My gaze stalked Danté until he settled into the driver's seat. All I saw after he drove off were buildings, people walking down the street, and trees. The black suede divider shielded my view of Mr. Fine Ass Danté.

What would Seven do? I texted her, Girl, this man is so fine.

No reply.

I texted her again.

U forgot your laptop at my house. Want me 2 send it 2 U?

I prayed she'd tell me where she was. I wasn't comfortable not knowing where my best friend was. Was she safe? The picture she'd texted me was beautiful. Although she should, Seven would never cheat on Maverick. He'd changed her like no other man we'd talked about. Wished I had a man that attentive who didn't want kids.

Was this how Seven lived? I had no idea. She drove herself everywhere. She never told me, but I couldn't imagine a limo picking me up for dinner with Maverick and not doing the same for her. My girl could've set me up with Danté. She probably figured I wouldn't go out with the limo driver. The one time Seven had invited me to a game, Maverick had emphatically told her, "No."

Danté cruised along the lake, parking at the docks. When he opened the door, it was like a scene straight out of *Coming to America*. Rose petals had been strewn along a rich ruby red plush carpet leading to a huge white yacht. Holding my hand, a guy dressed in a tuxedo escorted me aboard.

I didn't get another glimpse of Danté as he drove away. I wanted to see him again. Go out with him. Get to know his story. Fuck him once a week or at least once.

My jaw fell when I saw Maverick dressed in an off-white blazer and slacks, a blue and red silk scarf neatly tucked at his neck, an off-white fedora tilted on his head. The only item missing was a cigar. His smile was warm and inviting.

"You look absolutely beautiful, Zena. But I want you to look stunningly gorgeous," he said. "Leslie will help you prepare to my liking."

Prepare to his liking? Is this how he'd captured Seven?

Following this strange woman, Leslie, I understood how my girl had fallen in love with Maverick and why she wanted to drop the twenty-five pounds to please him. Would Seven lie to me about possibly being pregnant?

Leslie interrupted my thoughts. "Once you finish showering, your attire will be over here. When you're properly prepared, Mr. Maxamillion will join you on the top deck."

I showered and lotioned my body with Ecstasy Shea Soufflé. Prada perfume rested on the vanity. Dare I spray on Seven's favorite cologne? Obviously, he wanted me to, otherwise there would've been more options, unless this was her private room. Exiting the bathroom, I took a deep breath when I saw, suspended from a hanger, the white dress Seven had bought for her wedding reception. We'd picked out that dress a year ago, together. I stood still, closed my eyes, then sighed heavily. Seven looked absolutely gorgeous in that dress from Bloomingdale's.

Sitting on the edge of the bed, I retrieved my PDA. No text messages from Seven. This was her second day away. Maybe she was busy working out. Perhaps her phone had died. It wasn't like her not to text me back. I texted her, U okay, girl? then sat my phone on the bed.

My fingers danced along the pearled and sequined knee-length halter dress, which fit me perfectly. "Wow. I had no idea Seven's life was so elaborate. She was so modest. Humble," I said aloud.

Glancing at my phone, I saw there was no response from Seven. "Oh, well," I exhaled. "I can't keep my new client waiting. Besides, Seven can't fit in this dress, anyway. Maybe Maverick didn't want to waste his money."

Zipping up the dress on the side, I stepped into Seven's slip-on diamond stilettos. This was probably the only day of my life I'd be a true princess. I was sure my best friend wouldn't mind letting me step into her world for one night only.

Tap. Tap.

"Are you ready?" Leslie asked, peeping inside the room.

"Lord, forgive me." I inhaled deeply, then quietly exhaled. "Yes, I'm ready." *For what?* I had no idea.

Maverick's wide smile indicated his approval. "Come. I want you to watch the sunset with me. You work so hard. I bet you don't take time to enjoy the view. And for me, you will spend lots more time working, so let's maximize this moment," he said, not waiting for a reply.

"Maximize? Huh, I like that. Maximize your money with Maxamillion," I said.

He smiled, nodded, then replied, "I like that, too."

Joining the captain at the helm, Maverick took control of the wheel. Coaxing me in front of him, he placed my hands on the wheel, wrapped his hands around mine, then pressed his pelvis into my ass. The yacht swayed with our departure. I felt his erection nudging the crevice of my ass, his nose nestling in my hair.

Lord Jesus, this is so wrong, but it feels so right, I thought as my ass involuntarily jerked into his dick. "I'm . . . I'm so sorry," I said. Embarrassed, I stepped aside.

"Don't be. We're going to have to spend lots more time together over the next few weeks, until our business plan and contract are solidified. You have to get to know me in order to represent me, respect me."

I wanted to say, "But what about Seven? Your fiancée? Remember her?" Maybe I was the foolish one. I'd witnessed business tycoons with huge egos bartering contracts with sexual favors. There was no way I could fuck my best friend's fiancé. I'd die first.

Maverick motioned for me. "Come closer. Stand behind me. Grip my hands," he said, snuggling my arms at his waist. "Hold me like your life depends on it," he said seductively.

My life? Was he insane? I was too far out on the lake not to take him seriously. What if this was some sort of test to see if I was loyal to Seven? What if I'd failed already?

"I'm a bit hungry," I lied. "Haven't eaten all day, and the motion is making me queasy." *Of your madness, not the boat.*

"Let's eat then." Maverick snapped his fingers. The captain reappeared, taking control of the wheel.

Did Maverick act this way all the time? As though everyone was beneath him. His authoritative undertone ignited a chilling bite that could leave one frostbitten on Chicago's hottest day. Faking a smile, I followed Maverick below deck to the dining area, wondering if Seven had texted me back. Maverick pulled out my chair, then softly kissed my neck before sitting across from me.

Chills penetrated my body. I had to say something. "Maverick, I'm not sure what I'm bargaining for here, but honestly, it doesn't feel right. Aren't you concerned about where Seven is?"

"Honestly, no. Are you?" he asked, gulping his Scotch.

"Seven leaves with no clothes. She leaves her laptop at my house, and you don't care?" I asked him.

"You're ruining my appetite with all this talk about Seven," he said.

That's it. I'm done with this creep. I pray Seven doesn't marry him.

"You can return Seven's laptop to me. I'll have Danté pick it up tomorrow," he said.

Infuriated, I said, "What? Did she ask you to ask me for her laptop? Do you know where Seven is?"

He sat there, staring through me.

"Answer me," I insisted.

Maverick's lips curved into a captivating smile that slowly sucked me in. Exposing his incredibly white teeth, he scratched his head, then casually said, "Since *it* doesn't feel right, *then* you're not the right one to represent me. After dinner I'll have my driver take you home. Our business here is done."

Wrong questions. Wrong answer. Wrong every damn thing. I didn't want to seem desperate, but this was a prime opportunity to elevate my business, my social status. To be able to say, "I represent Maverick Maxamillion Incorporated," would triple my clientele. If I did an excellent job for Maverick, he'd give me great referrals. I could stop relying on Deuce to pay my mortgage every month. While I tried to figure out a way to get back into Maverick's good graces, I sat quietly eating my salad.

The entrées came, then dessert, then the driver, without further conversation between us. I'd messed up big-time this time.

"It was nice seeing you, Zena. I'll have my personal assistant drop by and pick up the dress and shoes tomorrow, and don't forget the laptop," Maverick said, excusing himself from the table.

Leslie approached me, placed her hand on the back of my chair, then politely said, "I'll escort you back to the car, Ms. Belvedere."

There was no red carpet, no roses, no limo, no sexy-ass Danté. A wooden deck, a town car, a mediocre-looking driver, and me all dressed up headed home, with no contract. Who knew what Maverick had planned for me tonight? Obviously, I'd messed that up. I sat in silence, pissed with the way my evening had ended.

Parked in front of my home, holding open the car door, staring down at me, the driver said, "Ms. Belvedere?"

"Yes?" I exhaled, terribly disgusted with myself.

"Mr. Maxamillion said that if you'd like to reconsider his offer, let him know, and Danté will pick you up to join Mr. Maxamillion in his owner's suite at the football game tomorrow night," the driver said, reaching for my hand.

Of course, I wanted a second chance . . . to meet Danté and to work for Maverick, but I refused to betray Seven. I sat there, speechless. I was no fool. If I accepted Maverick's offer, I'd have to fuck him or cross him at some point. I'd be risking my loyalty to Seven.

To say yes might cost me my best friend.

To say no might prove to be the worst business decision of my life.

Chapter 10

Seven

Restless in Punany Paradise. I hadn't slept well last night.
The two escorts had offered to massage me at the same time.
They'd said the traditional welcome relaxation treatment would set
the tone for my stay. I was probably the only woman who'd refused.
Too much on my mind. Not ready for another man's touch pleasur-
ing my body. Slightly self-conscious, remembering Maverick's insult,
"You might as well be on the field, helping out." Undeniably, my feel-
ings of inferiority complicated things, making me feel unworthy.

Mama used to say, "Seven, always love yourself first. *First.*"

I know. I know that, Ma, I thought, lying in bed, with my eyes closed.
In time I'd get back to loving me first.

Wasn't like I loved Maverick more. I simply hadn't felt good about
myself, about us, since our last conversation. Before turning off the
lights, easing into bed last night, I'd turned on my phone, lowered
the volume, then placed it on the charger, not wanting to miss a call
or text from Maverick or Zena. No intention to respond, just wanted
to know if either of them was thinking . . . about me.

"Let it go, Seven. Let it go," I'd cried, scrambling my legs in the
sheets. Hadn't slept alone this much in two years. No one to hold me.
Brush against. Wake up to. Even if what Maverick and I had wasn't
perfect the last few days, he was home with me every night.

Inside my quiet beachfront suite, a king-size bed centered on a two-step, two-foot platform faced white wall-to-wall curtains. Turning onto my side, I sat up, placing my feet on the floor. Somberly, I sloped to the window, gripped the long clear handles, and slid the curtains apart.

The Atlantic Ocean spanned endless miles, sweeping in every direction. Opening the sliding-glass door, I stepped out onto my private patio. The sound of waves crashing against the shore curved my lips upward a bit, with peace and joy struggling to break through. If I allowed, Mother Nature was there to nurture me in a way that my man couldn't, wouldn't.

Going back inside, I browsed the bookshelves adjacent to the computer. Dammit. I wished I'd brought my computer. Couldn't ask Zena to send it to me; then she'd know where I was. I had documents and files in my laptop that were private. Pictures of me that I wasn't proud of, that were taken of me in college. One too many drinks had landed me in a few very compromising positions, naked. Some with multiple guys. Others having sex with women. Then there were my financial statements and wedding plans, stored away in marked folders.

Zena knew my code. I'd given it to her once to check the follow-up date for the caterer while I was in the kitchen, cooking dinner for Maverick. Right now I didn't trust Zena or Maverick. Both would judge me harshly if they knew the type of party girl I used to be.

I refocused on the books in front of me: *Up to No Good* by Carl Weber, *Dying for Revenge* by Eric Jerome Dickey, *Erotic City* by Pynk, *Single Husbands* by HoneyB, *She Comes First: The Thinking Man's Guide to Pleasuring a Woman* by Ian Kerner, and *Opening to Love 365 Days a Year* by Judith Sherven and James Sniechowski.

Ordinarily, I'd choose an African American–authored novel, except I'd read all my favorites, and now I wondered when Zane was coming out with her next outlandish novel. Hoping I'd learn something new about love, I selected James and Judith's book to see if they'd prove me wrong, then went to the kitchen. To my surprise, there were three carafes on ice. I read their labels: raspberry juice, mango-ginger juice, and papaya juice.

I poured a glass of raspberry juice, headed outdoors, and reclined in the hammock. Swaying slowly, ankles crossed, sunglasses blocking the rays, I delved in. The book started as I'd suspected, telling me the other person wasn't me and that I should remember that my partner's feelings, beliefs, and behavior were just as valid as mine.

"Yeah, right. Says who? I don't need a book to tell me that no one is perfect," I mumbled at the pages, reading on. By the end of the book, the sun was fading, and my heart was softening. Maybe I didn't know Maverick as well as I'd thought. He certainly didn't know me. But how much was too much to tell your mate, and how little was not enough?

Closing the book after speed-reading to the end of the last chapter, I decided one day I'd write my life story. Not for the world. For me. For the baby that might be inside of me today or in the future. Why wait? Tomorrow wasn't promised. I decided I'd e-mail my life story to Maverick, asking him to do the same.

One day, not today. Maybe before I left Punany Paradise.

I could stay here forever and ever, appreciating that no one at the resort bothered me. But I wasn't here for isolation, I reminded myself. I was on holiday.

"Let me see what's in that database of Serenity's." Rolling out of the hammock, I went inside.

Checking in with Serenity via instant messaging morning, noon, and night was the only requirement for guests choosing to stay in their suite. I e-mailed Serenity. Oops, I just read this. I'm good. Why hadn't anyone checked on me? Maybe they'd seen me outside reading. How could they? Maybe whoever had delivered my juice had sent her a note.

Heading to the bathroom—which was more like a personal in-room spa, with steam and dry saunas, a six-person Jacuzzi, a sunken tub filled with mineral water, a separate shower, and a private room for the toilet and bidet—I noticed the flashing light on my PDA, indicating I had a message.

Backing up to the computer desk, I read, Girl, this man is so fine. In separate messages, Zena had texted, U forgot your laptop in my car. Want me 2 send it 2 U? then U okay, girl?

"Nah, nah. You bold enough to say my man is so fine, and you want to know if I'm okay?" I said, placing my PDA back on the computer desk.

More concerned with why Maverick hadn't contacted me at all, I sat in the chair and browsed the last profile in the group of men.

I clicked on Jagger: Twenty-two years young, native of St. John; six feet five; 205 pounds; loves sailing, music, dancing, surfing, snorkeling; the best in cunnilingus delight. That man intrigued me once more. My pussy had the hots for this Jaggerman.

Why not do him? I thought. Oral sex wasn't cheating. Jagger might give me the sultry, bubbling personality I'd had before meeting Maverick, helping me to forget about what Zena was doing with my fiancé.

I typed in my request to Jagger. Can you meet me in the community area in two hours? Figuring I'd have to wait a few days to get on his calendar, I browsed the next profile at the bottom of the list.

Jagger's instant message popped up. Certainly. What took you so long to ask? I've been waiting to taste you, and I'll come ready. Your pleasure is my only wish.

I said, "Damn." Fletcher was caramel suckalicious. The imprint of his snake slithering down his muscular thigh, threatening to poke that plump, juicy head of his out of his chocolate boxers, lit up my pussy and my eyes.

I instant messaged Jagger. Looking forward to you. Then I sent Fletcher an instant message. Can you bathe me tomorrow at midnight?

Fletcher's message came back. I can do whatever you'd like me to do, Seven. Can't wait.

My pussy was on high beam! I was beginning to like this place. I walked over to my closet. Inside it, there were at least fifty colorful sarong, with the tags on but no price. When they said, "All-inclusive," that was what they meant. I gathered the tags were just to let me know the items were new. A rack of one-piece swimsuits and bikinis stretched wall to wall. Beach sandals lined the shelves above. Slip-on stilettos in my size were in a row below the evening dresses. Why so many clothes for a nude resort? Probably because no one had worn them.

Selecting a simple red sarong, I opened the dresser drawer filled with vibrant panties in lace, Lycra, and satin. "I won't be needing any of these," I said, deciding at the moment to let my pussy be liberated.

I showered, poured myself a chilled glass of mango-ginger juice from the carafe, then added a shot of rum to relax. The tip of my big toe eased into the Jacuzzi, leading the way for my naked body. "Ah," I exhaled. Being alone suddenly felt heavenly.

Resting my head on the inflated pillow, I closed my eyes, opened my legs, and let the jet shoot up from the bottom of the Jacuzzi cleanse my pussy and pleasure me with multiple orgasms while I sipped my drink. Drinking with my eyes closed, I could smell the mango and ginger, taste and feel the flavors trickling down my throat. Bubbles blasting behind me massaged my back.

Setting my glass aside, I whispered, "I could stay here forever."

Shriveled fingertips wiped away the sweat from my forehead. If I paced myself, I could experience all twenty-six guys by the end of my stay. Only this experience would be better than when I was in college.

The plush white towel, almost longer than my body, absorbed the excess water from my body. Carol's Daughter body products lined the vanity. I layered my skin with Sweet Honey Dip . . . Chocolate Brown Sugah Body Butter and the Ecstasy Shea Soufflé, tied my red sarong under my arms and around my breasts, and let it flow over my hips, snuggling up to my ass.

Finishing my drink, I reached for an unopened bottle of 16.9 ounces of water, then drank the entire contents. That should do until we returned from the community area where I was headed for an evening of pleasure.

Seven, keep an open mind. Enjoy yourself. Be happy or you'll have to leave, I thought right before Jagger greeted me with a warm smile, which sent a tingling sensation throughout my body.

"Hello there, beautiful. How are you?" he asked, opening his arms, waiting for me to accept his hug.

I did.

He held me firmly. His strong hands embraced my shoulders.

I took a deep breath, then exhaled. When was the last time Maverick had held me with such conviction, such patience? Momentarily, I wished Jagger were Maverick, praying Maverick wasn't holding Zena in his arms.

"Wow, you're really tense," Jagger said. "Let me relax you."

Looking around, I asked, "Where?"

"Wherever you'd like. The entire island is yours to enjoy."

"Let's walk for a while," I suggested, trying to relax on my own.

I'd met lots of men in Mississippi. Most of them conservative, up-tight, minimalist, and happy with barely getting by as long as they could pay the bills and have a little money left over to drink. My mother had insisted I explore men outside of Webster County, cities outside of Mississippi, countries outside of America. My mother had encouraged me to relocate to Chicago for undergrad school, then advised me to move someplace other than Chicago for grad school. Then she left me before I got my college degree. Daddy must've needed Mama more than me; he left shortly afterward, leaving me to walk across the stage with Zena.

"You're so beautiful. Want to talk about what bothers you?" Jagger asked, holding my hand as we strolled along the beach.

I exhaled. "There are so many things right with my life, I hate to complain about what's wrong."

"Seven, it's only complaining if you don't either do something about it or let it go. I had it hard in St. John. Lots of tourists coming from all over the world. Men and women wanting me to service them like I was a piece of meat, a sex machine."

Suddenly I felt guilty.

Jagger continued. "Not appreciating me for me. Not knowing or caring to know my last name, how I grew up, or if I cared about them," he said. "I like this place because the women who come here, they're genuine, you know. No more explaining to men that I'm not bisexual. I've never had sex with a man. These women here are like you, Seven. They care about living a better life, and they're doing something about it. Whatever that is for them, you know. I get to help them do that. In return, they actually care about me and the other guys here. Many of them write us. Some come back just to visit us. I like that. I hope you come back to visit me."

Just to visit? Yeah right. For a moment, I felt selfish. I hadn't asked anything about Jagger. But I'd only been with him for a few minutes. And he wanted me to come back and visit him?

"Well, I'm here for six weeks," I said. "I have a question."

"Anything for you, Seven. I'm not just saying that. I mean that," he said.

"Have any of the women at Punany Paradise fallen in love with you?"

Smiling, he answered, "Not really."

"What kind of answer is that? What do you mean, not really?"

"It's not me they fall in love with. They fall in love with themselves, not only because of what I do, but because of what all the men here do . . . We adore each and every woman. We respect you. We treat you like the queens you are."

"Is that because we get what we pay for?" I asked.

He nodded. "True. And because you are beautiful inside and out. I tell you, every woman that comes here loses at least ten pounds if she stays for just one week."

My lips tightened. *Impossible.* How could that be? "Now you're straight lying."

Frantically, he shook his head. "No, seriously."

"How?" I asked.

"You arrived two days ago, right?"

"And?"

"And when was the last time you thought about food? I mean a full-course meal, like breakfast, lunch, or dinner," Jagger asked, kissing the back of my hand.

Silence consumed my thoughts. Not once had I thought about food in that way. I had reflected on my life a lot, had spent way too much time imagining what my fiancé was doing with my best friend, had read a book, had talked to my mom's spirit, and had slept.

"You see, Seven. When our worries turn into happiness, when we are happy like the Creator intended, food sustains and vitalizes us. Food does not consume or console us. Punany Paradise is about connecting with the chi energy in your womb that feeds your soul. Your creative energy. Chi drives your passion. I guarantee you, by the time you leave here in six weeks, you will be a sizzling size six."

The smile on my face could not be erased with a Brillo pad. "No way," I said, cheesing ear to ear. "I haven't been a size six since high school."

"I want to make you feel like you're in high school again. Let me please you, Seven," Jagger said. "I know you don't know me, not yet, anyway. All I ask is that you trust me."

Unwrapping my sarong, Jagger laid it over the sand.

"Lie down," he said, guiding me to a horizontal position, parallel to the waves washing ashore.

"Ooh, nice. I love your punany. You have a beautiful pussy, Seven. Your shaft is thick, and it's protruding," he said, lightly kissing my clit. "Yes, she's excited for me. I like that." He kissed me again.

Oh my gosh, I thought. *What am I submitting to?*

Lightly grazing my pubic hairs with his teeth, he massaged me, softly stroking my nipples.

"Is this okay?" he asked.

"Yes," I agreed, breathing rapidly.

Spreading my outer lips, he knelt between my legs, twirled my hairs with his fingers, then his tongue. Licking his fingers, Jagger teased my clit. I wanted to scream.

"Relax," he said. "Don't hold it in. Let it out. Release yourself. That's why you're here. We will never recapture this moment. Let go for me, Seven. It's okay to be vulnerable with me. I won't hurt you."

I heard a few women screaming in the distance, giving me permission to join them. "Yesss!" I yelled, releasing the energy.

Jagger placed his wet, hot lips on my shaft, then whispered, "ABC," licking the capital letters. With each letter, he passionately grazed my clit.

"Oh, God," I moaned, cuming just a little with each stroke.

Light flutters and gentle, subtle licks pleasured me. The sea breeze swept against my skin, nudged my hair. The moonlight stared into my eyes when Jagger traced the letter *E,* ending with that middle stroke, then passionately sucked my clitoris into his mouth.

I swear, by the time Jagger got to *Z,* easing his middle finger inside of me, stroking my G-spot while sucking my clit, all I could do was cry a river of tears, which cleansed my spirit.

Chapter 11

Maverick

Overcast.

Dark clouds swept down on the Windy City. Rain poured down in the middle of the workday, drenching the unsuspecting, the ill prepared. A funnel of darkness swirled, skating along North Michigan Avenue, snapping umbrellas inside out, the sound of microwave popcorn frantically approaching its peak. Dirt, debris, leaves, rain stuck to the five-thousand-dollar, hand-stitched, tailor-made suit cloaking my body; an unsavory residue permeated my skin, making me want to slither out of my clothes, shed like a snake.

Parting the pack, racing across East Chestnut Street from Water Tower Place, I darted into my office building, bypassed the line of people waiting to buy tickets to gain access to the Hancock Observatory, located on the ninety-fourth floor of the John Hancock Center.

Shit! Where'd that storm come from, man? I thought, plucking dirt from my jacket. Weather conditions around the world were becoming less predictable with each passing year. First, a tornado in Brooklyn, now one in Chicago.

Blame the man-made wind tunnels on the politicians, the city planners, and the architects that created this eclectic monstrosity after the Great Chicago Fire of 1871, which killed hundreds of people. Sometimes a mass of people had to die to give birth to innovative ideas. Or sometimes just one person needed to be laid to rest to make the world a better place for another. For me, that one person was my father.

After the fire, Chicago was resurrected. After I moved out of my dad's house, I was reborn, wishing my father would've died shortly after I'd left so I could've returned home to my mother. He hoarded her all our lives; I was an unwelcome kid in his home.

Refusing to soak in childhood trauma, I curtailed my negativity, instructing my secretary to call my driver. Then I asked, "Has Ms. Stephens called?"

"No, sir. Not yet," Amanda replied. "But Ms. Belvedere phoned. Said if your offer still stands, she'd love to join you at tonight's game."

Took her long enough to respond. I knew she'd call me. I wondered what Zena was like in bed. For certain, she wouldn't become Mrs. Maxamillion until I found out. The sooner she gave in, the better.

"Is my new house near ready for inspection?" I asked Amanda.

"They're on schedule, sir. Three more days. The floor plan for your new home is fabulous. Ms. Stephens is going to love it. My favorites are the rooftop Jacuzzi and swimming pool. I hope you don't mind me asking, but why did you let your fiancée make all those reception plans, then build her an estate, where you plan to surprise her with an all winter-white wedding reception?"

"Because I can afford to."

All was not in vain. The only thing that had changed was my bride. My grand plans had somewhat backfired. But with no contact information, for all I knew, Seven could be gone for good. I didn't want to be alone. I didn't want to live with Danté, and I had been kept from my mother all my life. I would perish if I had to live without a wife.

Amanda smiled, then asked, "Is it true? Are your football and basketball players going to be there?"

"Yes, the players will be there. Is Ms. Belvedere's contract ready?"

"It's on your desk, sir," Amanda said, with a smile.

Perfect. The contract was a test. One, to see if Zena would sign it without reading it first, a sure sign not to hire or marry her. Two, to determine her level of competence.

Closing my office door, I removed my clothes, placed everything, including my underwear, in a laundry bag, then showered. After easing on a gray tailored suit with hairline purple vertical stripes, a hand-stitched lavender shirt, no tie, I stepped into my gray ostrich shoes.

I sat at my desk, reading the final contract. My lawyer had added in a few clauses, like: "Grantor agrees to pay Grantee the sum of one hundred thousand dollars, $100,000, per month." The following clause read, "This is a performance-based contract whereby Maverick Maxamillion Incorporated, the Grantor, reserves the exclusive right to rescind at its discretion, without cause at any time, and the Grantor shall be held harmless under all circumstances, without obligation for restitution of any kind to the Zena Belvedere Agency, the Grantee, if the stipulated outcome, as determined by the Grantor, is not achieved."

I'd taken advantage of most of my female clients by allowing an "out" clause for me while obligating them to perform.

Amanda's face popped up on my office iChat. Mr. Maxamillion, your driver is here. Don't forget your cashier's check for Ms. Belvedere so she can finalize your wedding plans.

Check? More like a surprise gift of fifty grand to Zena basically to plan her own wedding. All the work for the real reception, I'd done.

"Perfect," I said, leaving my office immediately. Passing Amanda's desk, I said, "Have Danté pick up Ms. Belvedere from her home."

I had to scale back on spending time with Danté. I'd devised a plan to keep him busy and out of my space for a while.

"Okay, sir. Enjoy the game," Amanda said, smiling.

Amanda was a sweet girl. Sharp. Efficient. Obedient. Perky. Attractive. Twenty-one, straight out of college. A bit too young according to my personal preference. Girls that young weren't women yet. I wanted only grown folks in my bed.

My driver was waiting for me outside my office. As I slid into the backseat, I noticed that the dark clouds hadn't dissipated. The inclement weather might work to my advantage, forcing Zena to stay the night at my place.

I called Danté.

"Yes, Mr. Maxamillion," he coyly answered.

I chuckled at his tone, then asked, "Where are you?"

"I'm on my way to Ms. Belvedere's."

"Good," I said. "Flirt with her. Make sure to give her your business card with your cell number, and tell her you'd like to take her out.

You know how we do it. You take care of her, and I'll take care of you," I lied.

"Will do," Danté said. "Anything else?" he asked, with enthusiasm and extra bass in his voice.

"Yeah, when you drop her off at the stadium, you're free to go home. She's going home with me," I told him, sure my mixed messages would fuck him up.

"You know what? Fuck you! I helped your ass when—"

I interrupted, "Tell me a thousand fucking times so I don't have to hear it again?"

Danté hung up.

I glanced out the window and saw that we were passing my dad's house. My mother was sitting on the wet porch. What had caused her to be outside after the rain?

I told my driver to back up to the house. After getting out of the car, I stood at the fence. "I love you, Ma."

My mother looked up at me for a moment before standing. She brushed off her blue floral print dress, and came to me. As she hugged me over the three-foot fence, she said, "I love—"

"Get your ass in this house!" my father yelled at her from the porch, holding the screen door open.

I held her tight as she struggled to free herself. "Mama, why?" I cried.

Slam. The screen door closed.

My father disappeared into the house. I knew I had only a few moments before that punk would shoot at me again.

Getting in the car, I instructed my driver, "Let's go."

As he drove through the streets of Chicago's South Side, I wished my tears could bleed my father's DNA from my body.

"Asshole!" I yelled, kicking the passenger seat. "I hate you! I swear that motherfucker gon' make me *kill* his ass."

Chapter 12

Maverick

My ego wanted Zena butt naked on her knees, sucking my dick. My pride wanted a wholesome wife. My heart wanted Seven. My dick wanted to be buried six feet deep in Danté's ass. Complications with all three. Zena I could never love the way I loved Seven. Seven I wouldn't be faithful to the way I could be faithful to Danté. Danté, one word, *unacceptable*. He could never give me the kids I desperately craved.

After parking in front of Soldier Field, my driver opened my door. Staring up at the stadium, I was proud of my accomplishments. Adding kids would be the icing. Now that I was thirty, it was time to start a family. Have a few of my seeds trampling in my new backyard, learning to play football on the field, play tennis on the court, shoot hoops indoors, or hit a few rounds of golf on our private eighteen-hole course.

I said to my driver, "Wait here for me until after the game."

Danté texted. B there shortly . . . She's hot . . . I want to fuck her in her ass.

Wait for my permission, I texted back.

Don't need it.

I replied: Ur right . . . after u drop her off, ur fired.

Love in my life went more than it came. How was I supposed to give Seven what I never had? When I first met her, I rescued her from the college rat race and made her a model. Putting her on the cover of my promotional brochures, on Web site advertisement banners, and on television commercials for my Bentley dealerships should've been an incentive for her to stay sexy. There was something special about Seven that I hadn't expected. She was so unique that I had to make her my wife.

Seven was the first woman to make me fall deeply in love with her. I still couldn't figure out how she'd done that shit. I hated being vulnerable.

Seven didn't give up her body on the first few dates. She wasn't a virgin, but she told me she was tired of casual lovers. She was saving herself for someone worthy. That someone happened to be me. Seven was a challenge.

I called Danté.

"Everything is good," he answered.

Thought so. "One more thing. I'll personally meet Ms. Belvedere when you pull up to my VIP space, and I'll escort her to the owner's suite."

"No problem. You got it, man," Danté said, driving up. A fake smile was plastered across his succulent lips.

I opened Zena's door, then complimented her as she got out of the car. "Excellent choice of attire, Ms. Belvedere."

A tangerine beaded halter exposed the right amount of lickable cleavage, a shawl draped her naked shoulders, wide-legged pants caressed her perfectly round ass, and three-inch open-toe heels made her two inches shorter than me. Zena would fit in flawlessly with the women and wives in the suite. Like Seven, she was not allowed to socialize with the athletes.

As Danté drove away, he texted, Do NOT fuck her. She's mine!

Possession was ten-tenths of my law. "Put this in your purse," I told Zena, handing over the envelope with the check.

A wide smile preceded a lingering stare. "What's this?" she asked.

"Your compensation for the wedding. Finish the details for me, and I'll give you a PR contract." *And this big dick.* "Did you bring Seven's laptop?" I asked, hugging Zena's waist. She didn't pull away.

"Gosh. I left it in the car, with Danté. Remind me to give it to you when he picks me up," Zena said, with a warm smile.

Good. Once again, Danté had done his job well.

As we entered the owner's suite, a smile wide enough to block my view of the entire football field crossed Zena's face. "This view of the fifty-yard line is unbelievable," she said.

"Believe it, like I believe in you," I said, introducing Zena to my other guests. "Seven had an emergency trip. Zena is taking over until Seven gets back," I lied.

The smile disappeared from Zena's face. "Nice meeting you both," she said, walking away.

Approaching Zena, I asked, "What was that about? Is that how you're going to treat my clients?"

"Clients?"

"Yes, they are team owners, too," I scolded, grunting between my teeth.

"Seven is my friend. My best friend," Zena said, teary eyed. "I miss her."

Women were so fucking emotional. I hated that shit.

"I haven't heard from her since she left. Her trip wasn't an emergency. Why did you lie? You forced her to leave, didn't you?" she said loudly.

"Lower your voice," I commanded. "She's my fiancée. I love her, too. That's why I want you to take over. Come. Let's watch the kick-off."

The game couldn't hold my undivided attention, not with Zena's head leaning on my shoulder. I'd put it there to help her relax. She hadn't resisted. With another win on the record, I accompanied Zena to my limo.

"The weather is bad. Stay at my house. My driver will take you home in the morning," I said.

"Your house? Where will I sleep?" Zena asked.

"Wherever you'd like," I told her, hoping she'd make the right decision and the first move.

Chapter 13

Seven

Stress revisited me like an old acquaintance, making my stomach churn, grinding away my appetite for love, food, sex. Worrying about everything, at the same time caring about nothing. The sun rose gradually, dissipating into the ocean. Seven in the morning to seven in the evening, white satin sheets, a white linen comforter, the silkiest down pillows cradled me as though I were an infant in my mother's womb again.

Other than making my way to the kitchen for papaya-ginger juice, an untouched fresh crab pasta salad, which I tasted only with my eyes, and occasionally water, I lounged in my room. "I could stay in this bed, this space, forever and ever." No one at the resort bothered me.

Earlier this morning, I'd checked in online, as required. Jagger instant messaged me around noon. Seven, your spirit is captivating. Can't stop thinking about you. Hope you let me pleasure you again.

I hadn't bothered responding. I was exhausted, and he'd probably sent that note to all the women he'd licked into cosmic paradise. My focus wasn't on Jagger. No text messages or calls from Zena or Maverick. I questioned what was I doing with my life. A part of me desired to have Maverick's baby growing inside me. The other 80 percent knew best not to have a baby out of wedlock.

Did I want to be a stay-at-home mom, homeschooling my kid while keeping another infant or two to help out a couple of single moms?

I'd like that. I wouldn't charge them to give their babies a safe, clean, loving environment ten hours a day, five days a week. Working single moms needed people they could trust with their pride and joy.

Mama used to say, "Seven, if the women take care of the women, the world will be okay. Everybody deserves a break in life. Always give back. Always help yourself first."

Passing time, I sat at the computer, reflecting on what Serenity had said about names having meaning; then I Googled *Maverick*. According to the Wikipedia definition, his name meant "a motherless calf, a non-conformist or rebel." Consulting the dictionary, I found "a person who does not conform to generally accepted standards or customs." Searching Maverick Maxamillion via numerology, I couldn't believe my eyes as I read, "Your number is seven. The characteristics of seven are analysis, understanding, knowledge, awareness, studious, meditating." Nothing about being compassionate, loving, or faithful.

I read about my name. "Your number is nine. The characteristics of the number nine are humanitarian, giving nature, selflessness, obligations, creative expressions."

"Whoa, Serenity was right. I expected to find some generic zodiac type of definition," I said aloud.

Mama had told me, "Anyone who unconsciously names a child without understanding the meaning of the name may one day open Pandora's box. I named you Seven because God rested on the seventh day. The seventh day is holy. There are seven wonders of the world, seven gates to the other world, seven wise men of the ancient world. Not three. Not eight. Seven has special symbolism in universal philosophy and religion. And, baby, if you ever get a seven-year itch, scratch it."

I composed an e-mail to Maverick.

Although our parents are dead, they named us appropriately. I now realize that you hold true to the meaning of your name, as do I. Question. How did we get here? Why did I trust that you'd love me forever? We haven't made it to the altar, and you're already treating me like I don't matter. Maverick, as much as I do love you, I love myself more. I'll have professional movers pick up my car, my clothes. Keep your ring. Keep the wedding and reception dresses. I'm letting go, letting you go. I won't step foot in your home ever again.

Tears plopped onto the keyboard as I clicked on the send button. I felt better and worse at the same time. Didn't want to use my baby for bait, so I didn't mention the possibility of having his child. One day at a time was all I could deal with right now. Babies were lifetime lifestyle changers for the mothers.

Sitting on the toilet, I wondered aloud, "What is Mr. Fletcher going to do to me . . . um, um, um?"

I wiped myself, then stared at the white tissue. Disappointed by my missing period, I cleansed my hands, then went to the computer to send Maverick another e-mail, apologizing for being inconsiderate of his feelings. Maybe I was too conforming. Wanting things a certain way, my way, expecting Maverick to be more like me, less like himself. Surprisingly, he'd replied to my earlier message. Anxiously I read.

Zena said hello. We're headed to Big Sur for a few days. The Place at Esalen. I'm not going to waste my money that you've spent on this wedding. Sure you won't mind Zena wearing your engagement and wedding rings since you just kicked me like a damn dog. I see you've grown balls since you've abandoned me. Where in the hell are you?

The Place at Esalen, where he proposed to me at two in the morning in the outdoor mineral bath overlooking the Pacific Ocean. No one could get in for a treatment or tour without a reservation. He was taking Zena there? Was that why my so-called best friend hadn't tried to contact me?

"Do whoever the fuck you want, you . . . you . . . nonconformist, egotistical, blackguard bastard!" I yelled at the screen.

Slam! I snatched a book, then threw it to the floor. *Slam!* Another. *Slam! Slam! Slam!*

Forget them. "I'm the one in paradise," I said, angrily clicking on the picture of Quin. His calming profile was hypnotic. I took a deep breath, then sat on the edge of the chair in front of the computer. Quin was the first in a set of identical quintuplets, seven feet tall, 245 pounds, broad shoulders, small waist, loves to swim, best underwater lover.

Underwater? Me? Or him? I sent Quin an instant message, hoping he'd preserve my sanity. Would love to go deep under the sea with you anytime tomorrow.

He replied, Lovely, Seven. I'm all yours at noon, provided that you promise to feed me.

Me? Fish? Food? What? A song by Tony! Toni! Toné! popped into my mind, so I IMed back, Whatever you want, singing the lyrics "Girl, you know I will provide whatever you need . . . call . . ."

Grinning, I said, "This place is too frickin' good to be true."

No matter how down I was, my sadness didn't last once I got on this computer. Men I'd never imagined were at my fingertips, at my convenience, willingly. A text appeared on my phone.

Seven, please, I'm worried. Let me know you're okay. Maverick demanded I give him your laptop. I lied and told him I left your laptop in Danté's limo. That way I can act dumb and keep your laptop safe at my home until you get back. He's a super nice guy, Danté. I've got the pussy throbs for his fine ass. Wanna straddle his face. Ride his dick. I bet it's pretty, too. He asked me out, but I don't want to give it up on our first date. I need your advice, girl . . . quick! BTW, I have your car. Drove it to my house last night.

Drove my car to her house? *O-kay.*

I placed my phone on the computer desk, then walked away. Was I supposed to be stupid? Zena was really playing me. She was driving my car, had my laptop and my man, and she was headed to Big Sur with my fiancé. I went back to my phone, texted, Don't you mean your date's name is Maverick? then walked away without pressing the send button.

Backstabbing bitch! When it comes to a big dick, women have zero loyalty.

I stepped into a cold shower, too upset to cry. I had to freshen up.

I scrubbed my body, head to toe. Dripping, freezing inside and out, I tucked the towel underneath my armpits, then fell backward across the bed. Toes numb. Hands tingling. *Better calm down before I suffer a broken and betrayed heart attack.*

My eyes closed. I exhaled, trying to forget that Maverick and Zena were becoming a happy couple. Zena didn't need my advice. She needed my foot in her ass. The chimes softly ringing in my suite were a relief. Fletcher was here.

Holding on to my towel, I went to the door. "Hi," I said seductively, melting into his strong arms for a much-needed caring hug. Right now, I needed someone other than me to care about me.

The sheer black fishnet, collarless shirt and boxers clung to his body. My lips curved downward, not with sadness. The boxers draping his big, juicy dick looked like a bigmouth bass trapped in a fishnet. His thighs, oh my. His ass, unbelievable. His tasty, tempting, protruding nipples found openings in the net. The eye of his dick puckered at me. I wanted to lick him all over. Give his super head mouth to mouth.

"You already bathed?" he asked.

Shaking my head, I said, "Uh-uh. A little refresher shower. Oh, no, I didn't bathe. That's what you're doing for me."

Grinning, he said, "Oh, indeed." He placed his hands on my shoulders, and his fingers magically meandered up my neck. "You seem uptight. I want you to relax. I'll prepare the Jacuzzi," he said, escorting me to my bed. "Lie down."

That I could do. Crawling into my bed face forward, I stretched out, then curled my arms under my pillow. "I'll be right here," I said, sinking into the silkiness against my cheek.

What was it that I loved about Maverick that kept me mentally attached to him? Common sense would've let go of that jerk the second he'd said, "Lose the weight, or the wedding is off." Maybe I just needed time to get him out of my system. Zena wouldn't lie to me, would she? That was my girl, and we knew one another too well. A man had never come between our friendship. Was she really going out with Danté, our limo driver? If I had to choose between marrying Maverick or staying friends with Zena, that would be an easy decision.

Fletcher returned to my bedside, gently nudging me. "Seven, you can relax, baby, if you want. We have lots of time for me to do you. We can cuddle, take a midnight stroll on the beach, or I can give you your space."

"Huh? What?" I said, turning over. My towel escaped from my body. Naked, yawning, I said, "I'm ready."

Holding out his hand, Fletcher said, "I'm ready for you."

Lowering my palm into his, he led me to the Jacuzzi. I stepped into the heat of the water as he held my hand. Fletcher got in with his clothes on, if fishnet was considered clothing.

"We have fresh pomegranate juice and water right here. Which would you like?" Fletcher asked, gesturing toward the chilled carafes.

Day three. No solid foods. I caressed my stomach. There was a noticeable decrease in what Dr. Oz referred to as my omentum. I wasn't happy like Jagger had mentioned. I should be . . . I was getting there.

"You," I wanted to say, but I honestly didn't want another man other than Maverick penetrating me if I was pregnant.

Studying my face, Fletcher asked, "You mind if we talk . . . dirty?"

My lips curled as I shyly stared toward the ceiling for a few seconds. What was happening to me? I was not shy. I took a deep breath, then said, "I couldn't help but notice how incredibly big your dick is," leading the conversation.

Fletcher moved closer, sat facing me, then said, "Can I teach you how to verbally seduce me?"

What was wrong with what I'd said? Defensively, I replied, "Okay, I guess I'm not doing it right."

"Seven, you can't do sex, sex talk, or sexy wrong with a man. But you can do it better. Most dicks are on automatic pilot. An experienced woman knows how to get inside a man's head and take control of his dick. Men want women to take control. I want you to take control of me." Fletcher paused, then asked, "What do you do for a living?"

No way was I professing to be a well-kept woman. That wasn't my truth anymore. "I'm going back to school for my master's in architecture."

Fletcher held my hand under the bubbling water. Slowly, he massaged my fingers.

"Almost finished your master's, huh? Impressive. That means you've completed undergrad. Let's just say you've gotten your master's degree, but you have not designed your first building or home for a major company or client—"

I interrupted, "I've already designed my dream house on the water." I wished I hadn't shown my plans to Maverick.

"Business intellect is great. I bet you'll alter your design by the time you get your master's. My point is, love and sex also require education and on-the-job experience," he said, lightly stroking my palm.

Trying to be cool, I took a deep breath. His nails gently gliding along my palm made my pussy twitch.

He went on. "Foreplay starts well before great orgasms. The best foreplay starts outside of your thinking about my dick or my being obsessed with sticking my dick inside your pussy. That will automatically evolve as we progress, if you'd like. At Punany Paradise, all the men think outside the punany. We want to connect with all of you. We want to please every part of you. And we like teaching and helping you to discover what you like."

Wow. As simple as that seemed, Maverick and I had never spent quality time to spiritually bond. Looking into Fletcher's eyes, I saw crystal clear white surrounding sincere hazel irises. "I love your eyes," I said, trying to get it right this time.

"You don't love body parts. You love people. Seven, your eyes are so beautiful. You send chills through my body when I gaze into your eyes. I feel connected to you."

"And your lips, the fullness, the wetness," I said, kissing my thumb before smoothing it over his mouth. "I want your energy . . . to kiss me."

Lifting my hand from the water, Fletcher kissed my palm. His tongue traced the lines of my wetness, and I swore the nerves were connected to my pussy as she puckered with each stroke.

"May I kiss you, Seven?" Fletcher asked, gracefully circling his tongue over his lips.

I whispered, "Yes," as I closed my eyes.

Gently, he pressed his lips to mine. "Look at me, Seven," he said, and then he kissed the side of my mouth. Then the other side. Trailing kisses down my neck, then behind my ear, Fletcher made his way back to my mouth, this time parting his, nibbling mine. "Your thick, juicy lips taste like nectar," he said, passionately sucking my tongue.

Fletcher guided my hand to his chest. The sensation of the wet fishnet strumming beneath my wrinkled fingertips made me want to rip off his shirt. "Your chest is strong, smooth," I moaned, circling his nipples between the knitted strands. "You're making me wet all over."

"And you've got my dick hard as a hammer," he said, lifting me onto his lap. "I want you to feel me pressed up against you. Feel my energy travel all over your body. Give me your energy, Seven. I want all of you."

My clit brushed against his dick head. Gripping his shoulders, I bore down on him. I couldn't stop cumming. I felt his shaft throbbing. I screamed, "Oh, my God," so loud, I swore everyone in the world, including Zena, heard me.

Fletcher held me close. My cheek firmly rested against his cheek. Fletcher had mentally seduced me to an orgasm without any penetration. Maverick had never done that.

"Seven, you are one special lady. I want to dry you off, then put you in the bed so you can relax. The night is young, and I'm not done making you cum. I am just getting started. I hope I get to share my bigmouth bass dick with you so I can deeply pleasure you and your pretty punany."

"Fletcher?"

"Yes."

"Talk real dirty to me this time."

Chapter 14

Zena

Friends forever.

I missed my girl Seven. Kind of took her friendship for granted. Figured she'd always be in my life. Talked daily, several times a day, about everything, sometimes nothing, holding the phone while watching the presidential debates, *America's Next Top Model,* or *Boston Legal* until she fell asleep on me. The things we'd done together, I hated doing alone. Wasn't sure if she was safe, dead. Worried all the time now. Replayed her voice in my mind. *I'm leaving in the morning.*

Couldn't report her missing. She'd been gone long enough. Seventy-two hours. My concern was I was the last person seen with her. Crazy cops would investigate me first. Didn't need them snooping into my personal and professional life.

"Zena! Who give you this piece of shit?" Deuce asked, storming into my bedroom.

"What?" I asked, staring at the contract. "Oh, that. Maverick Maxamillion wants me to do his PR. I thought you were resting on the sofa."

"He thinks my baby is a fool! Have you read this?" Deuce asked. Veins popped on his forehead and neck.

"I'm not signing it," I said, reaching for the contract.

"You're damn right you're not signing it!" he said, refusing to let go. "I'm going to take this to him personally and make him wipe his ass with it!" Deuce stomped out of my bedroom.

"Deuce, wait," I called out too late. I heard my front door close.

Deuce had stopped by, crashed on the sofa, then left with my contract. I exhaled. I had to get ready for my date.

With the fifty-grand cashier's check Maverick had given me, I could solicit new business. But until then, the check would be in my safety-deposit box at my bank. I laid the check on my desk, removed Seven's fiery red laptop from the bag, powered it on to see if the password she'd shared with me worked. Typed in her user name: Seven Stephens. Entered her password, a combination of alternating letters and numbers: p8n2n9p2r2d4s3.

Log-on successful.

When I clicked on the drop-down box, no links appeared. I double clicked on the Memoirs folder, expecting to find baby pictures of Seven with her parents, high school and college graduation snapshots.

Frowning, I whispered, "Are you serious? Is that Seven? Naked? Having sex with *four* men?"

Zoomed. Zoomed again on the first photo in the gallery. Two men standing on opposite sides of her, titties meshed together, pinching her nipples between their fingertips. One lay underneath her, his dick deep inside my girl. In another photo, a woman with her face buried in Seven's bush, licking her pussy while staring up at the guys. Seven's back was arched, her head tilted, eyes shut, mouth wide open, as she firmly gripped two thick dicks, those of the guys to her left and her right.

Zoomed again to see if my girl was on drugs. Couldn't tell with her eyes closed.

My pussy twitched. Lust consumed me as I wondered what her sex-capade had felt like. The next pic, girl gone. Replacement, a guy. His dick in Seven's pussy.

"I thought the guy on the bottom was in her pus . . . aw, hell no." Maybe the man on the bottom wasn't inside her ass but had his dick stuck between her butt cheeks.

WARNING. LOW BATTERY. POWERING OFF.

"No," I yelled. There were 298 more pictures in the gallery.

Digging in Seven's laptop bag, I grumbled, "Oh, my god." No power cord. Did she always carry a gun?

Wished we had identical computers instead of matching cars. Both parked in my garage. My fingerprints on her steering wheel, her laptop, and her gun. What if she'd . . . *Zena, don't be stupid.*

I placed the gun and her laptop inside her bag on the floor next to my desk, looked at the cashier's check on my desk. Shaking my head, I exhaled, "Whew." Then I got in the shower.

Loyalty didn't have a price. I was glad and pissed she'd left her laptop with me. Had Maverick seen those XXX photos? "Of course not," I said aloud. I had to buy a power cord. Had to see the other pictures. Maybe the gun was a sex prop. I aimed the showerhead directly at my pussy, and my thoughts traveled to sexual nooks and crannies, making me cum.

"Focus, Zena, focus . . . okay, I'm good," I told myself, wiping my eyebrows, swiping my eyelids. Patting my pussy with a towel, I went to my desk, gazed at the check.

The fifty thousand from Maverick was tempting, as was the hundred grand a month, until I'd read that ignoramus's contract. Enough to pay off my mortgages and business loan in two years, but I might work my ass off and end up getting paid nothing. I understood why Deuce was pissed.

Why was it necessary for men to undermine women in business and in bed? Did Maverick honestly think I'd entertain letting him stick his dick in me, like Zena Belvedere could be bought?

Fuck Maverick and his money.

Now Danté, that was who my pussy was so wet for. I fantasized about having him in my bed, his smooth, sexy head between my legs. His dick throbbing in my pussy as he fucked the shit out of me. If I had a hole in my head, I'd let that man stick his dick in it. "Indeed I would." I danced from my bed to my closet, preparing for our date. A short strawberry red designer dress with a scoop in the back would grant him access to my radiant skin—back, arms, thighs, and legs.

Dialing Maverick's number while staring at the shoes in my closet, I clenched my teeth, despising him. *Scumbag.*

"Hey, Zena. For a moment I thought I had bad breath or something. You should've slept in my bed last night, not yours," he said. "You didn't have to leave in the rain."

"Have you heard from Seven?" I asked.

"Nah, have you? You're the one with her car and her computer."

"I wouldn't have asked you if I had. Don't seem like you care much about her or me," I said flatly.

Maverick yelled, "Don't tell me how the fuck I feel about my mother, you got that! Stay the fuck out of this, punk!"

"Excuse me? Are you okay? I didn't say anything about your deceased mother." I was capable of being a bitch when necessary, but not toward the dead.

Maverick is crazy! Oh, God, I hope Seven is all right.

"I meant to say fiancée, not mother. I'll have Danté pick up the computer, the signed contract, and the car. Bitch, you stay the fuck away from me before you get hurt. It's all your fault Seven didn't tell me where she's at. Your ass knows where she is."

Maverick was truly insane. Not my problem. Karma was his bitch. Wait until Deuce showed up at his office. We'd see who was the bitch.

"I told you the computer was left in your limo yesterday. Danté has it." I hated lying on Danté but had no problem lying to Maverick. "I believe Seven said there's a hard copy of your wedding plan somewhere in the library at *your* house."

"Zena Belvedere, do not fuck with me. I will shut your little agency down overnight. Get over here tonight," Maverick demanded.

I played along. "Mind if I stop by tomorrow? I can bring your PR contract with me. Can I suck your dick?"

"Suck my dick? Tomorrow? Sure. Can't wait. See you then," he said, ending the call.

Maverick was about to have his nuts blown off if he kept playing mind games with me. I wouldn't dare let him stick his dick in any part of me. He was either scheming or borderline schizophrenic.

Not me. Not this time. Crazy or sane, no man would use me to justify ending his relationship with my girlfriend. Been there before. Refused to betray another friend. I had to regain access to Seven's laptop. There was something more important on her hard drive than those pictures. More important than her leaving town to lose weight. I felt a chill, then shivered.

I draped three strands of elegant pink pearls around my neck; the longest strand discreetly tapped the area in front of my pussy. The other strands outlined my cleavage. Easing my toes into my leopard slip-on heels with pink trim, I stood before the full-length mirror, admiring myself. It'd been months since I'd invested three hours in preparing for a date. I prayed Danté didn't show up at my house, driving his limo. When I released the clamp from my hair, silky curls flowed over my shoulders.

Puckering my moist lips, I brushed on strawberry and cream glitter gloss seconds before my home phone rang. Eagerly I answered, "Hello."

"It's me," he said in the sexiest voice. "I'm at your gate. Let me in."

Damn. I exhaled, entered my code to open the front gate, then peeped out my window, waiting to see what car would arrive in my circular driveway. "Damn." My hopes went unanswered when I saw that limo.

"Oh, well . . . Wait. Being chauffeured on a date could make for interesting role play."

After returning to my bedroom for a final overview of my attire and to get my handbag, I strolled to the door, my bright smile leading the way. When I opened it, Danté stood there, with a gorgeous bouquet of yellow and pink roses, which widened my smile.

"For a lovely woman, with gratitude and appreciation for allowing me to share your company this evening," Danté said, standing outside my door.

No gesture from him for a hug or kiss. Maybe his driving the limo wasn't so bad. I could sit in the front with him. Close to him. Close enough for him to have one hand on the steering wheel, the other touching me. Regardless, I'd have a great time. It'd been too long since my last date and humanly assisted orgasm. In case we didn't get together again, I'd fuck him tonight. Why not?

"Come in," I said, leaving him the foyer.

I went to my bedroom, arranged the flowers in a tall purple vase, and then we walked outside. A driver got out of the limo, opening the door for us.

I smiled. What would sex in the back of a limo feel like cruising seventy miles per hour on the freeway, with the top open?

"After you," Danté said.

Hopefully, that applied to everything we'd do tonight.

Chapter 15

Zena

Danté looked like the type of man who could fuck me ruff and hard, then nice and slow. He probably didn't want kids, but he'd make beautiful chocolate babies. He was probably like me, married to his job. And it wouldn't surprise me if he had several women in his life, whom he'd fucked right here in his limo, on these black leather seats. Who cared? Not me. I wasn't interested in marrying him. I wanted to suck his dick, then spit out his seeds.

"So," Danté said, "what do you think about me?"

He'd left room for an entire person to sit between us.

"Charming," I said, crossing my legs, stretching them in his direction.

"Charming. That's it?" he asked, smiling.

Matching his smile, I said, "Don't know your middle or last names, address, dating history, the real reason you invited me out, or your mother. Charming is appropriate."

"Middle name, Danté. First name, Demarcus. Last, Davis."

Prejudged that one incorrectly.

"Dating history. Haven't been out with a woman in over six months."

Liar.

"Haven't had sex with a woman in over six months."

Double liar.

"I'm a workaholic." He smiled as he gave me his address. "And I asked you out because you're beautiful, sexy, brilliant, and you're perfect," he said, touching his nose to the back of my hand, then inhaling.

Shaking my head, I placed my hand in my lap, then replied, "You don't know that."

"Haven't been wrong about a woman since my divorce."

Sounded bitter. My pussy didn't want to hear any ex-wife drama. Not tonight. "How long have you worked for Maverick?" I asked, staring into his eyes.

He stared back. "Don't work for Maverick. Work for myself. Own my own company. Been driving Maverick and his clients around for seven years. Before he had real money, I took care of him. Gave him a break. Two-for-one discounts. He's loyal to me. I'm loyal to him. Strictly business," Danté said. "If I knew there was going to be an interview, I would've applied for the job."

The driver parked in front of the House of Blues.

"Why here?" I asked.

"Love the drinks. Like the food. Can't beat the entertainment. We can go somewhere else if you want," he offered.

"This is good," I said, getting out of the limo, thinking about the last time I'd been here with Seven. Missed her terribly.

I drank more champagne than I ate of my Voodoo Shrimp or spinach and strawberry salad. Danté ate more of his Southern Seafood Bake, with shrimp, crab, rice, mushrooms, and red bell peppers, than he drank.

He leaned forward, then whispered across the table, "You're incredibly gorgeous. I want you. I'm asking. Please say yes."

I leaned back against my chair, not wanting to anxiously accept his offer. "To do what?" I asked.

"Nothing. I don't mind doing all the work tonight," he said. "You ready . . . for me?"

I nodded.

A few minutes later, the tab was paid and we were back in the limo headed to . . . I wasn't sure, but I would shortly know.

Cuddling in Danté's arms, I relaxed all the way to . . . my house. Actually, my place was better. I'd be more comfortable with him in my space.

The driver opened the door; I led the way straight to my bedroom.

Danté held my face in his palms, gently looked into my eyes, then said, "Thanks for a great evening. Thank you for letting me into your home. I promise I won't disappoint you."

His muscular hands slid my straps over my shoulders, down my arms, easing my dress and thong over my hips. Scooping me into his arms, he carried me to my bed, then laid me atop my leopard comforter.

"Keep on the shoes and the pearls," he said, parting my legs and placing the pearls in his mouth.

His wet lips grazed my clit. His tongue swiped first over, then under, the pearls, making me wetter, hornier, on the verge of cumming. His tongue slowly slid up my shaft, returning to my clit.

Yes, Lord. My body shivered with pleasure. The snapshot of Seven having sex with four men came into view. For a moment I imagined I was Seven. Every part of my body sizzled. I moaned, "Finger fuck me, Danté."

He did. Stuffing my pearls inside my pussy with every stroke.

As he strummed my G-spot with my pearls, his tongue fluttered along my wet pussy.

"Fuck me, Danté," I said, sliding closer to my headboard, popping the pearls out of my pussy one at a time.

He followed me to the top of my bed. Big dick in hand, swollen head leading the way. He slid his dick in. Which was hotter, his dick or my vagina, I couldn't tell. I didn't care. I gripped the pearls in my fist, along with the comforter. My pussy greedily tried to swallow his throbbing dick. His muscles contracted. My muscles contracted.

"Damn, woman," he said, holding me tight. His body jerked several times. "Come with me, Zena," he moaned.

I hung the pearls around his neck, then exhaled. "Wait." I braced my hand on his hairy chest.

Frowning, he shivered, then whispered, "What's wrong?"

"Nothing," I said. "I want your dick in my mouth. Lie down for me." Had to get his dick out of my pussy. Abstinence, oral sex, and condoms were my contraceptives.

Trading positions, Danté was lying on the bed, with legs spread wide.

My tongue traced the protruding rim of his dick, easing down his shaft to his balls, then up to the ridge right underneath his head. Softly, I wrapped the pearls around his slippery shaft, sucked his head into my mouth, holding my hand tightly around the base of his penis, locking in the blood. I savored his sweet thickness. Letting the pearls fall to his balls, I held his head against the G-spot in the back of my throat, held my breath. My pussy dripped cum with overdue pleasure.

"Umm," I hummed. Felt so good having a dick in my mouth. I loved giving head. Loved having my lips wrapped around his shaft. I paused, closing my eyes. A long, steady flow of air filled my lungs. "Yes." Taking him deeper into my mouth, I sucked, licked, came, sucked, licked, and came some more until I could taste precum oozing out of his dick. Eyeing him, I asked, "You have a condom for this deliciously big, pretty-ass dick of yours?"

He exhaled, "Yeah, in my pocket. Put it on for me, will you, baby?"

Baby. The word danced with my spirit. Wished he were all mine. It would be heavenly to come home to a man, a husband, who didn't want kids. Cuddle with him in front of my wood-burning fireplace. Wake up with him in my bed every morning instead of every once in a while. Hoped this wasn't my last time with Danté. He felt so damn amazing. If Seven wasn't using her wedding gown, if Maverick wasn't marrying Seven, Danté and I could star in our own version of *Madea's Family Reunion* and get married.

Tossing the pearls to the floor, I got up, got the condom, opened the pack. Sucking the tip into my mouth, my lips tight, I gradually rolled the condom over his head, down his shaft, then mounted him.

Curling my fingers, I swear I wanted to scream, "Lord, Jesus!" when I sat on his dick. I eased up, held my hips above his, keeping the head in, trying not to cum right away with his head throbbing against my G-spot.

"You okay?" he asked, placing his hands on my hips.

I nodded. "Better than okay."

"I love your energy, Zena. I can tell you want me as much as I want you. Thank you for sharing your beautiful body with me."

He lifted me off of him, slid from underneath me; we traded places again. This time his tongue circled my areola. Narrowing in on my nipple, he bit hard enough to evoke submissive pain, sucked firm enough to please me, making me cum again.

The next three hours I'd cum, he'd cum, and I'd cum over and over until I surrendered to the uncontrollable orgasms auditioning for matrimony in my vagina.

The last words I recalled hearing before falling asleep at three in the morning were, "Baby, I see why I was intimidated by you. You are a real woman."

The sound of my front door closing awakened me at seven-thirty. The sunlight was in my eyes; the pearls were in my bed. I hurried to the living room, opened my door in time to see Danté's limo cruising toward the security gate. Maybe he had to pick up a client and didn't want to wake me. A kiss on the cheek, lips, or a quickie would've been considerate.

"Oh, well. My pussy feels great," I said, skipping to my bedroom.

Glancing around, I noticed that my dress and thong were on the floor, beside my bed. I picked them up, headed toward the bathroom. Passing my desk, I stopped, took a few steps back, then stared.

Seven's laptop, and the cashier's check, were gone.

Chapter 16

Seven

Blue skies. Teal waters flowing deep inside my soul.
I reclined in a lounge chair, looking out over the ocean. Been sitting here since before sunrise. Watched darkness turn to dawn. Fletcher offered to join me, but I didn't want the company. Quiet time with my mother's spirit would end soon. Boats would drift out to sea. Naked swimmers would dive into the ocean.

The woman with the auburn locks walked nude along the shore, her hair arranged in a ponytail. Smiling, she waved, then shouted, "I want to spend time with you. Let's get together tomorrow."

Her body, less than perfect. Cellulite, a few stretch marks, protruding belly, round butt, thighs rubbing, and plump breasts that begged for a bra. She seemed confident and almost a size smaller than when we'd met. I wasn't sure I could be that bold if I had her body.

I almost nodded back to her. As she kept going, I realized I hadn't checked my mail at the front desk since I'd checked in.

Punany Paradise was much more than a sexual resort. It was a place to sit still, to cleanse my heart. Would anyone miss me when I was gone, the way I missed my mother, my father? What had I done to make me believe anyone should care if I was dead or alive? Would spirits welcome me into the ever after?

Journaling in the book Serenity had given me, I wrote how I wanted my life on earth to culminate:

Seven Stephens never grew old. One day her bright light transitioned into a peaceful space. Greeted by her mother with open arms, a beautiful smile, and a gentle touch, Seven floated on air into the universe the Creator had prepared. She defied gravity, like her body was filled with helium, and the air in her lungs gave way, thrusting out the energy in her body. Survived by two beautiful children—one daughter, one son—two grandchildren, and a host of people she'd helped along her journey through life. Seven Stephens lived. She never died. Seven Stephens's legacy dwells in the hearts of her survivors, truly a reason to smile, celebrate, and rejoice in her goodness forever.

A teardrop splattered on the page right before a familiar voice whispered, "Hey, you."

Looking over my shoulder, I saw Jagger. I smiled up at him. "Hey back at you."

"Mind if I join you?" he asked. Feet planted in the sand, he hadn't moved.

"I'd like that," I said, happy he'd asked.

The huge orange ball of energy had made its way into the blue cloudless sky, absorbing warmth from the ocean and reminding me of my date with Quin. Contrary to what most people believed, the heat from the sun dispersed into the ocean upon sunset, warming the midnight waters. Best not to break my date with Quin to spend time with Jagger. A lump lodged in my throat. I swallowed, placing my sarong over my stomach when Jagger reclined in the lounge chair next to me.

Gazing at my waist, then out to sea, he asked, "What are you journaling about? Wanna talk?"

I swallowed again, then asked, "You ever wonder, what's the purpose of life? Why some people are happier than others? Why babies cry when they come into the world? Why loved ones break our hearts?" The lump in my throat choked my vocal chords, trapping my next words in my head.

Jagger interlocked his fingers with mine. "Yes. Just like you, I do wonder about many, many things."

Blinking away tears, I asked, "Like what?"

Jagger softly said, "Like, if we're created equal, why don't we treat one another as such? Man feels superior to woman. White man believes the color of his skin makes him superior to all races, yet his spirit is often vexed, perplexed, and plagued with ill intentions. Americans remain arrogant, even though their country is going bankrupt and China is quietly taking over. Russia is making a move for dominance over Georgia. Nuclear weapons are being designed to wipe out millions of men, women, and children. Man won't be satisfied until he self-destructs. Yeah, I do wonder, Seven. Mostly, lately, I wonder about you. Are you happy?"

Wasn't expecting that last part. Quietly, I exhaled, squeezing Jagger's hand. "Not right now. But soon," I answered.

Jagger smiled, pulled away my sarong, picked me up, carried me to the ocean, then tossed me into an approaching wave.

Scrambling in shock, I stood. Before I opened my mouth, a wave crashed against my back. The current pulled me under. I struggled to stand again. Got swept under again. This time I was dragged out a little farther. Panicking, I reached for Jagger. He didn't know that I didn't know how to swim.

Walking backward, Jagger watched me battle the waves slamming into me. As I gulped salt water, my obituary scrolled in my mind. I hadn't given birth to my two children. Hadn't seen the birth of my grandbabies. This was not my time to go. Digging my feet in the sand, I fought the next three waves with all my strength, with every step, until I reached shore.

Gasping, I wanted to yell, "Motherfucker, are you crazy?" but I could hardly breathe.

Jagger lifted me to my feet, then said, "Without consciousness, you are drowning your spirit. I threw you in to show you how it feels to fight for life. You're a fighter. Get over him, Seven. Your spirit is fighting for freedom. If you let him drown your spirit, you have no life." Jagger kissed my lips, then said, "I love you, Seven. I care about you. Let *me* be your life support."

Slap! My hand landed across his face. "Don't you ever throw me in the ocean again," I cried. "I can't swim."

Jagger held his open palms toward me. "No problem. Won't touch you again," he said, walking away.

I hated how practical he was. Too bad love wasn't logical. His for me or mine for Maverick. Perhaps I should let go of Maverick and learn to love Jagger.

Salty wetness saturated my body. I felt an extra gush of wetness ooze between my thighs. I smiled. Tied my sarong around my waist, not sure if I was happy or disappointed that my period had finally arrived.

Chapter 17

Maverick

Danté never let me down. When we first met, I was a young man with a vision, with determination to become successful. Danté helped me out. My four years in college, I owned two expensive suits, which I'd bought with part of my student loan funds, along with six shirts, nine ties, and three pairs of dress shoes. I'd coordinated at least fifteen different looks out of that wardrobe. I was always neat, clean, and professional, and clients, professors, and students respected me. No one, except Danté, had given me anything.

Quietly, I sat at the bar in my entertainment room with Danté, admiring him. Danté was a real man. A selfless man. Not many men would generously help another man to make it in this world. My own father would kill himself before teaching me how to be a man. There were some things in life I could never repay my best friends, Chad and Danté, for. Chad hadn't given me what Danté had. Chad had faith in me when I didn't have faith in myself.

Having Danté pick up my clients, chauffeur them to and from meetings that I arranged at country clubs, restaurants, and hotel lobbies when I had no office, had allowed me to minimize my business expenditures on the front end. Back then I'd skip a meal a day in order to pay the barber to cut my hair frequently, style my beard, and to get regular manicures and pedicures.

I asked Danté, "Man, how did you manage to get Seven's laptop out of Zena's house without her eagle eyes noticing?"

"I have my ways. It wasn't complicated," he said, pouring two glasses of Scotch, handing me one. "A toast to one less bitch in our lives."

Standing in front of him, clinking my crystal glass against his, I stared into his eyes and said, "I hope your way didn't include fucking my Zena." Then I picked up the bottle of Scotch. "Let's wait in the living room. Chad will be here shortly."

We sat on the sofa, where Seven and I had had our last conversation. I missed her.

"Zena was easy," Danté said, smiling. "Real easy. She was so wide open, I could've had her any which way I wanted. Front, back, down her throat, in her ass, any which way."

He was too fucking assured. What had happened between them? "Could have? Did you or didn't you fuck her?"

Casually, Danté said, "Chill out. Not like she's your woman. You're not going to marry her or Seven, so stop trippin'."

"No, you're right. I might not marry Seven, and Zena isn't my woman . . . but you, I love you from my heart," I said, downing my glass of Scotch.

He shook his head, gulped his drink, then said, "Ditto. But I must admit I like pussy as much as you do, maybe more. I've held off for six long-ass months, while you've had the luxury of a fiancée, who, might I remind you, you're building a damn house for, when I'm the one who deserves that house."

Not this shit again. I loved and hated making Danté mad. The veins in his forehead protruded. That usually meant the veins in his dick were protruding, too. "I told you, you can have this house after I move out."

"I don't want this damn house. This is the house that you fucked me in longer than you've known Seven. Let her move in here permanently, and we can share the new house now that it's finished." Danté poured himself another drink, then said, "I'm not asking, Maverick. I've earned the right to be your husband."

Husband? Indeed, he could be my husband if I weren't worried about repercussions from my clients, losing business, or being castrated by the media. His threats had grown old.

The character he'd possessed—loyalty, friendship, dedication, discretion, and trustworthiness—when we first met was now tarnished by his love for me. Why did we have to fall in love? I wanted to marry Seven to remain acceptable to society. I wanted to marry Danté because if I had to choose who I'd spend the rest of my life with knowing that the world would embrace us, I'd undoubtedly choose my man.

Danté removed his shirt, tossed it on the back of the sofa, and moved a little closer to me. His knee touched mine as he said, "Ain't shit gon' be right in your life until you deal with your old man. We're going over there again today. We need to curse him out, beat his ass, and move your mother into our new house. She can live with us. I hate seeing you suffer like this."

That was the kind of shit that had made me fall in love with him. "Miserable as she is, my mom don't know any other way to live. He's got her fucked up in the head."

"Yeah, like you're trying to do with Seven, but that shit backfired on your ass. You honestly believe she's going to have your baby and mine? Like your recommending in vitro fertilization to her is going to work? They can't combine your sperm with mine. That's insane. Your problem is you don't think shit all the way through."

I saw Danté's nipples harden, making my dick harden. His eyes traveled down my abs to my crotch.

"Yeah, that's why I fucking pay you. You don't pay me," I retorted. He need not get shit twisted.

Danté countered, "Don't forget who helped your ass get what you've got. I'ma get mine from you, you best believe that, *before* Seven gets hers."

I'd heard enough of his truth. "Shut up and suck my dick," I said, unzipping my pants.

Danté slid a few inches on the apricot sofa, then pressed his lips to mine. Mustache to mustache, our mouths parted. First, I sucked his tongue, and then he sucked mine. His mouth covered my nipple, the second most sensitive part of my body. My dick agreed as precum rose to the top, spilling over my head.

Once I started fucking Seven doggie style, the only time my nipples got attention was when Danté and I made love.

He kissed my neck, held me close.

I found comfort in being with him. We took care of one another. I could be myself with him. He was easy to talk to. Outside of my home, we never displayed our intimate relationship. Inside my home, we never discussed business.

What in the hell was I doing with Seven? Leading her on by building a house that I prayed would keep my love affair with Danté a secret. I feared that if my father discovered I was bisexual, it would validate his hatred toward me.

Seven had to have my baby, our babies. One for Danté, one for me. Then I could divorce her, and Danté and I could raise our kids without a woman. But divorcing Seven would mean exposing my relationship with Danté. Not marrying Seven would mean I'd have to find another wife. Zena was too angry to be an option. Or was she? If she'd fucked Danté, and if she didn't mind fucking me, maybe we could barter her into our lives.

I stood, then walked to the bedroom. My lover, my love, followed me. By the time we made it to the bed, we were completely naked. I lay across the bed; his body covered mine. He took my dick into his mouth while I sucked his beautiful erection into mine.

Sixty-nine was our favorite position because we both loved oral sex.

Mouth wet, jaw strong, he sucked me so fucking good, I felt the cum inside of me stirring inside my balls, creeping up the wall of my shaft, yearning to explode inside his mouth.

His strong hands cupped my ass, squeezing my butt. That shit felt fucking fantastic. His head bobbed like my dick was a sweet candied apple lollicock on a stick.

Fuck! Normally, I could hold out for at least an hour if I focused on not cumming. Not this time. My toes started to curl. Legs, ass, and back tightened. My spine curved.

With determination, Danté took more of my dick—his dick—into his mouth. Deep, long, strong strokes.

Fuck! I forced his dick deeper inside my mouth. Grunted. Thrust down on him, nestling his head in the roof of my mouth, like a baby sucking its thumb. That was how I felt. Vulnerable. A long stream of cum left my body, taking my love and energy for Seven along a trail that led to Danté.

"Turn over," he insisted.

I was now joyfully in the submissive position I'd used to fuck Seven from behind.

I felt him releasing my cum from his mouth onto my asshole; then bright lights flashed as his dick entered me raw. Neither one of us liked using condoms. Most of the time we did when fucking women. I trusted Seven wouldn't cheat on me. She was my fiancée; we didn't need condoms. That would change when she got back, until she got tested again.

More women had HIV and AIDS than men. In reality, that meant more men were probably contracting the disease from women rather than the other way around, especially if they were diving face-first into a female's pussy when she was on a light day of her menstrual. Only a fool would suck a woman's fluids like a vampire, granting her possibly contaminated blood direct access to his body.

I loved Danté inside my ass raw. I wanted him to make me forget about Seven, forget about my father. She was probably giving my pussy to some man who didn't give a fuck about her.

Thrusting his shaft deep inside of me, Danté shivered. He thrust, then shivered, alternating his motions until his climax subsided.

Opening my eyes, I saw the bright light again. Looking over my shoulder at him, I saw Zena watching us both.

"You bitch!" I yelled, scrambling from underneath Danté. We both raced after Zena's ass. I yelled, "Bitch, give me that fucking camera."

Zena raced downstairs, then out of my house. Both of us desperate to catch her, we chased her as far as the hallway, then stopped, staring out the window. That bitch hopped into a red Lexus—I knew it was Seven's from the license plate—and sped away.

"This shit is all your fucking fault," I told Danté. "You fucked that bitch, didn't you?"

"No, you fucked her when you told me to take the computer and her check. That's the fucking reason she showed up here. I bet you'll lock your damn doors from now on, mister. I live in an elite neighborhood," he countered.

"My door was locked," I said, walking away from the window.

I picked up the phone and called the doorman.

"Yes, Mr. Maxamillion. How may I help you?"

"Did you let Zena Belvedere up?" I asked.

"Yes, sir. She's on your all-access list. Ms. Stephens added her over a year ago," replied the doorman.

I hung up. "That bitch."

"You're the bitch," Danté countered.

We stood in the foyer, yelling at one another, until I saw Chad parking at a meter across the street.

Racing upstairs, we headed for separate showers. I deodorized my room, picked up our clothes, tossed them into the library, and closed the door. Quickly, I opened the door and looked at the desk in my library. My fucking computer was gone.

Not Seven's computer. Seven's laptop and charger were in her laptop bag in my living room, waiting for Chad. Zena had taken *my* fucking computer. The information on my computer, in the wrong hands, could sentence me to consecutive life terms in a federal prison. Now Zena was truly out of her league. I had no choice but to hire someone to kill her before the media and Danté discovered my other life.

Chapter 18

Zena

Terrified of going home, I went into hiding for three weeks. Posted up at a small hotel in Peoria, Illinois, on Conference Center Drive. One phone call to my receptionist, Donna, when I'd gotten here to inform her I had an emergency, wasn't sure when I'd be back, and to tell her to take off until further notice. I told her I'd continue her pay; her job was secure.

A few unanswered calls to Danté and I decided it was best not to call his gay behind again. No texts or e-mails to or from Seven. No leaving the hotel for food, although the Granite City Brewery was within walking distance, as was Steak 'n Shake. Wasn't going out for clean underwear, yet I saw a Wal-Mart three blocks away. Made a deal with an employee named Hannibal to deliver everything I needed to my room. He was friendly and extremely accommodating.

If I'd found Seven's laptop at Maverick's house, I could've entertained myself instead of being bored. I did, however, manage to get away with Maverick's laptop, and as soon as I bought a charger for it, I'd find out his secrets.

All was quiet, including my cell phone, which had died two days into my stay. Car charger wouldn't do me any good because I refused to leave my room, drive around, or sit in the car, waiting for a charge that wouldn't last long. Could look out the window and see Seven's

Lexus downstairs. Enough of holding myself hostage. It had come time for me to leave the hotel. I wasn't going to die here.

I put on my hand-washed panties that had hung over the tub, drying, overnight. I removed the plastic laundry covering from my clothes, got dressed. Opening the hotel door, I peeped my head out. After looking left, right, left, right, I exited the room and quietly closed the door behind me. The hallway was empty. Elevator empty too. That might have been the norm, but it felt eerie as hell, like someone was right behind me, breathing on the back of my neck. Constantly glancing over my shoulders, I saw no one was there, except my conscience. Not guilty. Cautious.

Exiting the elevator, approaching the lobby, I quickly checked out. Running through the parking lot, I got in my car, hcadcd north on Interstate 55, with my cell phone recharging. No text. No voice mails. Nothing from Seven, Donna, Danté, or Maverick, that lying bastard. He probably had had no intention of contracting with me. I prayed Deuce had beat Maverick's ass by now.

There was light traffic through Bloomington all the way until I hit heavy traffic on the Dan Ryan Expressway, then merged onto Interstate 90/94, exiting at 50B, onto Ohio Street.

Catching Maverick and Danté fucking wasn't at all what I'd expected. Not in a gazillion years! That was why Danté's ass hadn't answered my calls. He'd set me up for Maverick. That, and he was busy having link sausage for breakfast. Maverick and Danté sexing one another hard like a woman and a man—that messed me up, made me consider becoming a lesbian. I phoned my doctor's office, made an appointment to go in for a blood test to make sure I hadn't contracted any diseases.

"Yes, indeed," I said, driving on autopilot straight to the pleasure store on North Halsted in case I didn't leave home until Seven returned. She had about two weeks left at that weight-loss camp. Storming through the doors, I passed the handbaskets and grabbed a shopping cart. Rolling down the aisles, I tossed in a silicone vibrator, a rabbit vibrator, a waterproof vibrator, a classic vibrator, a butt plug, a glass dildo, a magic wand, a beehive vibrator, a clit exciter, the pure gold clit stimulator, a few gold bullets, a double dildo, and a hundred

condoms for my take-home dicks. I was done with these undetecta-
bles.

Three thousand eight hundred dollars later, I was in transit to my
doctor's office for an HIV test. Entering my doctor's office, I requested
an oral swab and a blood test. Gave my oral sample. Waiting for the
results, I sat impatiently, my heart pounding against my chest while
they drew blood.

A half hour later, I heard, "Ms. Belvedere."

I stood and followed my doctor into a private room. Before I sat in
the chair, she said, "Your oral is nonreactive. You're probably fine.
We'll call you in a day or so, when we get the results of your blood test
from the lab."

I left without speaking a word to her. I drove home in silence. No
music. No talking on the phone. Who could I tell that would understand? Deuce would definitely not feel me on this. He'd probably divorce me early, not caring about his U.S. citizenship.

This was a fucked-up situation. "Thank God we used a condom," I
mumbled, parking Seven's car in my driveway. Tossing the toys on the
floor in the doorway, I ran to my bathroom off the foyer, knelt over
the toilet, and vomited.

"Ugh, yuck!" I jammed my finger in my throat, damn near regurgi-
tating the lining of my stomach. If I could, I'd puke out my womb.

"I can't," I panted, "believe I sucked his dick." Danté did not look
or sound or act gay.

He had no gay tendencies. Zero. Nothing about him was feminine.
After wiping my mouth with the guest bathroom towel, I went into my
bedroom and picked up the pearls he'd put inside my pussy. Breaking
each strand, I snatched them apart until they scattered over the floor,
bouncing, then rolling, like marbles.

"Lying motherfucker! Why me? Why did that son of a bitch have to
choose me?" I cried.

I splashed cold water on my face, showered, brushed my teeth,
then slipped on a pink hooded jogging suit, along with my white and
pink tennis shoes. I had to warn Seven.

I texted her, YOU NEED TO CALL ME RIGHT NOW GF.

I got back into her car, drove to a computer store, purchased a charger for Maverick's laptop, then drove to an intimate boutique inn on Ohio Street. I set up the laptop on a table in the back of the bar area, plugged it in. Sat where I could see everyone coming my way.

I signaled to the bartender, ordered a glass of merlot. "I'd like the fried calamari as well, please," I told him.

There were a few patrons; the bar was almost quiet, like a library. Sipping my wine, I sat with my back against the wall so no one could accidentally see the pictures I'd taken of Maverick and Danté. Seven's X-rated photos were innocent in comparison to what I'd captured. How much money would the media pay for this scandalous love affair?

Danté's dick was all the way in Maverick's ass in one picture. Halfway out in the next, with no condom. I wanted to slam my camera on the floor, but instead I sat there captivated, grinding my teeth, heaving with each frame.

"As soon as I download these pictures, I'm e-mailing them to Seven," I whispered, dropping the camera in my purse.

When I opened the laptop, the sleep mode awakened.

RECOVER or START NEW options appeared.

"Recover, of course," I said, clicking the button.

The words *Maverick Maxamillion Incorporated* popped up on the heading of a document.

Dear Mom,

Every day I read this letter. Again, I cannot send it to you. Again, I cannot stop by to see you. But each day I get a little closer. When I drive by your house, I stop because I want to hug you again. Kiss you. I so desperately need to hear you tell me, "I love you, baby."

I wish Dad were dead. I know that's wrong. Probably why I can't mail you this letter. I'm positive that he doesn't let you access the Internet. One day, hopefully sooner than later, I'll see your face. That's if one of Dad's bullets doesn't kill me first.

I'm marrying the woman of my dreams. Problem is, there is also a man that I love very much. The closer I get to making a commitment, the less I want to decide. I sent her away so I could work things out with him. I'm building her a beautiful twenty-nine-thousand-square-foot home, which he wants us to live in. I'm all fucked up in the head. Dad's fault. But if I could talk to you before I get married, I know you'd tell me what's right before I . . . before I . . . I love you, Mom.

Inserting my memory stick in the USB drive, I saved a copy of the letter to send to Seven. Maverick's ass had lied about everything, including his parents being dead. I double-clicked on a file that was minimized on his toolbar. I covered my mouth, then whispered, "Oh my god."

There was an official-looking contract for hire to assassinate . . . Demarcus Danté Davis and Frank Maxamillion on the same day, on Seven's wedding day. I froze, holding my breath, wanting to throw up my calamari and red wine. Exhaling, I felt my body tighten. This was more than I'd bargained for. I texted Seven: YOU NEED TO CALL ME RIGHT FUCKING NOW!

Saving the document to my memory stick, I quietly closed the laptop. Leaving it on, I packed the laptop in my oversize purse, then tiptoed out of the bar. Looking to my left, right, left, right on Ohio Street, I realized that Seven's Lexus was gone.

Chapter 19

Seven

Love at first sight. Possible? Impossible?

I was getting Maverick's money's worth out of my vacation. Forget Zena and all of her lying text messages. I was not contacting her.

What was Jagger's motive? First, he said he never fell in love with any of the women; then he couldn't stop professing his love for me. Men. I wanted to believe Jagger but I'd learned I had to fuck them over before they royally screwed me. My heart was hardening. Toward Maverick and Zena. My pussy was balling out of control. I had reverted back to my old days of taking charge. Seventeen days left and I had a different guy lined up for every night, except tonight. Finally, the woman with the auburn locks was coming to my suite in two hours.

I checked my e-mail. Shocked when I saw I had an e-mail from Maverick. Subject: I Apologize, I'm Wrong, I LOVE You Just The Way You Are.

I felt tears bubbling up, so I cautioned myself, "Don't you dare fall for his pitiful attempt to get you back." I clicked on the message.

Dear Seven,
      Please forgive me. I need you. I have to marry you. I'll do any-thing to prove my love to you. I never did anything with Zena. I was trying to make you jealous because you were the one who left me without telling me where you were. I don't care anymore. I just want you to come home as soon as you get this message.

I clicked on REPLY, then typed, You don't deserve me. I deserve better than you. Every woman deserves better than you. I inserted one of the nude photos Jagger had taken of me—breasts firm, stomach flat, thighs tight, and ass just right, with a perfect hook. Perfect size seven. What a difference a month of happiness had made in my life. I wasn't happy every moment of each day, but I was definitely happy more than I was sad.

Sent him another picture of my punany, with the caption, "Your lips will never taste my sweet pussy again," clicked SEND, then walked away from the computer, like he'd walked out on me.

The last two years being with Maverick, I'd forgotten how liberated I felt being in control. I had my mother to thank. She'd spoken to me every day at Punany Paradise. I'd learned to sit still each morning, allowing her presence to feed my soul with unconditional love.

I poured a glass of pineapple-ginger juice, filled my Jacuzzi with warm water, stepped into paradise, and relaxed.

"I could stay here forever," I whispered. Not physically. Mentally.

Closing my eyes, I recalled my dive with Quin. Reluctant to scuba dive, I'd confessed to Quin I didn't know how to swim.

"No problem, Seven. I'm the best. I'll teach you how to swim like a fish," he'd said.

Three days later, our boat had sailed to a private cove. While I'd floated on my back, Quin had eaten my pussy in the shadows of the cove. Each of my orgasmic screams had echoed. As he'd dog-paddled behind me, his dick had entered me and his hands had teased my nipples, and we'd drifted together.

"Lean back," he'd instructed, floating under me. "I got you, Seven," he'd said, stroking my pussy to the rhythm of our buoyancy. At that precise moment, my only wish had been that every woman would experience Punany Paradise at least once in her lifetime.

I spread my legs in front of a jet stream in the Jacuzzi, kept my eyes closed, swayed my beautiful hips until I came. I stepped out, energized. After toweling off, I lathered my body with Almond Cookie Shea Soufflé.

Checked the computer to see if Maverick had responded. He had.

Seven, that's my pussy. He'd inserted a few pics of his own. Of a home, one based on the drawings that I'd created. My heart softened.

"Was that why he'd asked me to leave? He was trying to surprise me," I said aloud.

A tear fell. I couldn't reply in a weak moment. Best to wait until my head cleared.

My date, dates, for the evening arrived in time to save me from emotionally falling. Opening the door naked, I said, "Come in."

I made my way to my closet, wrapped my body in a peach sarong, and said, "I'm ready."

I'd insisted that Jagger join us. Wanted to see him interact with another woman. Sense if his energy was the same as with me or different with her. We strolled the beach, Jagger in the middle.

"I don't want to exchange names. Just want to bond, enjoy some female energy, get fucked real good, and go back to my suite. That's cool?" asked the woman with the auburn locks.

I replied, "Perfect," before Jagger responded, "I'm here to please you both."

Jagger squeezed my hand. Had me trying to figure out if he'd done the same with hers. *Whatever.* I was having a good time regardless.

"Got an idea. You ladies game?" Jagger asked.

"Of course," I said as she replied, "Certainly."

He led us to the yachts, helped us aboard one; then we sailed out to sea.

As we floated under the moonlight, Jagger turned off the engine, reminding me of when Maverick and I used to go out on his yacht on Lake Michigan. Shaking my head, I fought to erase Maverick from my mind, my heart.

Jagger kissed me, then whispered in my ear, "Seven, let him go. Now."

Turning me to face her, the woman with the locks untied my sarong, cupped my breasts, kissed me softly, then whispered, "Women are better than men."

Her lips trailed behind my ear. She stood behind me, held my hair over my shoulder, then French-kissed my neck, her tongue dancing on the nape. Gently. Seductively. Making me cum in a way I hadn't realize I could. My body shivered as Jagger enclosed my areola with his wet mouth. Tongues dancing on my flesh in the night. Sea breeze whistling against my clit. Stars. Not the ones above. The ones circling in front of my eyes.

She moved to the front, again taking control of both of us. "Stand behind her," she told Jagger.

He did as he was told.

"Spread your legs," she said to me.

I did as I was told.

She took his dick into her hands, dipped his head in and out of my pussy as she laid soft kisses on my clit.

Looking up at me, she said, "Men are human dildos, you know. That's the way a real woman sees him, them. There's nothing a man can give you that a woman can't give you better. We're softer, sexier, smarter." She planted those pussy-dripping kisses on my clit again as she dipped Jagger's dick inside me.

He held my breasts, teasing my nipples as if in disagreement with the woman licking my pussy.

Taking it all in—Jagger's dick was now in my ass, and her licks were now on my shaft—I came hard. Legs trembling, I stepped away from them, then dove into the ocean.

I'd swim my way back to sea or die trying to understand what life was about. Love at first sight? Blind faith? Jagger was winning my heart, but that woman made me feel things I'd never felt before in my life.

Chapter 20

Maverick

Had a lot of shit on my mind this morning. Dick protested Danté's touch trailing down my spine to my ass. My back inches from his chest. His kisses on the nape of my neck made my face squint, lips scrunch up. Inside of me, my anger was suppressed, threatening to break through. Agitated, annoyed, I pulled away from him. I could've punched him in his face, repeatedly. Hatred—for Danté, Seven, Zena, my dad, all except my mom—boiled in my veins.

"You've got to get out of my house. Can't take us spending time together every night. You've got to go," I told Danté firmly, unwrapping his hand from my limp dick. His heated breath burst against the back of my neck, circling my throat. I couldn't face him.

I got out of bed. Dressed. Loose-fitting jeans, no belt, snug black wife-beater, outlining my chest, highlighting my biceps, shoulders. I'd lost a few pounds since Seven had left. Missed her cooking. Seeing her pictures, I realized she was finer than when we'd met.

Fuck!

Left him in the bedroom, in the bed, buried under my black satin sheets. Went to the third floor, closed the door. I sat alone in my library, scrolling through the e-mails in my PDA. Used to rely on my computer for access to my e-mails. The computer could be replaced. My hard drive couldn't. Too-sensitive data. No backup data anywhere.

My jaded past was in a woman's hands. A woman who didn't give a damn about my future could send me to jail or straight to hell, destroy me. Had to depend on Zena not doing something stupid, like sending those fucking pictures to my clients or releasing my contracts to the police. Could lie and say she created the documents to frame me for not marrying her. Tried resetting my password. Each time, she still had access, sending me empty e-mails from my own address. Bitch was in control. Wouldn't log out of my account from my laptop.

I called her from the cordless in my office.

"Yes, Maverick. What is it now?" she answered, sounding annoyed.

"Zena, you need to give me back my laptop. You're fucking with my business. My livelihood. And make sure that punk who calls himself your man, Deuce Callahan, stays away from my place of business. I'm willing to give you back the fifty-thousand-dollar cashier's check in exchange for my computer."

"You can't buy me. Shouldn't you be sucking on a bone? You two liars deserve one another. My only question is, which one of you is the man?"

Biting my bottom lip, I exhaled, pounding my fist on the glass-top desk. "I'm trying to be nice—"

"You can have your laptop back when Seven gets back."

"Bitch! I'm tired of fucking playing games with you! You've got forty-eight hours, or your ass is dead! You hear me!"

Bam! My fist hit the desktop again. The phone base fell to the floor. I left it there.

"You're a reckless man, Maverick Maxamillion. Why don't you focus on one thing at a time? Follow through with your hit on your lover, Danté, 'cause I want his ass dead, too, and then I'll tell you what to do next. And just so you know, you don't want to fuck with Deuce. He's a real man."

Bam! Bam!

"Fuck! See what you made me do! Fucking around with you, I've cut my hand," I shouted. *Click.* I froze. Bitch hung the fuck up on me?

Click?

Aw, shit, a second click. Closing my eyes for a moment, I hung up. "Bitches," I whispered, staring out the window. Forty-two degrees. Lake Michigan was chilly. Morning dew clung to each pane, partially hindering my view. Wish I were on my yacht, standing with Zena near the edge. I'd pick her up, toss her ass overboard into the lake, then speed over her body.

I saw Chad's car turning the bend onto Lake Shore Drive.

Zena had me, had Danté by the balls, too, could ruin us both with a . . . click.

Getting my fucking laptop from Zena was my number one objective. Finding out exactly where Seven was, was urgent. Confronting my father today was necessary. Making sure Danté left my house when I did was mandatory. He'd gotten too comfortable. Hadn't left my house without me since Zena caught us making love. His trying to come out of the closet and replace Seven wasn't happening. Pressuring me to take him to the games. No damn way. I wasn't gay. He was.

"Wanna talk?"

"Shit! Don't creep up on me like that, man," I said, my heart thumping. I hadn't heard my library door open.

Chad parked in the driveway, in front of my garage. He'd arrived in time to save me from myself. Save me from Danté's narrowed eyelids, oozing hatred. Since Zena had crept in on me, I had to grant Chad and all visitors entry. Good neighbors were fine. Trespassers would get shot. Should've shot Zena while she was in my house.

Danté stood behind me. His hands were jammed in his robe pockets, close to his thighs. I saw the imprints of his knuckles.

"You've gotta go back in the bedroom and stay there until Chad leaves," I insisted, attempting to pass him. I didn't want to find out how much he'd heard of my conversation with Zena.

He blocked the doorway. Watching him ease his hands out of his pockets, I held my breath.

Our eyes met. We exchanged energy. Love. Hate. Love. Regrets. Fear.

Danté opened his mouth, embraced me. His tongue parted my lips, invaded my mouth. Passionately, he sucked my tongue as though my dick was in his mouth, then said, "Yeah, you should be scared."

He turned. Slowly walked into my bedroom, closed the door.

So, he'd overheard my conversation. I'd handle him later. I trotted downstairs to my first floor and opened the door for Chad. "Hey, man. Good to see you." I meant that shit.

"Same here. Got what you want. Maybe," he said, hiking his shoulders toward his ears.

"Let's go upstairs to the formal dining room," I said, leading the way to the second floor. I had to be in ear range of Danté's footsteps.

"You'd better sit for this one, man," Chad said, sitting at the table. He powered up Seven's laptop. "You sure you want to know where she is?"

"Got to," I said, sitting next to him. "Before we get started, tell me, how do you bypass passwords to access systems?"

I had to get into Zena's personal files. See if I could incriminate her. Get into her business files as well. Wipe out her bank accounts, all of them. Crash her system. Let her know I could destroy her ass, too.

Chad shook his head. "That info in the wrong hands is dangerous. Let's just say I know how to reset passwords on practically every account that has one."

Chad and I had an interesting relationship. We were friends. Hadn't hung together much in college. I'd been hustling my way to success. He'd taken school way too seriously, studying, cramming for the bar exam, dating one girl since high school, whom he married after he'd passed the bar. I'd given him four tickets to the football game. He'd brought his wife and another couple, like they were on a double date. No more tickets for his henpecked ass. Our worlds, different. Friendship, unchanged. I'd do anything for Chad, if he asked.

He went on. "I tap into other people's accounts to give my clients an edge over the opposing counsel's clients in the courtroom."

I was more concerned with getting those pictures and my laptop back. Zena was too dangerous, potentially lethal. I'd hoped that when I got Seven's car back, my computer would be inside. Not. But Seven's car was locked in the garage to stay. Eventually, Seven would have to come and claim her property.

Danté and I had tailed Zena to the boutique inn on Ohio Street. Like most women, she'd been oblivious to the fact that we'd followed her from her home. Danté was too aloof about the pictures Zena had taken. Hadn't mentioned them. Was he hoping she'd ruin me? Had they partnered to set me up? I couldn't trust anyone.

"This is where your fiancée is," Chad said.

"What the . . ." My bottom jaw dropped. Blood was instantly diverted to my groin. Almost naked men on the home page. Gorgeous bodies. I bit my bottom lip. Jealous. I wanted in.

Chad clicked on a few more buttons. Each screen was more provocative. My dick got hard when I saw Jagger. My mouth watered. *I could suck his dick.* He could do me . . . if he were on my team. He wasn't. His firm stance; the flexing of his bicep; his standing sideways, showing off his long, thick dick; the stern body language mirroring his eye contact—these said, "Females only."

I slid my chair farther under the table, hiding my erection with my hand. "What else is on there?"

He double clicked on the Memoirs folder, and that shit fucked me up. The woman I had proposed to was a slut. A whore. A tramp. Worse than a prostitute. I sucked in my lips, stared at my boy, Chad.

"Now what? You're going to go get her or leave her there?" he asked. "Sometimes we're better off not knowing. Once you know, you can't forget that shit, man."

"I need another favor," I said, staring at pictures of Seven maneuvering four dicks at once. Bitch belonged on the corner in a short skirt, or in a damn circus.

"I'm listening," Chad said.

"Can you make someone's PDA, laptop, and office systems crash if I give you the e-mail address and cell phone number?"

"Better if I had an e-mail address. Why? You want to destroy Seven?"

"No, not Seven," I said. Hadn't thought about that. "Zena."

"Her best friend? What's up with that? She got something you need?"

"I'm trying to protect Seven. Zena might have those pictures," I lied.

"That's a stretch, don't you think?"

"Just do it," I said.

"Not sure if I can help you on that one. If I weren't married, I'd ask Zena out. What are you going to do about Seven? That's the question."

I begged Chad. "I need for you to do this, man." Then I said, "The wedding's off."

"Why?" he asked. "You're going to be like your old man. Follow in his footsteps. Heart of ice. Unforgiving. You love Seven. We've all done some dumb shit in our younger days. Marry her," Chad said, turning off the computer, pointing to a piece of paper. "That's the password for her computer."

So much shit. So little time.

"You're right. I should marry her," I said, thinking about Seven's new body. Tight. Slim. Fucking fantastic. Why should another man get to fuck her? "I've gotta go see my parents."

"Whoa," he said, rubbing his hand on his chin. "That's cool, man. You want me to go with you?"

"Nah, I gotta do this alone. Shit might get crazy."

"Exactly. That's why I should go with you," he insisted.

"I'm good. I'll call you tonight," I said, standing. "Thanks for cracking into her system. Hope you can help me out with Zena."

"No problem. I'll take care of it for you. Get me all her e-mail addresses. Hey, man, don't lose your cool when you confront your old man. If you get pissed, don't touch him. Leave immediately," Chad said, standing.

I followed him to the front door, locked the door behind him, then headed back upstairs. Danté wasn't in my bed. Searched the house. No Danté. Looked in the garage. His car, gone.

I returned to the dining room and Seven's computer, logged on to the Internet, checked my e-mail.

Seven had written: As I discover the true me, I fall deeper in love with Jagger. It wasn't planned, but your asking that I leave was the best thing that ever happened to me. Since you're happy with Zena, I've moved on.

I shouted at the screen as I replied, I told you I didn't fuck her! Seven, don't make me show up at Punany Paradise. If you're not back home within seventy-two hours, I'm coming after you. I inserted a few of her slut photos, then continued. Bet lover boy doesn't know you're a tramp. Come home in three days, or your pictures will be all over the Internet. No one will ever hire you.

I had to go see my old man. Get the dumb shit off my chest. I hadn't done anything wrong. Wanted, needed, to see my mother. But my old man wasn't going to have the advantage this time.

Walking into my library closet, I removed the black shoe box from the top shelf, opened it, stared in disbelief. My gun was gone.

Crash! Crash!

I fell to the floor, crawled under my desk. Some fools outside doing what? I waited a few minutes. Silence. I crept to my third-floor window, peeped outside.

Danté had a brick in each hand.

"What the fuck are you doing?" I yelled.

Danté yelled, "You told him not to let me up! I made you! If I can't have you to myself, you don't have to worry about your old man killing you. I will."

Crash! Crash!

He hurled the bricks in his hands through the foyer windows. Sitting, I propped my elbows on the desk, closed my eyes, then exhaled, "Why me?"

Chapter 21

Zena

Men. Why did women need them? Why did I need any of them? The men I'd met, they'd requested more of me than I'd ever asked of them. "Zena, can you help me out with my cell phone bill? I have to talk to you every day, baby." Or "I'm short on my rent. I'll pay you back in two weeks. My baby's mama is always in my pocket. Can you take care of this round? I'll catch the next."

The lame, senseless, repetitive excuses from men who dodged being responsible for themselves had made me tired of dealing with them. That had been my college dating experience. How Seven met Maverick, I hadn't understood until now. She hadn't. Maverick had met her. Courted her. Treated her well, then isolated her. The less she knew, the safer his secret.

Had a few secrets of my own. Seven had no idea I was already married. To a man who'd have his citizenship in one more year. I met Deuce Callahan at Chicago's city hall, said, "I do," signed the marriage certificate, had sex with him once and hadn't fucked him since. He'd brought the witness. He'd paid off my college loans, given me a lump sum in cash.

I was comfortable; he was consistent. The most handsome, reliable man in my life had been nowhere in my life since he'd showed up at Maverick's office. I sat on the edge of my bed, dialed his number.

"Hey, baby. Things are crazy. Stock market out of control. Sorry I haven't been by. I took care of that Maverick maniac. You good?" he asked.

No, he hadn't taken care of Maverick. I smiled, then answered, "Yeah, I'm good. You?"

"Zena, listen to me. I really want you to have my babies. Say yes." Deuce sounded anxious.

After all the nonsense with Danté and Maverick, I said, "Yes."

"Oh my. Are you serious? Please tell me you're not just telling me what I want to hear," he said.

I felt his smile. "Yes, I will have your babies," I said, not believing my own ears.

"I will be by tonight," he said. "Zena?"

"Yes."

"I love you, woman."

"I love you, too, Deuce," I said, ending the call before I changed my mind.

Found one man I liked other than Deuce, and what happened? I caught him dicking down another man with more passion than he'd fucked me. Glad I found out before I'd done the unimaginable, fall in love. I'd never been in love. My relationships hadn't lasted that long. How much time was required to fall in love? One month, six months, a year? Six years? Citizenship?

I was pissed off. Maverick should have Danté killed. Do women a favor. Do me a favor. Make sure Danté wouldn't deceive another female. Keep me from going to jail for killing Danté myself. For Danté's sake, I had better not test positive for HIV.

Did Seven know about Maverick's double-agent lifestyle? Was that why he hadn't wanted me hanging out with Seven? The reason he'd leave whenever I came around? What team was he on? She on? Were their secret lives another reason Seven hadn't responded to any of my text messages? Friend or not, it was best to let her be, deal with this situation my way. Like in a relationship, sometimes friends had to give friends fifty feet of space instead of three. I was done texting Seven.

I picked up my cell phone, speed dialed Donna to see how her first day back was going.

She answered right away. "Hey, Ms. Belvedere."

"Hi, Donna. How is everything going?"

"Everything on this end is quiet," she replied. "Can hear a pin drop. Phone's not ringing much. It's real quiet."

I listened. Couldn't hear background noise. "Any new inquiries?" I asked, scanning the toys I'd bought. Two remained unused. Those orgasmic mechanical assistants I'd used had exceeded my expectations.

"Not yet. Not today. I had time, so I designed a new e-flyer ad—"

"Yeah, I saw it. Looks good."

"I e-mailed it today to repeat and potential clients. I'm surfing the Net, adding you to major search engines. You may want to consider banner ads on a few sites. The recession is slowing business for everybody. Three of your top clients terminated their contracts today. Said they had to cut their marketing budgets, downsize their staff. I hope you come in soon. Your mail is piled up on your desk. I've put it in bundles," she said, sighing heavily in my ear.

She was right. I had to go into my office. Afraid Danté or Maverick would confront me at my workplace, I'd stayed away. For the first time, I considered carrying a weapon. Crime up. Unemployment up. Dow Jones down. Way down. If Maverick would have Danté killed, he surely didn't give a damn about me.

I needed to check my office mail. No electronic business deposits had been registered to my account the last few business days. That was odd. My reserves were getting low. No new business. Losing long-term clients. Heating my bedroom with a portable to avoid warming the entire house. Not good.

Raising the temperature on the thermostat, I almost forgot Deuce was coming over. "I'll see you next week. The mail for today come in yet?" I asked.

"About an hour ago."

"Any checks?" I asked. I briefly entertained selling Maverick his laptop for the fifty grand he'd offered. Or I could close my business, have Deuce's babies, and become a full-time housewife.

"Not today. Maybe they'll come in on Monday," Donna said. "Ms. Belvedere?"

"Yes?"

"Be honest with me. Do I need to start looking for another job? I'm concerned about your meeting payroll."

Meeting payroll? She was the only one on my payroll. And she was worried? Was Donna stealing from me?

"Donna. Do you have another job? Is there something you're not telling me?" I asked, holding the clit stimulator in one hand, a vibrator in the other.

"It can wait until I see you next week," Donna said, backing down.

Not in the mood to interrogate her, I said, "Fine," ending the call.

If she quit, I wouldn't have to pay her unemployment, and I'd save almost eighteen hundred a month. Staring at the unopened thirteen-hundred-dollar clit stimulator, I placed it on my nightstand. Might have to take it back for a refund.

I opened the vibrator, rubbed it down with toy cleaner, followed by a hot, damp towel. Peeling the gold package away from the condom, I placed the condom in my mouth, sucked the tip between my teeth, then placed my lips over the head of the vibrator. Keeping up on my skills, I tightened my lips around the head, then unrolled the condom down the shaft, almost to the base, finishing with my fingers.

"No more blow jobs or gay men for me," I said, turning on the cordless dick. I'd just fuck myself until Deuce and I lived together. That way I didn't have to guess who was straight.

The pearls rotated; the head vibrated. I climbed into bed, lubricated my dick, spread my legs, then reclined on a pillow, bending my knees. Slowly, I inserted the head, closed my eyes, and exhaled out my mouth.

I switched a button, and the head rotated clockwise, thrusting the pearls along my G-spot. I clamped my thighs together, holding the vibrator in place. I reached for the clit stimulator and opened it, rubbed it with toy cleaner. Wiped it with the damp towel. Inserted the batteries. Turned it on.

"Goddamn!"

The vibration shot throughout my entire body. Head buzzed. Feet tingled. I took a deep breath, placed the tip against my clit. Instantly,

I came. The vibrating dick in one hand, the clit stimulator in the other, I came so hard, I damn near passed out.

I limped to the bathroom, preventing my thighs from brushing my clit. My body jerked as I showered, water streaming on my shaft.

"That combination is lethal. Better not do that again anytime soon," I said, turning off the water.

My cell phone rang. Not knowing if the call was close to going to voice mail, I grabbed the towel, dried one ear, slipped on my earpiece, then answered, "Hello."

"Ms. Belvedere?"

"Yes. Who's calling?" I asked.

"I'm calling with your lab results," she said.

My knees buckled, and I nearly slumped to the floor. If she said I had to come in, I'd expect the worst. If she told me the results over the phone, I was good.

"Hello?" she said.

I whispered, "I'm listening."

"Your AIDS test is nonreactive. It's negative," she said.

A heavy sigh escaped my lips. "Thank you so much. So much."

"And," she continued, "congratulations. Your pregnancy test is positive."

"No, no. You've got me mixed up with someone else. I didn't request a pregnancy test. I'm not pregnant yet. You sure you know what you're doing?" I asked her. "I'm Ms. Zena Belvedere."

"Yes, ma'am. You're pregnant. If you want confirmation, you can get a home test. If you want to terminate the pregnancy, we can assist you with referrals for an abortion."

Ending the call, I raced to the bathroom, kneeled over the toilet, and vomited, as if I could regurgitate the baby, then flush it. Holding my stomach, I cried.

What was I going to do? Have an abortion? Or birth a baby into this world for a man who loved men more than women? I cried until my body ached.

Wait a minute, I thought.

Deuce wanted babies. Demarcus Danté Davis was tall, dark, and handsome. So was Deuce Callahan. Deuce would never know the truth.

I showered, preparing my already conceived child for its new daddy.

Chapter 22

Seven

Living my life like it's golden.

Thanks to Punany Paradise, my pussy was walking on sunshine. Cruising on orgasms. I could come anytime, anywhere, without touching myself. My mind, my masterpiece. My body, my temple. My life, my life.

Today was my last day at Punany Paradise. My time here wasn't indefinite. I had to go back home. Get my things out of Maverick's house. Clear my conscience. Bring closure to whatever it was we had.

"Thank you, Mama," I said aloud, knowing she'd help reveal my troubling truth. Like an addict, I had to rehabilitate myself, get Maverick 100 percent out of my system. Come clean. Become sober.

Ten days remained on my reservation at the resort. I'd be back. Soon. No refund requested. I wished Zena had come to Punany Paradise with me. We'd still be friends. I missed her so much. When I got back to the island, I was going to explore my relationship—if that was what I could call it—with Jagger. See if he was worth pursuing or if his advances were a façade.

Staring out the patio window, toward the ocean, I slid open the door, stepped onto the sand, and did jumping jacks while watching the sunrise. Blinded by the rays, I ran in place, fast. Arms pumping. Titties jiggling. Thighs burning. Mind racing faster than my thrusting fists. Back and forth. Forth, then back.

Invigorated, I returned inside and sat naked at the computer. I saw Maverick's demand that I return in three days, and I saw Zena's messages about Maverick and Danté. Outraged, I screamed, "Maverick, go straight to hell. Detour, motherfucker, detour. Do not pass by this good pussy. Don't think about blowing a kiss at my bootylicious ass."

He wasn't better than me in business. More than half of the ideas he'd implemented were mine. Mine! He truly couldn't outmatch my boardroom or bedroom skills. I was taking over Maverick Maxamillion Incorporated. I'd show him my freshly waxed pussy, cuddled between two lean, cellulite-free thighs, and introduce him to the bitch in me. Omarosa didn't have shit on Seven. I had the handle on the bitch switch.

My nails fiercely clicking against the keys, I typed: I wasn't seeking your sorry-ass approval. I DON'T need your permission to be a woman. The same as you don't need my permission to be homosexual, be bisexual, gay, or whatever you consider yourself. I enjoyed fucking twenty-six guys in one month at your expense.

Do whatever you'd like with my pics. Don't forget I've got pics of you, too. I'll be by tomorrow to get my things . . . Don't touch my shit!

Wait until I get to Chicago. It was his turn to be pissed off and pissed on, and not a little. A whole fucking lot. *I will drown that motherfucker in his own misery.*

"If I say shit, Maverick had better drop his drawers, squat, and give me a full load," I yelled.

I glanced at the time, 7:11 a.m. Six hours before my departure to the airport. No bags or baggage to pack or check. I headed to the Jacuzzi; I turned on the cold water only.

I lay on the living-room floor, interlocked my fingers behind my head. Closing my eyes, I felt tears escape the corners, streaming toward my ears. I really missed my best friend. I owed her an apology. Replying to her messages was insufficient. She deserved what I was going to give her, a face-to-face apology. A hug. A kiss. A thank-you for her being more of a friend to me than I'd been to her.

Mama used to say, "Friends don't let men come or cum between them. If you have a healthy relationship with a girlfriend, keep it that way. Men envy the relationships women are able to sustain. The close-

ness. The sharing. The caring. The heartfelt love. Seven, baby, like diabetes, an insecure man will deliberately kill everything and everyone
in his veins. Keep your girlfriends close, because when a man does
not have your back, a true girlfriend will look out for you, no matter
what. Just make sure you look out for her, too, when she needs you."

Getting up, I grinned, turned off the water. Happy I was sharing my
last moments with Jagger. Sad I'd be in transit to O'Hare before sunset. Jagger wasn't accompanying me back to Chicago. I wanted Maverick to believe I had someone better than him. Actually, I did. But
my heart wasn't 100 percent convinced about Jagger.

I heard a tap at my patio window.

Sliding open the door for Jagger, I smiled, tugged at his white linen
drawstring pants.

"What's up with all the clothes?" I asked, wanting to invite him into
my personal space, my heart.

Jagger's finger traced my hairline, my jaw, my chin. Lightly touching the center of my forehead, he ran his fingers between my eyebrows, swiped each one, continued down my nose, outlined my lips.
Then he cupped my face, taking my entire mouth into his. Jagger's
tongue penetrated my lips, sucked my tongue into his wet mouth.

I couldn't breathe. I didn't care. I could stay here forever. Love, the
pentacle of life. His love overwhelmed me. Moved me to tears that
wouldn't stop flowing.

He whispered, "Seven, I love you."

More tears. Strangling words trapped in my throat. A lump of compassion compelled me to hold him. Tight. Tight as I could so he
could feel what I couldn't speak. Love. Not lust.

"I . . . I . . ." I exhaled.

"Tell me," he said. "I need to hear you say it. Look in my eyes and
say it, baby."

Batting tears on my breasts, his chest, I cried, "I love you, Jagger,"
not wanting to disappoint him. I loved so many things about Jagger,
but I wasn't in love with him.

Rip!

He tore his linen pants off his body and his hard, beautiful dick
sprang forth. The head greeted my clit. He tossed the cloth to the

floor. Made his way to the bath area, dipped his hand in the water in the Jacuzzi. Upon returning to me, fingertips wet, cold, he pulled me to the floor, on top of him. Jagger held me close. Kissed my face, my cheeks, my forehead, my chin.

"Seven, don't go. You have ten more days. Give me each day. I'm afraid I may never see you again," he said.

My legs around his waist. His pubic hairs under my ass. He searched my eyes for confirmation that I'd stay.

Softly, I said, "Why don't you take a week off? Come with me."

"What?" He smiled, gripped my shoulders, leaning me backward. Searched my eyes for confirmation.

Uncertain, I looked away. What was I saying? I could ruin Jagger's feelings for me if I dragged him into my unpredictable forecast. Windy. Gloomy. Overcast. Thunderstorm watch. I had no idea what to expect when I arrived in Chicago.

"That was my heart speaking. Going with me isn't a good idea. I'll come back. I need to go home alone for right now."

"No, no, I want to go with you. I want to protect you. Keep you safe." His grip tightened . . . loosened. His steady gaze locked with mine. "Stand up," he said.

One arm braced my back, and the other was under my knees. Jagger carried me to the Jacuzzi.

"Oh, no, you don't," I said, laughing. Scrambling out of his arms. "That water is cold!" I yelled.

Too late. I'd planned on gradually adding in hot water to warm the water before I, before we, got in. I couldn't drown in the Jacuzzi. Still didn't want to get tossed in the water. Jagger got in the Jacuzzi, extended his hand.

"You don't have to control everything, Seven. Sometimes it's good to let go," he said. "Seven, please. Let me come with you. It doesn't matter where we are, as long as we're together."

I blurted, "How do I know you're not trying to get American citizenship?"

Shit! The water *was* cold. I shivered. Hugged myself.

"You don't know. And you don't know me very well," he said. "If that was all I wanted, I could've been an American ten times over. Many American women have proposed to me. America is the freest country in the world. At the same time, the people are enslaved. Like you. Americans thrive on revenge, determined to drag one another down before they let go. You cannot let go of a man that you know is bad for you. You must like drama."

I laughed. He didn't.

Emphatically, I said, "Fine. Come with me. But don't blame me if you don't like what happens. Don't depend on me to take care of you financially, either. And do not expect me to be with you all the time."

"I don't have a visa," he said.

My eyes narrowed. Why was this man putting me through this?

"I need time to get one. Serenity can expedite the process. Wait for me," he begged.

I didn't want to wait another hour, minute, second. Another day might make me stay several days, ten days, or forever. Perhaps that was his plan.

He held my hips in his palms, guiding my pussy over the jets. Not too close, yet a perfect distance for the streams to tease my clit. His lips grazed my shoulder; he kissed my ear.

Lord Jesus, what are you trying to tell me?

Then his dick floated into my chilled pussy.

I closed my eyes. More tears. More aches. More love pains found their way to my throat. Holding on to the edge, I felt his hands cover mine. His tongue danced on the back of my neck, slowly making its way to my opposite ear.

"I love you, Seven. Why won't you let me love you in every way possible? Beyond your imagination."

"I will. I promise. But I can't give you all of me . . . Ah, that feels good. Let's not talk right now," I pleaded, thrusting onto his dick. I squeezed my pussy as tight as I could, clamping his dick inside.

Jagger pulled out, picked me up, carried me to the bed, laid my dripping body atop the white comforter, spread my legs, then softly kissed my clit. Again and again, his lips gently touched mine.

Salty streams flowed into my mouth, my ears.

"I want to satisfy you so good that when my lips are not on your sweet pussy, I want you to cum thinking about me," he said, resuming his clit-a-thon.

Jagger climbed atop me missionary style. His dick was wedged against my shaft. He kissed me. I kissed him, held him close.

"I could stay here forever," I whispered.

"Don't tease me, baby. You're not staying. But if you say it's okay, I will be in Chicago as soon as I can," he said.

Men. Vulnerable. Warm. Loving. Caring. Until they got what they wanted from me. What did Jagger want? What did Maverick want? I wasn't sure, but I was determined to find out.

"I would love to say, 'Let me know when you're arriving. I'll pick you up from the airport. You can stay at Zena's house. I'll give you all my contact information,' but I can't." Tired of talking, I added, "Baby, make love to me like you'll never see me again."

No sooner had I spoken those words than for the first time, a man cried in my arms.

Chapter 23

Maverick

I'd read in Barack Obama's *The Audacity of Hope,* "Someone once said that every man is trying to either live up to his father's expectations or make up for his father's mistakes." That man was me.

I rolled over in an empty bed. First time I'd slept alone in years. The house was empty. No Seven. No Danté. As insane as Danté was, breaking out the foyer windows, screaming at me from downstairs, he was more sane than me.

Love made people do the incomprehensible. My lying to Seven, lying to Danté, lying to myself. Time for me to think sensibly. My life wasn't mine. Headed in a tunnel loaded with dynamite. I felt it. The ache in my bones.

I lay awake, staring at the ceiling.

Hadn't planned on missing Danté. Never believed Seven would lose the weight. I got out of bed, went into the living room, sat on my sofa, staring out the window. The way I felt right now, I'd shoot myself in the head.

I jumped to my feet. "Fuck!" I had to devise a plan to regain control.

Sitting back on the sofa, I stared at the cell phone in my hand. Needed to call off the hit on Danté. Couldn't. Something compelled me to call Seven instead.

"Hello," she answered cheerfully.

"Where are you?" I asked softly.

"Where are *you?*" she asked.

I overheard an announcement in the background. "Last call. All passengers for San Francisco must board for an immediate departure."

I said, "I'm at home. Waiting for you, baby."

"Good. I'll be there shortly. Thirty minutes tops. To get my car. I'll hire movers to get the rest of my things tomorrow or the next day," she said.

"I miss you so damn much," I said, forcing back tears. "I'll be here waiting for you. We need to talk."

"Gotta go. My driver is here. Bye." She hung up.

I hung up. Went to my bedroom. It was messed up. Clothes scattered. Comforter on the floor. Picking up my suit and tie, I tossed them in the laundry. I sat on the toilet. Shit. Then showered and shaved. I put on a splash of cologne. Sweatpants, black wife-beater. Straightened up my bedroom. Changed the sheets. Put her favorite red satin sheets on the bed.

Pacing in my library, I stared out the window, eyes following every town car that went by. Thirty. Forty. Fifty minutes. One hour. Two.

I called her phone. No answer. Redialed the speed dial. No fucking answer.

I went to the garage, got in my car, and sped off down Lake Shore Drive. Took a left on the Magnificent Mile. Drove to the end. Kept going. Found myself parked in front of my mother's house.

I got out of the car. *Slam.* Closed the door, almost shattering the driver's side window. I didn't care. Today I was prepared to kick my father's ass or die trying. Didn't know which was worse, not living up to a father's expectations or having a father with no expectations of me.

Ding-dong, ding-dong, ding-dong, ding-dong.

Relentlessly, I jammed my finger against the button. Fed up with his bullshit. Balled my fist, prepared to knock his ass the fuck out the second he opened the door; step over his body; tell my mother how much I missed her, loved her, needed her in my life; then carry her out of his house in my arms, for good.

My mom quietly opened the door, then walked away.

No plan B. Uneasy, I entered, looking around for him.

She sat in the old familiar rocking chair, swaying back and forth. Knitting.

"Ma," I said, standing in front of the coffee table. Wasn't going to let my old man sneak up on me.

No answer from my mom.

"Where's your husband?" I asked her.

That was appropriate. Always her husband, never my father.

Knitting needles clicking, softly she said, "Your father is in the hospital, fighting for his life. I'm home fighting for mine. Don't know what I'd do without him," not looking up at me for one second.

He treated my mother like shit on the bottom of his shoes, and she was fighting for her life when she should've been praying for his death. She'd let him control her all my life, most of hers. How could I free my mother? I knew what I had to do.

I sat at my mother's feet, placed my head on her knees. "I'll take care of you, Mom. I promise. You can move into my new house with me."

The needles stopped clicking for a moment. She looked at me. Looked down at her lap, started knitting again.

"What's wrong with him?" I asked, not giving a damn, wishing he'd die.

"Can't say. He told them not to release any information. Didn't want me to worry. I think his cancer is flaring up again." Her eyes remained fixed on the yarn, which was unraveling from the spool.

"Can't say or won't? You're his wife. You have a right to know. You must know, Ma. You shouldn't have to guess what's wrong with him."

"Why don't you go see?" she said. "Then come back. Let me know if he's going to die in that place or come home. I'd appreciate that." Her eyes closed, then opened. Why wouldn't she look at me? I was sitting at her feet. How could she not see me?

My mother had no idea what she was asking. "For you, Ma, I'll do anything," I said. I stood. Kissed my mother on her cheek, then headed to the hospital. The same hospital on the South Side where I was born.

* * *

Bypassing the busy nurses at the desk, I swiftly strolled down the hall, scanning the patients' names on the doors. When I got to his room, I refused to knock. I entered.

Stood over him. His body, skeletal. Flesh clung to bones. Tubes flowed. One tube connected to the needle in the back of his hand. The other, clamped inside his nose, lay on his sunken chest. Oxygen tank beside his bed.

"Why?" I asked, waking him up.

Slowly, his eyes, almost the size of golf balls, opened at the command of my voice. He didn't scramble. Lay there. No response.

"Wish I had my gun right now. I wouldn't shoot you. I'd beat you with the handle until your fucked-up head caved in. Wouldn't be here if my mother hadn't asked me to check on you."

Feeble, he reached toward the call button.

Bam!

I knocked his hand away. "If you know what's good for you, you'll listen. I asked you a question. I demand an answer."

Gasping, he fumbled to adjust the tube in his nose; his arm trembled. He mumbled, "Had to protect you, son."

"Me? Don't give me that bullshit! Protect me?" I grunted, one inch from his face. "Your sorry ass didn't give a fuck about me, and I want to know why. Are you my real father?" I asked, wanting to push the needle deep into the back of his hand. But I couldn't.

Whimpering, tears streamed down his face. Nodding, he whispered, "Son, I'm gay. I haven't had sex with your mother in over twenty years. I lied to her. Told her I had prostate cancer. Didn't want to infect her." Closing his eyes, he said, "I'm ashamed of how I treated you. I wanted to protect you. Better for me to disown you than to have you find out about my secret life and disown me."

That fucked me up. *Infected? Gay?* "Please tell me you're lying."

He pressed the button connected to his IV, administering what I assumed was a painkiller. He held his finger there.

I snatched his finger away.

His head wavered. "Don't touch me, son . . . I . . . I . . . I have full-blown AIDS. Didn't want your mother or you to know." His mouth opened wide. "I want to die. I'm ready. Don't want to live this way. I deserve to die," he pleaded, closing his eyes.

How would I have felt knowing? How would my life have been different?

He'd fucked up every day of my entire life. The first day he called me son, he mentioned AIDS. How could he do that to me?

"Take the pillow. Cover my face," he pleaded. "I'm useless. Don't want your mother to have to take care of me. Tired of suffering."

Ain't this some shit. He was tired of suffering?

Before I got here, I thought I could kill him. Now that I knew we were more alike than different, I couldn't hurt him. I sat beside his bed. I had so many questions. Didn't know where to begin. "When did you first know you were gay?" I asked him.

His voice was weak. He struggled to say, "For certain, when I was sixteen."

"Did you love my mother?"

"Still do love her," he said, closing his eyes. "Best thing that ever happened to me was your mother."

My mother, not me.

"I need you to look at me," I said, giving him a moment to reopen his eyes. "Why did you want to kill me?"

He shook his head. Closed his eyes. Opened them. I stared, waiting for his response, praying he'd help me to understand why I was so angry.

"Misdirected anger. Don't be like me, son. Accept the fact that you're gay. You deserve to live your life with whomever you'd like. Don't marry that girl. Marry the man you love. Don't ruin her life like I ruined your mother's by hiding my sexuality. And whatever you do, don't birth innocent kids into your confusion."

So now he had a fucking conscience? Probably found the Lord since he'd been hospitalized.

I fluffed the pillow behind his head, then walked out.

Stopping at a pay phone, I dialed his number, filled with dread.

"You make up your mind yet?" he answered.

"Yeah. It's a go. On my wedding day. At exactly twelve noon," I told him. "One small change of plan. Don't kill him. Kill me," I said.

"Can't do that. You're confused. I'm canceling the contract," he said, then hung up.

I was relieved. I didn't want to die at my wedding. Leave Seven with haunting memories. I desperately wanted to be loved for who I was, a gay man.

Couldn't face my mother. She'd get the call about my father soon enough. I went home, found Danté sitting in his limo in front of my building. Foyer windows still boarded up from his outbreak.

I parked in the garage. Met him outside. "Come up. We need to talk."

Quietly, Danté followed me onto the elevator. He reached into his pocket, pulled out a gun. Whatever he had planned, I was not resisting.

"Found this in Seven's laptop bag," he said, handing the gun to me.

Unlocking my front door, I said, "You don't have to lie on Seven. She'd never touch my gun. If you want to shoot me, go ahead."

Danté placed the gun on the table in the foyer.

Angry all over again, I held open the door, told him to leave. He passed me, went upstairs.

I followed him to the fridge. He grabbed two beers, sat on the sofa, bit his bottom lip, turned on the television. If he stayed, he'd get what he deserved. At the moment, I hated everyone, including myself.

Danté slid his hand inside his sweatpants, pulled out his dick, held it in one hand, his beer in the other. My dick hardened instantly.

I took his beer; poured it over his head, his chest, his dick; dropped to my knees; then wrapped my mouth around him. Tears streamed down my face, blending into the beer. Danté remained silent.

Holding his hand, I stood, led him to my bedroom. Undressed him.

Quietly, he undressed me.

"Ride me rough," I insisted, submitting to him.

Danté pushed me face forward against the wall. Grabbed his dick.

"Maverick, you asleep? Oh, damn. I didn't mean to interrupt," Seven said, standing in the doorway.

Glancing over my shoulder, I said, "Could my life possibly get worse?"

Seven replied, "Maverick, I already know. You need to stop lying to yourself. Carry on. I just came for my car. I'll be back to get my things tomorrow."

Chapter 24

Zena

"Hello! Surprise! I'm back."

I'd recognize that voice anywhere. Seven was in my living room, and Deuce was asleep beside me.

Scrambling to find my robe, I rushed to greet Seven.

"Don't tell me you're in the bed, too," she said, sitting on my white sofa.

I was so happy to see her, I couldn't stay upset. I fell on her, hugged her like we hadn't seen one another in years.

Leaning back, holding her shoulders, beholding a true goddess, I said, "Hot damn! Where the hell did you go?"

Golden complexion. Seven's ankle-length cotton dress was tapered to her perfect body. Her grin stretched across her face.

"Come with me. I'll show you where I went," she said.

"I've never seen you so happy. Let me get us something to drink," I said, disappearing into my kitchen. I stood in the middle of the kitchen floor for a moment. *That bitch looks fucking fantastic!* I knew I should've gone with her. I wouldn't be trapped with this baby inside me if I had.

I poured two glasses of cran-apple juice, then made my way back into the living room. "Girl, we have so much to catch up on," I whispered.

"I hear you have company. I'm going to get out of your way," Deuce called from the bedroom.

Seven's eyes widened. "Girl, who is that? Seems like I'm not the only one who has a few lifestyle changes going on."

Deuce entered the living room. His eyes froze; he stared at Seven. "Hello. I'm Deuce Callahan. How long have you known my Zena?"

Seven cut me a look, then answered, "How long have you been knowing my best friend, Zena?"

"Oh, yeah, that's right. You are the one with that gay fiancé," Deuce said.

I interrupted, "Baby, don't. That's not proper. Seven is my friend, not yours."

"Well, she is one hot, sexy friend who doesn't have to marry a gay man, that's for sure. I will find you a husband," he said sternly.

"I'm good," Seven said. "Real good. Don't need a man to define me."

Grabbing his bicep, I ushered Deuce out the front door. He was infringing upon our time. After closing the door, I sat on the sofa with Seven. We hugged for a long time. "I seriously missed you. I'm so glad you're back," I said, crying.

"I missed you, too. Sorry I wasn't much of a friend while I was gone, but, girl, I had the most amazing time. But what I want to know is where you've been hiding that fine-ass Nigerian man."

Quietly, I said, "He's my husband."

"Your what? How long? Wait. Reverse. I missed a whole lotta shit," Seven said.

"That's the least of my problems. I'm pregnant." I said, sipping on cran-apple juice, wishing it was a magical abortion serum.

"Preg . . . what? When did this happen? You don't want kids. You never wanted to have kids. You did this for him?"

"Accident," I said. "Not his baby. Danté's." My stomach churned.

"Whoa. What? Wait. Back up to the very beginning. I'm all ears," Seven said.

As best as I could, in between tears, I gave the overview of how and why I'd married Deuce. How I had ended up in bed with Danté and was now carrying his child. How I planned to let Deuce believe it was his child.

"Stop crying," Seven said. "Right now we have to think. First, do *you* want to have this baby? If you do, I'll be here for you. If you don't, we're going to the abortion clinic in the morning. It's your body. The one thing you can't do is let Deuce take care of another man's child, believing it's his. That's trifling. You'll ruin your life, his life, and your child's life. Lying is the one thing you are not going to do, you hear me?" she scolded.

Terribly confused, I asked, "Should I divorce Deuce? Does Danté have a right to know I'm pregnant?"

"Hell no, girlfriend. On both. What they don't know won't hurt them. My mother used to say, 'Better to ask the Lord for forgiveness than to ask a man.' And that's exactly what you are going to do."

"Would you say that if I hadn't sent you those photos of him with Maverick?"

Seven smiled, then said, "I just walked in on them booty grinding again. Danté had Maverick pressed against the bedroom wall, getting ready to ride him. I walked in by accident. I didn't trip. I got in my car and came over here. I'll get my other things from Maverick's house tomorrow. He wants to talk, but there's nothing he has to say that I want to hear. I wish him well. Them well."

"I'm going to have an abortion," I blurted, not believing the words I'd spoken.

Seven smiled at me. "See, aren't you glad you voted for Obama? McCain would've made you have that baby." We laughed as she continued, "Zena, your body is your temple. There's nothing wrong with not wanting to spend the rest of your life regretting one night of pleasure. Don't trip. I'm your best friend forever. After you recover from terminating your pregnancy, I'll take you to this new spot I found. We're going to D.C. for six weeks."

"You're not getting off that easy. Where did you go?" I asked.

"I went to Punany Paradise," she said, grinning. "Met this guy named Jagger. He is absolutely wonderful, but I'm not ready to get serious with anyone. You know the shit men do to us. Fuck us. Kick it with some other chick. Travel all over, bragging about how they had sex with the finest woman in the world. Emotionally and physically detached, that's how I'm living my life, and it feels great. See if they can handle the stories I've got to kick back at them."

Forget all that. I had to stay focused so I wouldn't get left behind. "Oh, so you went to Punany Paradise, and you wanna take me to D.C.? I've been there too many times to count, and let me tell you, the men there are not all that," I said, frowning.

Shaking her head, Seven said, "We're not going to Washington, D.C. Girlfriend, we are going to Dick City. My treat."

"Hallelujah!" I said, kicking my feet in the air. "I'd better start repenting right now for my sins."

Suddenly, life didn't seem so gloomy. My best friend had changed my heart. I wondered if we'd run into Oprah and Gayle in D.C. Probably not.

All I knew was I could not wait!

. . . To be continued in *D.C.*,
Dick City

Are You a Maneater?

(Score yourself here.)

1. No
2. No
3. No
4. Yes
5. Yes
6. Yes
7. Yes
8. Yes
9. Yes
10. Yes
11. Yes

Give yourself 10 points for each of your answers that match the answers above.

- 0–50   You are close to becoming a maneater but have work to do.
- 51–80   Your maneating skills are good.
- 81–100   You are a true maneater.
- 101–110   You need to come with a maneater warning label. Congrats!

Acknowledgments

It's Monday, November 3, 2008.

First, I'd like to thank my Creator for blessing me with an honorable character. I live my life bettering myself while encouraging and helping others. In one hour, I'm heading to Obama headquarters here in Oakland to make phone calls to voters around the country. Tomorrow I'll do the same. Perhaps I will call you.

I love my editor, Selena James. Adore my agent Claudia Menza. Am grateful for my Kensington family: Laurie Parkin, who is never too busy for me, Karen Auerbach, Adeola Saul, Jessica McLean, Steven Zacharius, and Walter Zacharius.

My Grand Central Publishing family, Karen R. Thomas, my editor, Linda A. Duggins, my publicist, and LaToya Smith, you are absolutely beautiful. Thanks for your generous support. And to my agent Andrew Stuart, thanks for taking special care of me.

In *Character of a Man*, I allowed Seven, Zena, Maverick, and Danté to be true to themselves, hoping you will understand that our deepest internal struggles shape the core of who we are.

Do me a favor. Select one person in your life, open up to them, share with them who you really are. Share your fears, your goals, and your dreams. At the same time, get to know the same about another individual. I mean, *really* get to know them.

What I learned from writing *Character of a Man* is, like the characters, most people, myself included, don't have anyone who truly understands who they are. That could be because we don't open up, or the people we open up to don't hear us, or we simply don't understand who we are.

My pride and joy and love smile and shine through my eyes whenever I think of my one and only twenty-two-year-old, six-foot-nine, super-handsome, intelligent, and talented son, Jesse Bernard Byrd, Jr.

He's a young man of great character. I love my son with all my heart, and that's the same way I love myself.

I want to thank another man with upstanding character, Barack Obama, for giving me hope that Americans will become united throughout all the States. I've already noticed a positive change. Some of you have opened your hearts, shared your personal experiences with me, and I appreciate you. From Gary, an eighty-year-old white man who openly told me about his sex life, to my dear friends Ed Fitzpatrick (owner) and Bill Gaines (the man) @ Coliseum Lexus of Oakland (I have bought three Lexus cars and am looking at the convertible now), to the married woman @ the Blackberry Bistro who shared intimate details of her marriage. Each of you has helped me to grow.

Obviously, without my parents, there'd be no me or my wonderful son. I'm eternally grateful to Elester Noel and Joseph Henry Morrison. Both of my parents have made their transitions, my mother when I was nine years old and my father when I was twenty-four years old. For those of you who are blessed to still have your parents, give thanks.

My parents also blessed me with the greatest siblings in the world— Wayne Morrison, Andrea Morrison, Derrick Morrison, Regina Morrison, Margie Rickerson, and Debra Noel. I love my siblings.

I hate that one of my sisters stopped speaking to me because she didn't like the way I asked her to repay me. Truth be told, she has a husband, and if she accepts his doing less than his part, personally that isn't my concern. If he'd done his part, she wouldn't have needed to borrow anything from anyone. Bottom line, I'm always going to love my sister, no matter how she feels about me.

For Tasty Tuesdays in the HoneyB VIP Suite, we come together at Arsimona Lounge in my hometown, Oakland, California, every third Tuesday of the month to discuss relationship issues and challenges. If you find yourself in Oakland during this time, e-mail me and become my personal guest.

I want to thank the friends who support me: Carmen Polk, Malissa Walton, Bernard Henderson, Kim Mason, Onie Simpson, and Donna Jacobs. Lisa Johnson, Malissa Walton, Eve Lynne Robinson, Denise Kees, Deborah Burton, thank you for reading *Character of a Man* and providing great feedback.

We're working to bring you *Making the List,* a literary Web site and television series. My coproducer, Richard C. Montgomery, is the best. *Soul Mates Dissipate*, the movie, has not been forgotten. It's taking more time than I anticipated, but I do believe the universe is in order and the movie will happen when it's supposed to and the timing will be perfect.

A big hug, kiss, and thank-you to Noire for her contribution to our collection, *Maneater*. Noire is the absolute best!

Feel free to hit me up with a piece of your world at www.mary morrison.com. Peace and prosperity.

Discussion Questions

1. What's your definition of character? How important is a person's character to you? Why?

2. Did you take the maneater test? Are you a maneater? How do you feel about maneaters?

3. Could you marry a bisexual man or woman? Do you believe Maverick should marry Danté?

4. Did Maverick's father's rejection mold Maverick? How? Did Maverick's mother love him?

5. Would you vacation at Punany Paradise alone? What fantasy would you like to fulfill at Punany Paradise?

6. Should Seven have engaged in sexual pleasures with Jagger and Fletcher while she was unsure if she was pregnant?

7. Was Deuce Callahan loyal to Zena Belvedere? Should Zena have agreed to have a child/children for Deuce? Why or why not?

8. Was Zena a true friend to Seven? Was Seven a loyal friend to Zena?

9. Are you pro-choice? Do you believe Danté had a right to know Zena was pregnant with his child? Do you think Danté should have the right to approve or disapprove of Zena having the abortion? Why or why not?

10. Was Maverick responsible for Danté's emotional breakdown? Has

a mate ever caused you emotional trauma? If so, did you act out of character when you experienced this trauma?

11. Should weight loss (or gain) become a factor for marriage during an engagement? Would you lose weight to please your spouse?

12. If you found XXX-rated photos or a video of your fiancé or fiancée, would you still marry him/her? Why or why not?

13. Would you take a vacation to Dick City? Why or why not?

SUGAR-HONEY-ICE-TEE

Noire

This urban erotic appetizer is dedicated to B.D.G.C.
Yum, yum. You da man!

Chapter 1

Iain't never been the type of cat you would call fine or good looking or nothing crunk like that, but what I'm low on in the looks department I more than make up for with my earwax skills. See, I know shit. Secret shit. Scandalous secret shit. People must mistake me for their friendly neighborhood bartender or something 'cause they trust me with the type of shit they shouldn't be telling nobody but God.

For real. Let 'em pull some kinda dirty, nasty, diabolical stunt they too ashamed to talk about. Male or female, they take one look at me and all kinds of grimy, low-post skeleton bones start jumping outta their mouths.

You know my type. Never seen, hardly heard. I don't take it personal, I was born this way. Too chunky around the middle. Not quite tall enough. Thick legs. Nose on the wide side. Dark skinned, but dusty black, not pretty black. The kind of cat you can stroll past on the street corner or stand next to on the elevator and don't even see. Seriously. I could walk into a room with only two people in it and neither one of them would even notice me—until somebody shits all over 'em or they got a few guilt trips they need to unload. And that's when a nondescript, beer-bellied, can't-get-no-pussy anti-baller like me becomes a big fat earpiece in high demand.

Take Blow, my room dawg and fraternity brother from back in the college days. He's a real smoove nig, curly haired handsome, and got mad chick appeal. Me and Blow share a crib in North Jersey and his babe game is so foul he can stink up the whole damn house. Man, my nig's flow is so grimy that keeping his lips locked ain't even an option. Blow tells me *all* his dirty dirt, and I mean *all* of it. Shit. If Blow tried to keep half his rotten secrets in his mouth all his teeth would probably fall out.

So yeah. I'm a sound post for my boy, nah mean? Hell, I'm all ears. Twenty-five-eight I listen to his exploits, and then I keep everything he tells me right under my hat. C'mon. That's what homeboys are for. Right? Me and Blow are real tight like that, but if you thinking any of that, uhm, fluffy, fruity shit, you can just think again. I said I can't *get* no pussy, not I don't *want* none.

But Blow gets plenty, and we live under the same roof because it works out best for both of us. Blow draws chicks like he's got some kinda dick mojo, and he don't give a shit about none of them. They come up in the crib ready to strip butt naked at his command, and just like a heat-seeking leech I get off strictly through the association. And I mean I get *off,* too. All it takes is one good look at a sexy babe and I'm ready to grab some lotion, lock myself in the bathroom, and pay homage to the snake called Big Oscar who lives in my pants.

So like I said, it works out. Blow tells me his secrets, and I'm satisfied with living on the spare scraps he tosses off. If I start feeling a little low and unappreciated when he nuts up and clowns on me in front of all our boys, it's a small price to pay to be in his company.

See, Blow's a celebrity. He's a quarterback for the New York Giants. He's a Reggie Bush–looking cat with an outrageous cast of honeys constantly on his trail. We went to high school together and were roommates in college, too, but Blow ended up with a National League contract, and I ended up with . . . Well let's just say I ain't never had Blow's kind of luck.

But while Blow and two of our fraternity brothers, Nap and Tomere, got signed straight out of college because of their superior athletic skills, I had to fall back on my interpersonal groveling skills to get on the team, because no matter how much shit people liked to tell me, secrets didn't pay the rent and they sure didn't fill up my size 48 jelly belly.

I humbled myself and asked Blow for a hookup, and not long after my boys suited up in the blue and white, Blow put in a good word for me with the team's administration and I got on with the Giants as an assistant to one of the senior athletic trainers. It was a real sweet deal, too. I wasn't actually playing the game, but I was *in* the game, if you know what I mean. Working with the athletes was great, and the perks allowed me to indulge all my vices free of charge. I pulled in decent bank, grubbed down on somebody else's dime every day, and traveled all around the country first class with the team.

The senior athletic trainer was a fat Polish old-head who got hired back when icing knees and taping swollen ankles was about all an athlete could expect. He wasn't up to speed on MRIs and electronic nerve stimulation therapies and all that new technology, so he left me alone and let me do my thing.

And my thing was straight, too. But I couldn't say that about Blow, Nap, or Tomere. Those cats was superior athletes, but they were also borderline idiots who wilded out on the regular.

Especially Blow. I stayed by his elbow, kinda keeping an eye on him, ya know? It wasn't easy though, because Blow had been living dirty ever since I'd met him. He'd come real close to getting kicked out of college for taking a rival football player out, and not during a game, neither. If it was one thing Blow couldn't stand, it was competition. He had to be tops on every list, but especially on the football roster, and if he sniffed out somebody he thought might give him a little run, he'd take 'em out without even blinking. We were juniors when Blow got accused of masterminding an accident and ending the season for a second-string quarterback who was bucking hard to be the starter. The cat was just walking with his chick toward campus when a car jumped the curb and according to witnesses, deliberately sideswiped them, breaking the girl's collarbone and dude's ankle and his shin.

Blow wasn't nowhere around when it happened, but he laughed like hell when we found out ol' boy's season was through, and right then and there everybody knew he'd set it up. Blow was a master at getting somebody else to do his dirty work, and he had a crew of flunkies waiting on the sidelines who would do all kinds of shit just to be down with him.

Nap and Tomere were just as bad. Nap was a shady businessman who pulled Internet real-estate scams, and the stingy niggah was also taking bets and shaving points on games. Tomere was a bobby-sock bandit. He liked real young girls. Not babies, but not grown women, either. He was a fake mentor for young kids in the hood, but he also dropped a big bankroll as front money so the youths could invest in crack and then return him a real nice profit.

You wouldn't believe the kinda capers these cats pulled, then sat around and bragged about 'em like it was nothing. They punked the shit out of each other, devising stupid pranks and practical jokes that usually cost a whole lotta doe to pull off. Blow was the worst of the three by a long shot, but they had a one-man-up thing going on between them where they were constantly trying to outdo each other and Nap and Tomere were catching up to Blow pretty fast. I had nicknamed the three of them Dirty, Dastardly, and Depraved, and they laughed like crazy at that shit. I'd thought I was dissin' the nigs, but they wore the names like quality traits and then joked me to death because I didn't have none myself. They were right, too. I couldn't compete on that level of griminess and I didn't want to, neither. Them boyz told me things that made my ears hurt, and they slid through life dogging anybody they chose.

But in the second week of the training season Blow messed around and got his ass stuck in a hole for real. Him, Nap, and Tomere fucked around with the *wrong* niggah, and all their chickens started heading home to roost. I mean, they'd gotten away with some real grimy capers in the past, so some might say that payback was a mutha. But my boys couldn't have known what this particular stunt was gonna cost them. They just *couldn't* have! I mean, not even *God* could have prophesied that them three boys was gonna run up on something so sweet, so wicked, so tantalizing and formidable that not even a fat, loyal frat brother with good listening skills could save them.

So now you wanna know what went down, right? Well, I'm about to put you on, but don't blame me if your gangsta can't take it. I mean, I could pretty this thing up and make it sound real sweet for you, but that's just not the way it happened. It went down nasty and dirty, and that's exactly how I'm gonna give it to you, so chill for a minute and let me flow, because this is a story about three of the sexiest, most devastating chicks I've ever run across. These three gorgeous yummys rolled up in the joint with Blow, Nap, and Tomere, but they rolled back out like a cyclone or a tsunami, wrecking everything that stood in their way. Some guys would prolly call these gangsta chicks names like scandalous, grimy, or sheisty, but where I come from you reap what the fuck you sow, so for the purposes of this story I'll just call these three vicious babes Sugar and Honey, and the coldest and slickest of them all, Ice Tee.

It was training season. Go to it time. The only time in professional football when you're competing against cats who are wearing the same damn jersey as you. Everybody wanted to be a first stringer, so tensions were high on the team. There were all kinds of crazy contests going down. Pissing contests, biggest dick contests, heaviest nuts contests, hardest hit contests, you name it. Professional male athletes and extreme competition go hand in hand, and like I told you, Blow, Nap, and Tomere were some straight-up competitive nigs.

Blow was a real cocky mahfucka, too. Handsome, charming, and fast as hell on his feet. But he'd committed one too many errors in the last season and had single-handedly ruined the team's only chance at the ring. Taking responsibility for his shortcomings wasn't even in him. He blamed those sacks and fumbles on everybody from the towel boy to the franchise owner, so management figured they needed to teach him a lesson.

They brought in Charlie Baker. Charlie had been an outstanding quarterback on an extremely shitty team, and you can bet Blow wasn't happy when the handsome, light-skinned cat showed up on our field wearing a practice jersey.

Charlie was young and just as hungry as Blow was. He was a damned good quarterback, too, some said the best in the league, and to cap it off, unlike Blow he was a public relations dream. I mean, the cat was so clean he fucked all our heads up. He didn't drink, didn't smoke, went to church every Sunday. His handlers kept the groupies and the hoes a mile back, while the press followed him around cracking jokes and writing shit about him that made the public believe he could walk on water.

And from what we could tell, he prolly could. Charlie was a square. He'd been born and raised in Harlem, but there wasn't a speck of grime on him. He kept a smile on his face and his attitude was always positive. Sports analysts showed up to watch him on the practice field, and rumor had it that management was hoping he could lead us all the way to the Super Bowl.

But you know how it goes. Niggahs are dirty. Especially when you jockeying for their position. There's more than one way to crush a man's dreams, and when you fuckin' with crazies like my three homeys, anything was liable to happen.

I caught a glimpse of what was coming the moment Charlie stepped into the locker room. He was a real threat and the guys didn't like him. At least most of them didn't. Blow and his boyz bum-rushed him from minute one, like the big-ass kids they were. They put shaving cream in his helmet. Ripped up his equipment. Slid some itchy shit into his bottle of jock powder—you know how bullies do it.

But Charlie wasn't no punk. He didn't even get fazed. He was a handsome cat, and in better physical condition than any player I'd ever seen. No matter what kinda tricks Blow and them pulled, he rode that shit. He didn't cut up and wreck shit, and he didn't complain to nobody, neither. Charlie got all his get back on the field. He outran Blow like that niggah was standing still eating a Double Whopper. Charlie clocked stats and put out numbers that were unbelievable, and if there was any doubt in management's mind about which quarter-back had earned his place in our starting lineup, Charlie showed his ass on the grass and squashed that noise immediately.

We were still a couple of weeks away from our first preseason game, and Charlie's name was at the top of the shrinking roster. That shit pissed Blow off so bad he got sick. He kicked all his bottom bitches outta the crib, tossed off his entourage, and stayed on his side of the house all by himself for three days straight. He wouldn't even let me come over. Wasn't nobody welcome except Nap and Tomere.

"Get the fuck outta here, Ribs," he said, closing the door in my face. I was surprised, because for the first time that I knew of, Blow was keeping a secret from me. "Your square ass ain't in this shit."

That messed me up. Blow told me *everything*, didn't he? I didn't know what kinda scheme them cats was cooking up, but I know they stayed locked up in the huddle for a whole day. And when it came time to check back in at the stadium, Blow was one happy dude again.

*   *   *

They caught Charlie after the whistle.

I was kneeling on the sidelines, wrapping tape around Stanley Johnson's sweaty toes when it happened. I looked up, and I swear it seemed like the sun got a little dimmer. Almost like a dark cloud had eclipsed it as I witnessed the last play of Charlie Baker's professional football career.

I didn't wanna believe my eyes. Nap went at him high. Then Tomere charged in and clipped him low. And as a final coup de grâce, Blow's flunky Pierre Hampton somersaulted through the air and dove directly down on top of Charlie with his shoulder, landing hard and completely destroying Charlie's knee.

I heard the bone snap way across the field.

I was on my feet and running toward them before anybody could raise the alarm.

"Stand back," I hollered, breathing hard, big belly jiggling.

They were still laying on top of him. Holding him down. Charlie's face was almost blue as he held on to his knee and moaned through big gulps of air.

I knew the leg was done just by the angle of it. And later, Flint Tompkins would tell me he'd seen Nap grab hold of Charlie's ankle and twist that shit up just as Pierre landed on his knee.

My boyz were still on top of Charlie, and all I could see was the griminess in this type of thing.

"Get up off him!" I leaned my three-hundred-plus-pound body over and started tossing them cats across the turf like I was a paid linebacker.

"Yo!" Nap rolled over holding his shoulder. "Watch that shit, Ribs! What the fuck is wrong with you? You almost fucked me up, man!"

Breathing hard, I knelt beside Charlie. He was doubled over in magnificent agony, gripping his shattered knee in both hands. "Be easy, fella," I said, gently removing his hands. "Take some real deep breaths, man."

Blow came running off the sidelines. That fool stood over us cracking up.

"Be easy," I just kept telling Charlie as he tried to catch his breath. "Be easy, man."

"Nah." Blow laughed loudly. "Be *done*, niggah! Take a real long *vacation*, mahfuckah!"

I helped Charlie lay back in the grass and was careful not to move his leg. He was in indescribable pain, and tears ran from his eyes as he stared up at Blow. Just by the look of rage on his face I knew this wasn't the end of it for Charlie Baker. Blow must have seen the same thing in Charlie's eyes, because he walked up close, talking cash shit and stomping his big cleats just short of Charlie's twisted, swelling knee.

"What, mahfuckah!" Blow barked. "What? You got a problem? You wanna go to war with me? Then get ya fuckin' boyz! Get ya homeys, my niggah! Get any fuckin' body you wanna get, ya feel me?"

Something in Charlie Baker's voice made my blood run cold. His words came out real low and frigid, but I swear to God I heard exactly what he said.

Charlie Baker had muttered, "Fuck the dumb shit, niggah. I'ma get my sisters."

Chapter 2

Nap McAllister stood in the mirror modeling an eight-hundred-dollar off-white Chivaly leather cap, the newest edition in his Nappy Fade clothing line. Nap was a hat man, and he had some of the baddest caps in the country. Hats had been the first item of merchandise to come off his production line because he liked to feel something on his head at all times. He was short for a linebacker, and the few extra inches he gained up top meant a lot to him.

And so did the other thirty-seven items produced and sold by Nappy Fade for Men. Nap was a true menace on the football field, but he had a magic eye when it came to men's fashion. What had started out as a secret hobby of sketching men's clothing during the off-season in college had developed into a lucrative multimillion-dollar business venture that rivaled Phat Farm, Rocawear, and Sean John. But not only was Nap a master at designing trendy menswear, he wasn't too shabby when it came down to running a business, either. He'd started Nappy Fade for Men with five Filipino seamstresses sewing in the basement of his grandmother's house, and had parlayed that small venture into a crew of thirty workers sweating over sewing machines in a loft in North Jersey.

But Nap was cheap. Prices were high as hell in urban centers, and he'd discovered a way to increase his profits by outsourcing his operations to a remote village in India. He'd recently hired a guide and taken a trip over there in search of the cheapest labor, the shabbiest facilities, and the most economically deprived village he could find. Nap had no intentions of bettering lives or fixing shit up. Unlike in the United States, there were low taxes and very few labor laws enforced in the region of India where he wanted to do business, and as long as he made a monthly payment to the right people nobody would come bugging the shit out of him about how many hours his employees worked, or whether they were old enough to be sweating over his sewing machines at all.

Nap's initial investment was so small it was almost laughable, and he'd shaken hands with the Realtor and paid it with a smile. He was now the owner of a fifteen-thousand-square-foot warehouse with a dirt floor and broken windows, and as he stood there sneezing and coughing up tiny spores and residue floating in the air from years of accumulated dust, mold, and rat shit, Nap knew his dreams were about to come true.

The only thing left to do was finalize a few legal documents, hire a staff in India, then prepare his inventory for overseas shipment. When it came to money and details, Nap trusted very few people. He could have paid someone to take care of all this for him, but his motto was, "Why give someone money to do for me what I can do on my own for free?"

So Nap handled his own damned business. In addition to managing the four slum tenements he'd purchased for pennies in Harlem seven years earlier, he also supervised every aspect of his newest venture and looked forward to getting it off the ground. Since it was football season he couldn't make things happen as quickly as he would have liked, but working slow was fine with him. He was careful to keep word about the move from getting to his current employees. He didn't want them to get disgruntled about losing their jobs and start acting crazy. Nap was afraid they might get lazy or vindictive. They might start pushing out shoddy materials or sabotaging his shit. He couldn't have that, so he kept them completely in the dark, including his managers and suppliers.

Fuck all of 'em, he thought. He wouldn't even stick around to give out pink slips. They'd figure it out when they came to work at 4:00 a.m. and found the joint padlocked. Businesses folded all the time and people were always looking for jobs. It was a fact of life for the weak, and Nap's life was set. He had a college degree, a major National League football contract, and several largely unethical but thriving businesses. Whether or not his employees found other work when he closed shop was not his problem.

But Nap did have one problem. It had to do with his tooth, and it was the sweetest damn problem he'd ever met. Her name was Sugar, and not only did she have Nap's sweet tooth throbbing with desire, she had his nose and his wallet both wide open.

He'd met her at Feel Good, a twenty-four-hour gym right up the street from his house. Like the rest of the team, Nap used the training facilities provided by the NFL franchise, but he'd learned from his boy Blow that true superstars had to push a lot harder. Even when it hurt. Nap pushed his body way past the breaking point. His will was much stronger than his flesh, and he hit the weights like a madman after team workouts and on rest days, too.

That fat–ass niggah Ribs was watching though, and he was always screaming on somebody about overtraining and stress injuries. So Nap did his most brutal and punishing workouts on the sly, away from Ribs's bitching eyes. Feel Good catered to a high-profile clientele, and he could pound his body in privacy as hard as he wanted to.

The first time Nap saw Sugar he had just walked into the weight room.

"Yo! *Yo!* YO!" Nap had squealed in excitement, nearly backhanding a nearby towel girl to get her attention. Sugar was walking past him killing a pair of hot pink workout shorts and sporting crazy sexy cleavage in a white tank top. Her light perfume trailed behind her and infiltrated his nose, and her phatty rump had taken command of his eyes.

The towel girl stumbled, then looked around rubbing her arm. She'd been filling a small icebox with bottled spring water and bright red apples, and Nap's blow had nearly knocked her down.

"Who the fuck is *dat?*" Nap shrieked, pointing at Sugar's wiggling ass. "Yo, she working up in here now?"

"Er—she's our new manager."

"Well introduce me, goddamnit! I drop some heavy bills in this joint every month. She needs to know the name of one of her biggest clients!"

They were introduced, and Sugar had been cool on him at first, which only caused Nap to work harder.

"How can I help you?" she'd asked in a disinterested, professional voice.

Nap was bent. Everything about her was perfect . . . her eyes, her smile . . . she was beautiful. So beautiful, it made his muscles weak. With his mouth wide open and a puppy-dog look on his face, Nap had taken her hand to shake, then tried to hold on for a few seconds more.

"I'm sorry," she said, easing her hand from his grasp and turning away. "If it's towels you require, or beverages and a light snack, Lana here can assist you."

"Wait—" Her fingers had felt perfect in his large hand. Nap wanted to touch her again. Everywhere.

"Um, I know you know me. Everybody does. I'm Nap McAllister. New York Giants football."

Sugar blinked, unimpressed. In fact, her glare became one of extreme distaste.

"Sorry, I'm not a football fan. I find it a dangerous, violent sport. But pleased to meet you, Mr. McAllister, and thank you for patronizing Feel Good. If you have an administrative issue please make an appointment with my secretary. If not, then Lana can assist you in all other matters."

It took Nap two weeks, but eventually he got what he wanted. Sugar's phone number. He hung around the gym every available moment until he wore down her defenses and was treated to first a smile and then a short conversation about weight training. Sugar gave him her number and Nap memorized it, then sat staring at the phone for half an hour before he worked up the nerve to call her.

"Stop playing yourself," he said out loud, chiding himself for acting like a punk. "You a celebrity, niggah! You pull fine bitches all the time!"

But it was more than Sugar's gorgeous face and blockbuster body that had Nap open. It was everything about her, from the way she walked to the air of class and superiority she held in her eyes each time they met. Whether Nap was a rich celebrity or not, Sugar definitely wasn't sweating him. Unlike most chicks who found out he was a professional athlete and were ready to get naked in the middle of the street, Sugar didn't give a damn if she never saw him again. Nap liked that. He started visiting Feel Good on the regular. He autographed a few head shots and posters for her staff and found out Sugar's work schedule. Unless there was team business going on, Nap stayed in the gym like a big rat, following behind Sugar like she was running on the green with a football under her arm.

And when he finally caught her, Sugar proved that she was more than worth the chase. They'd been dating for a few weeks and even though he knew it sounded crazy, Nap thought Sugar might be the one to lead the dog in him off the porch and bring it in the house for good. He was catching all kinds of crazy warm feelings for her every single day, and for the first time in his career he'd found something more important to him than football. Nap had found Sugar, a smart, gorgeous bombshell with a body that was both fit and sexy at once. The first time they got it on Nap was taken by surprise. The girl was hungry. She had more energy and drive than a little bit.

"Slow down 'fore I come," he'd whispered, popping sweat.

Sugar was riding him damn near to death. Her big titties bounced and quivered above him, and a bead of sweat dripped from her up-turned nipple and landed on his nose.

"Deeper," she urged, and Nap grasped her slim waist and raised and lowered her onto him while thrusting upward with all his might.

Sugar bent forward and covered his lips with hers, growling deep in her throat as her ass bucked and quivered. Switching positions, she lay flat on top of him and squeezed her thighs together, trapping his dick in a grip so tight it made him yelp and spurt. Sugar fucked him like she was the one with the pole, and Nap lay beneath her, massaging her damp, gyrating ass and moaning her sweet name.

Laying there trapped in Sugar's deep pussy lock, Nap was a happy man. He thought about his boy Blow and screamed inside; *Suck my dick, niggah!* Nap and his boys had been competing for bitches for the longest time, and Blow always went for the baddest chicks and thought Nap and Tomere should take whatever was left. Well, there was no way in fuck Blow could outdo him this time because they didn't make 'em any better than the girl rocking her hips on top of him. Nap felt blessed and bankrolled. Sugar had a nice career going so it wasn't his money that she was after. She was business minded, too, even more so than he was, and that stunned him. He'd laid out his intricate plans for expanding his clothing line and was knocked off his feet when Sugar not only understood his angle but made a few suggestions that could cut costs even further and reduce his overhead. Nap was on cloud nine. Already he was thinking about introducing a new line for women called Nappy Dugout, and he wanted Sugar to be his model and his spokeswoman. She had it all, this girl did. Body, looks, and above all, brains! Nap couldn't stop feening for her, and he couldn't wait to introduce her to his homeys neither.

Chapter 3

Have you ever seen a chick so fine that you gotta run to the bathroom?

Well, that's what happened to me the first time I saw Nap's new hottie, Sugar. We were partying with the team in Newark and everybody there was hooked up with somebody soft and pretty, except me.

Nap's girl sure had the right name. Sugar was sweet, all right. Sweet enough to make you sick. Somebody introduced us and I couldn't stop staring at her. I followed her around on the sneak tip, bent by her low-slung blouse and the heart shape of her ass. Every now and then I positioned myself so I was standing in front of her so I could eyeball those thick breasts with the million-dollar nipples, that threatened to poke through her blouse. I knew the girl could feel me stalking her, but I couldn't get enough. Not even when Nap crept behind me and stepped deep on the back of my foot, then clowned me right in front of her.

"Man, pick up ya lip, and tie down ya dick," he laughed, pointing as I used both hands to try and cover the big piece of wood that was rising in the front of my pants. "C'mon, son," he said, shaking his head in disgust like I'd just dug up my ass in public or something. "Gone in the bathroom and take care of business." Nap pushed me toward the men's room. "Gone, Ribs. You got your lotion, right? Gone in there and take some of that pressure off, homey."

All them cats stood around and laughed. I didn't think that shit was funny, but Nap was right. There'd been more than a few occasions in college that him and the frat brothers had bust into the bathroom and caught me slapping the hell outta my ten-inch snake. I kept a small tube of lotion in my pocket because I had no dick control to speak of, and sometimes the sight of a real sexy broad could send me right over the edge. I was pitiful with that shit too, because I couldn't always dig out my lotion and make it to the bathroom in time. Like a young boy going through puberty, my dick would nut at the drop of a dime, and if I ran across the right girl it really didn't matter where I was. My man Oscar would jump up outta the basement and start spitting right in my drawers.

I stood there and took Nap's joking like a champ, but I wasn't pressed though, because every one of them hard-dick niggahs was feeling the same thing I was feeling. All of them shoulda got a tube of lotion and joined me in the can 'cause they was bent on the sight of Sugar, too.

Still, Nap didn't have to do me like that. Wasn't no need to shine that kinda light on my problem and embarrass me in front of his girl. He knew all about my situation and he knew I couldn't control it. I mean, it was a blessing to have been born with such a heavy package, but it would have been nice to have a little dominion over that shit! I was worse than a thirteen-year-old. If the wind blew too hard my shit jumped on rock, and believe me, as much meat as I was packing down there, my johnson was hard to hide. Let a fine chick so much as stand too close to me, I'd be in trouble. My snake would be so hard my tighty-whitey drawers would be restraining it like a straitjacket, choking it all around the head and cutting off my circulation. Damn right I'd have to find a private spot and deal with all that. I couldn't get a woman when I needed one, so what else was a horse-dicked ashy fat boy like me supposed to do? I got multiple erections all day long, and they didn't go away on their own. And hell nah, if you thinking something like that, you're crazy as fuck. I didn't wish for less dick. I wished for *more pussy!*

"Sh-shut up," I told Nap, then pushed my hands in my pockets and tried to make a quick adjustment. I glanced at sweet Sugar, and she was smiling. It wasn't one of them "oh shit, that nigga is so nasty" smiles neither.

"It was nice meeting you," she said, then held her head slightly to one side and waved with three fingers.

I eyed those hard nipples and round hips and almost bust one right then and there. Struggling for control, I pulled one hand from my pocket and waved back, then hurried toward the bathroom so I could moan Sugar's candy-sweet name into my lotion-slick palm.

The next time I saw Sugar, Nap had come by the crib to chill and she was standing in my kitchen, chopping vegetables with a big knife.

"Pork Ribs!" Nap shouted when I walked through the door. He was chilling on Blow's brown leather sofa with one of his muscular legs draped over the top. I stared down at him and shook my head. Nap looked swole. Like he was bulking up pretty heavy with muscle. I'd already been on him about overtraining, and from where I stood the niggah looked like he mighta been dabbling in 'roids or something.

"Man, tell me you ain't messing around with nothing, Nap. You looking kinda mean and pumped up, my man."

"It ain't about drugs," he said, jumping up and sliding up behind Sugar and making me jealous by biting on her earlobes. "It's about life, niggah. It's about good sex and a good woman. What you know about that shit?"

I frowned. He had me there 'cause I didn't know jack about any of it.

Embarrassed, I dropped my briefcase and opened the cabinet where I kept my stash. I took down a full bag of Doritos, some frosted lemon cookies, and grabbed a banana from the fruit bowl. I was pouring a glass of Diet Coke when I felt a warm hand touch me from behind.

"Close your eyes," Sugar demanded.

I turned around holding my glass. "Whattup?"

"Don't look, Rishawn. Just close your eyes. I promise you can trust me."

Nap laughed and I closed my eyes.

"Okay," she said. Her voice was warm. I would have trusted her fine ass with a butcher knife at my nuts. "Think about all the toxins you're about to put into your body. I can tell you're a sugar addict by the food choices you just made."

Uh-huh, I wanted to say. Damn right I was a sugar addict, and if I could just get a little taste of her I'd volunteer to be the poster boy for sugar diabetes!

"Open your mouth," she demanded, and I obeyed.

Nap laughed again. "Ribs, she got you lookin' real stupid standing there with your lips hanging open, my nig!"

She placed something cold and sweet on my tongue.

"There . . . Taste that. It's so much better for you than those empty calories you've been taking in."

"Stoooopid . . . ," Nap sang.

"Don't be silly," Sugar said. "Rishawn, you look just fine to me."

Sugar made me smile inside. I ain't never been one to go for fruits or vegetables, but I shocked myself as I stood there crunching a sweet hunk of chilled pineapple and digging it, too.

"How's that taste?" she asked softly, her fingers on my arm.

"Yo!" Nap bitched. "Why you over there hand-feeding the hog?"

"Tastes kinda good," I admitted. "Can I open my eyes now?"

Her laughter was real sweet and even though I couldn't see her, I was getting hot just knowing she was standing so close to me.

"Not so fast. Take a sip of this."

I felt her hold one hand under my chin like I was a baby, then press the edge of a cup to my bottom lip.

"Aw, hell!" Nap bitched some more.

"Sip it slowly," Sugar urged. "Enjoy the way it coats your tongue and slides down your throat."

Her voice was like a warm silk glove stroking me. My mind took me exactly where I didn't need to go, and I stood there in front of her with my dick growing bigger by the second, and with nothing except my hands to hide it behind.

The liquid in my mouth was fruity smooth. It had just the right amount of sweetness and a little pulp to it, too. I didn't know what the hell it was.

"Guava juice." Sugar laughed at the puzzled look on my face. "It beats the unnatural additives in that diet cola coming and going. You can open your eyes now."

I did, and the first thing I saw was her gorgeous smile.

I glanced at my usual afternoon snack and suddenly it didn't look so hot.

"I'm preparing a light snack for Napoleon, and there's more than enough here for you to have one, too. Nutrition and exercise are the keys to a long, healthy life, Rishawn. My workout partner moved to the West Coast, and I'm looking for someone new. I know you're a trainer, but sometimes our jobs just don't motivate us. If you're interested, I would love to work out with you and give you a few fitness tips. We could take a few walks outside or on the treadmill at my gym, and then talk about nutrition and health until we both work up a sweat. What do you say?"

"He says no," Nap said firmly. "Pork-ass likes to eat. He says no."

Fuck Nap. I was aching. In my heart and in my groin. A woman like Sugar had never even taken a second look at me. My ass stood there grinning like a chump and looking crazy–stupid with my hands trying to cover the lump rising in the front of my pants.

"C'mon, Rishawn." Sugar ignored Nap and put her hand on my chest, right in the middle of my two fluffy man-breasts. "It'll be a great opportunity to try something new. What do you say?"

What the hell did me and Oscar say?

I said, "Um . . . cool, Sugar. That sounds hot. But right now I gotta make a li'l run to the bathroom."

Chapter 4

". . . and we are proud and honored to present this award for the highest level of mentorship and service to . . . Mr. Tomere Williams, defensive end for the New York Giants!"

Stepping up on the stage and into the roar of clapping hands and flashing cameras, Tomere Williams smoothed his tailored French suit and approached the podium. He accepted the large gold and brown plaque from the director of S.O.S., then adjusted the microphone, angling it up toward his handsome face.

"Thank you. Thank you, everyone. It is sincerely a pleasure to be here today, and the honor is all mine."

He glanced around at the huge crowd that had gathered in the Schomburg Center's auditorium with smiling faces. It was always a big deal when a major celebrity put large sums of money back into the community, and Tomere Williams was not only a major financial contributor to S.O.S., he was also one of its beneficiaries.

"Back when I was growing up here in Harlem," he said, forcing fake tears to well up in his eyes, "sometimes the only meal I ate each day was the one fed to me by the volunteers at Saving Our Sons. If it wasn't for the kindness and generosity of the people who stand before me here today, I might have *starved* to death out there on those cold streets."

A huge round of applause broke out, and a couple of older women sniffed and wiped away tears of their own. Tomere glanced into the crowd and met the eyes of his latest diversion, a beautifully wild girl named Honey. How she'd known he was getting an award today was anybody's guess, but Honey was clever like that. She played cat and mouse with Tomere, and although he was fast on the football field, he was way too slow to figure this girl out. She sat there in the midst of the poor, struggling folks of Harlem looking chic, sexy, and seriously uptown. Tomere had wrestled with a moment of stark fear because he'd already made arrangements to hook up with a sixteen-year-old shawty with monster titties after the ceremony. Her parents thought Tomere was taking the girl to interview for an internship as a candy striper in a hospital downtown, but in reality he had made reservations at a West Side hotel where he planned to lick her candy and be up in some tight young pussy all day long.

But not with sweet Honey in the house. Fuck that teenager. Tomere's dick thumped just looking at his girl, and he had to fight with himself to keep from breaking out in a smile when he was supposed to be crying. All this mentoring bullshit was a front. A big fat front. The water falling unabashedly from his eyes was nothing but crocodile tears. His stifled sobs were really chuckles of laughter in disguise.

Sure, he'd hung out at the Saving Our Sons center in his youth and had even gotten himself a membership card. But he for damn sure had never eaten their slimy food or gone hungry a day in his life. Tomere's parents had been business owners who lived in a nice Harlem brownstone but owned a chain of dry cleaners up in the Bronx. He'd grown up wearing some of the best gear in town, and the only reason he'd hung around the S.O.S. posse was because that's where all the hottest and loosest young girls in the hood were.

S.O.S. had had a good football team, and every young chick in the neighborhood would turn out to watch the athletes do their thing. After the games stank panties would be flying through the air all over Harlem. Tomere was always first in line to get him some trim. He was an R. Kelly type of man. The younger, the better. He'd played basketball, football, and run track. As a fourteen-year-old, he gotten more pussy in the cut of Harlem's stairways and back alleys than most grown men got from their wives in their own beds.

Of course, naming Saving Our Sons as his favorite charity and making large cash donations to the center was more than just a way of giving back to the community. It was a grassroots effort to be connected to what was important to him. A way of financing his drug payoffs and staying in touch with all the hot young pussy on the ground these days, and even though he'd gotten a bit older and a whole lot richer, the neighborhood hadn't changed that much, and neither had the mentality of the kids. Tomere got almost as much young ass now as he did back in the day when he was pretending to be a hungry little ghetto boy.

Not to mention the tax benefits of it all. Shit, giving to S.O.S. meant he prospered coming and going. With no wife or kids, and making the kind of bank he made, charitable donations were almost mandatory. Saving Our Sons was a real good set up. A handy little write-off. It served Tomere's purpose in more ways than one.

"Today," he continued speaking into the microphone, biting his lip and wiping at an imaginary tear. "I stand before you as an example of what a community of determined people can accomplish. You fed me, nurtured me, and guided me . . . some of you even knocked me upside my head when I needed it, and that probably helped me do the right thing most of all."

Tomere held his plaque up high in the air and paused for effect as the crowd roared. He saw Honey smiling up at him with her long sexy legs crossed at the knee. He thought about how he'd dove between those legs earlier that morning, licking the inside of her thighs until he got to that soft creamy spot in the middle. She hadn't allowed him to penetrate her, but his mouth watered as he remembered how sweet she'd smelled down there, how she'd bent her knees and locked her ankles behind his neck and squirted her sticky juice all down his chin.

Tomere had met Honey a few weeks earlier and they'd gone at it hard and strong from the jump. Months earlier he had taken an elbow to his top lip during a pickup game of basketball that had required stitches and had left a noticeable scar above his lip. He'd been having lunch in a local Harlem restaurant when a pretty young waitress approached him with the name of a plastic surgeon who specialized in removing scars from pigmented skin.

Tomere hadn't thought twice about the damn scar until the girl mentioned it, and when she said it made him look old and scary, he had called the surgeon quick fast and gotten an immediate appointment. Honey had been the anesthesiologist in the office, and the last thing Tomere had seen before going out for the count had been her sexy smile and gorgeous big brown eyes. Her skin tone was radiant and her thick hair had some curl to it. You could tell she was a sister, but she mighta had some Latina in her too, and Tomere liked her combination. She was tall and slender, and not even them ugly green scrubs could hide the breasts and ass she was packing. The girl had so much umph to her that Tomere had hoped to have a wet dream during his surgery, but he'd been too heavily drugged to remember a damn thing. Afterwards, he'd struck up a conversation with her and was surprised when she handed him her business card and suggested he give her a call.

She'd been fucking him dry for weeks. Her sheet game was so unique that he couldn't get enough of her. Tomere was used to banging young girls who had no experience and even less backbone. They'd bend over whenever he told them, twist their young legs above their heads however he wanted, and give him wet, sloppy top following his specific instructions. But with Honey it was different. The girl was bad, and she was all up in his crib and in his mind too. She showed up in some of the damnedest places, and Tomere never could figure out how she always knew where to find him. The bottom line was, Honey was mysterious and exciting. She took charge of him like she owned his black ass, and as different as this kind of thing was for him, Tomere found that he really liked it.

It was Honey who decided when and where they'd fuck, and he always, always had to eat her pussy out very thoroughly before he was allowed to put his dick anywhere near her. For the girl to look so damn good and come across with such polish and class, she was real gutter in the bedroom and she liked her sex hard and nasty. She commanded him in every direction. It didn't matter if he was on top or if she was backing that ass up to his face. It was all about pleasing Honey, and he was required to do exactly what he was told.

This was some crazy new shit that totally fucked Tomere's head up. So many times he'd wanted to blurt out a confession to Blow and Nap about how this girl had him on lock like he was a real bitch. How he lost all his gangsta in her hands, and when she glared at him and told him to peel off her panties or stick his big thumb up in her wet pussy, or demanded he get on his knees and toss her pretty ass-salad, or open his mouth and suck her slim, polished toes, he jumped to it like a good soldier and followed her orders to the tee.

Honey was a joker in the bed, and sometimes she got mean too. But even when she was degrading him, it felt good. She'd laugh as she forced him to march around the bedroom looking totally ridiculous with a rock hard dick and wearing nothing but her high-heel shoes! She made him watch in the mirror as she smeared red lipstick around his mouth, then tongued him down deeply and licked it all off. He thought he'd have the strength to draw the line when she insisted he put on one of her pink thongs, then snatched his erection outta one side and proceeded to wet it up with her tongue, but he didn't. The truth was, Honey was the first girl who punked Tomere sexually and could make him do anything she demanded, and it was the way she absolutely dominated him, much in the same way that he had liked to control teenage girls, that turned him on to no end. Honey was so damn sexy and her body was so hot and banging, that Tomere could practically cum just by looking at her.

And right now, holding his gaze in her spell, Honey uncrossed her legs, then crossed them back again and winked. Just that subtle erotic motion was enough to throw Tomere off his microphone game, and as he stood before the crowd of rapt attendees he fought to drag his mind away from Honey's charms and focus it on the mission of S.O.S.

Tiny beads of sweat had formed on his upper lip and in his pants, his dick throbbed. Despite all the pussy he'd eaten this morning, Tomere wanted to fuck. He wanted to fuck Honey. Out of the hundred or so women in the audience, Tomere could smell *her* pussy, and his dick jerked like it could shoot a load off right there in public.

Instead, he shook his head and did his best to calm down and conjure up fake moments of painful memories for the crowd. It was all bullshit, and he knew it. Life had been good to Tomere, and he'd come through most challenges on top. He didn't have shit to stand up there and whine about, but if he really wanted to feel sad enough to cry, all he had to think about was the possibility of losing everything he had worked so hard to achieve. A thought like that could put him in the nut house for real. Tomere shivered as he pictured himself living in a cold Harlem roach trap with a stank, fat wife. Or worse, he got dizzy seeing himself as a pissy street bum, riding the subway from one end of the line to the other. Just envisioning himself as penniless and homeless was enough to make his dick shrivel up real quick, and that's just what it did as he brought his speech to a close by thanking the board of directors and their staff for the distinct honor bestowed upon him, then sniffing back a few more fake tears before walking off the stage and waving good-bye.

From the crowd, Honey caught his eye and angled her head toward the door. She'd be waiting for him somewhere outside, Tomere knew. If he was lucky she'd be in the backseat of his Maserati with her legs spread and her panties around her ankles.

Clutching his plaque like a prize, Tomere hugged the women in the crowd and shook hands with the men as he made his way across the room and toward the exit doors.

Kristina, the sixteen-year-old slut he had been planning to fuck all day, stood near the doorway with a dumb, expectant look on her face. *Let the ho wait,* Tomere thought. She'd be waiting all damn day because he was outtie. He wouldn't even bother to tell her nothing. Let her figure it out when she came outside and found out his whip was gone. He was losing his taste for young girls, Tomere realized. Being with such a strong, sexually domineering woman like Honey kept him on his toes. She was a challenge that he looked forward to each day, and after only a few weeks she'd managed to get his house keys, his car keys, and judging by the way he broke his neck to follow her swishing little sailor skirt out the door, Honey had also gotten the keys to Tomere's heart.

Chapter 5

It wasn't more than a few weeks after becoming Sugar's workout partner that I first laid eyes on Honey. We were coming out of a team meeting and she was standing against a wall opposite the door. I was near the back of the herd, and I wondered why the line filing out the door had suddenly slowed down. But when I got close enough to see what had stopped the fellas in their tracks and had them whispering under their breaths, I stumbled against Roger Boston and almost took our star running back down to the ground.

"Who's that?!" I squeaked. Her beauty hit me right in my gut. It hit me someplace else, too, but I was too embarrassed to check myself out. Wasn't no need. My man Oscar was already poking his big head outta his hiding place and pretty soon anybody who bothered to look at me would damn sure notice him.

"That's Honey. Tomere's new trick. I heard she's a VIP for some black surgeon over in Harlem."

The girl was a VIP alright. A goddamn Vixen in Practice! I mean, Nap's girl Sugar was *fine*, and I loved the way she was pushing me toward better health, but she didn't have shit on this chick right here.

My lips went loose as I watched her leaning back against that wall. She looked like a damn tornado. Curves just blowing circles around her curves. I could tell how she got her name, because her skin was the exact same color of bee honey and she looked even sweeter. She had bright eyes and that curly kinda hair. It was slicked back from her gorgeous face and hung down past her shoulders. She had on a slinky little white dress that was so sexy my eyes got crossed, and there was a crazy amount of ice glinting from her ears and around her neck.

"Goddamn," I moaned out loud, then got pushed hard from behind as Tomere tried to get out in the hall to greet his girl.

"Move it, Ribs," he said and knocked past me with a big grin on his face. He walked over to that thick piece of na-na leaning against the wall and slipped his arm around her tight waist. "This is all me, bro. You couldn't handle half of this if you fuckin' tried."

Trying had never been my problem. Getting the opportunity had! A bunch of guys were still standing around in the hall. Most of them was faking like they were deep in conversation, but almost all of them were really busting looks at Honey Baby on the sly.

"Yo, Ribs," Tomere said, nodding for me to come closer. "Get over here. This is my baby, Honey. Honey, this is one of my best nigs, Pork Ribs."

I glanced at Tomere, then snuck another eyeful of Honey from head to toe. She was a stunna alright. A true banga. Her teeth were snow white and she had smooth light brown skin, and dimples in her cheeks that set her whole package off just right.

"Ribs?" Tomere said, interrupting my fantasy with a questioning look.

"Huh?"

His gaze dropped down toward my dick, then he looked up again.

I looked down too. My shit was sticking out like a flagpole under my gym shorts.

"Oh!"

I'd taken a few notes in the meeting, and now I used my pad to try and cover the bulge of embarrassment that loomed larger than hell in front of me. "I'm cool," I said, even though the scent of Honey's perfume tickled my nose and had me sweating all down in my drawers.

"Man, we playing *football* in this camp, yo. Go find you a little nappy dugout so you can swing that bat."

"I said I'm cool, playa."

Tomere shrugged and laughed, then kissed Honey on her lips.

"Don't pay Ribs no mind," he told her, leading her away and leaving me standing there hiding behind a notepad and looking stupid with my dick sticking straight out in front of me. "He's one of them real soft niggahs who's too shy to get any play."

Honey grinned at me over her shoulder, then snuggled herself under Tomere's armpit and sauntered off beside him. I was mad, but that didn't stop me from watching her phat ass cheeks bounce up and down as she walked away.

I hated it when my boyz joked me like that, especially in front of a cute chick, but it was a minute before I could take my eyes off Honey's bomb figure and turn away. I made a mental note that the next time Sugar Daddy Tomere needed somebody to cover for him with one of them fifty-leven Harlem juveniles he liked to bang, he could find somebody else. I was tired of being a flunky and getting clowned like a fool. These dudes was gonna have to start respecting me, or something big was gonna happen!

Damn right, I thought as I satisfied my bruised ego with a little bull-shit mental swagger. Something big had already happened. Right down in the front of my pants. With butt-naked visions of Honey dancing in my head, I fled toward my locker to grab my lotion so I could lock myself in the bathroom and satisfy the crazy black snake that lived in my pants.

Chapter 6

Her pink slit glistened with juice as Byron Ford dug her out. She'd scooted her naked ass to the edge of the high-profile bed and was moaning and thrashing around like she was starring in a porn video. Blow couldn't even remember her name, but he stood beside the bed holding her left leg high in the air. He slid into her with short, hard strokes as he tried—without success—to hit the back walls of her pussy.

"Oh, you stud!" the pretty white girl cooed, with her eyes closed tight. "You're hurting me! Not so deep! Yes, screw me, you beast! Pound my cunt! Your cock is magnificent! You're the best lay I've ever had!"

Blow was bored. He gazed down at her pink nipples and blond hair and tried not to yawn. The girl had a decent body, but she was a poor liar. Blow knew damn well he had a small penis. Nobody had to tell him that. From the time he was playing junior high school basketball and taking showers after gym class, he'd been well aware of his inadequacy. Not that every guy on the team had a tree-trunk dick, neither. Blow was far from gay, but he couldn't help peeking at the competition. Some of the other guys were less than hung, too. They had what Blow felt would be considered average-sized dicks. Not too big and not too small. Looking down at his own equipment, Blow realized his was definitely on the short end of the ruler. It was thick enough to pass, but not long enough to do any damage.

Just one more inch on his pole might have made a difference to Blow's young ego, but even though he'd tried every dick-enhancement exercise he'd heard about and sent away for endless mail-order penis enlargers, in the end nothing had worked, and Blow had learned to accept his shortcoming and put himself in situations where it really didn't matter.

Like now, with the nameless white whore fronting beneath him on the bed.

Blow was a sister lover at heart, but every so often his ego needed more stroking than his dick did. At those times, he'd find him a white girl whose only goal in life was to make him feel big. In all areas.

Black girls were just too honest. They didn't give a damn about your ego. Fuck the fact that he was rich and a baller too, sisters wasn't trying to pull no punches when it came down to the package. Too many times Blow had gotten with a black chick who expected him to live up to the myth.

"Uh-uh. Uh-*uh*. Why you playing with me like that? Big as you is? All them damn muscles? Well what happened to the one down there? Man, you real cute and all, but you gotta come better than that!"

And even those who didn't complain out loud often made him uncomfortable just by their silence. He'd be on top working that wet hole like a football was stuck inside it, and they'd be laying there staring at the ceiling or examining their fingernails or some rude shit like that.

To compensate, Blow had become a pussy-eating fool, and these days by the time he stuck his dick in a sister he made sure she'd already come more times than she wanted to. That pussy would be so wet and slick when he got ready to stick his meat in there that the girl probably figured if she couldn't feel him deep enough then it was her fault that her pussy was loose, not his fault for having a short dick!

His cell chirped on his nightstand and the white girl moaned louder.

Still thrusting his hips back and forth, Blow reached for it.

The girl got louder. "Daddy, yes. You're fucking me so good! Your cock is amazing. You're making me cum . . . you're making me cum . . . you're making me—"

"Shut up," he told her. He looked at the caller ID, then slid his wet dick out of her and turned away.

"Hey, whassup, gorgeous?" Blow spoke into the phone. "You got something good for me?"

Behind him the girl lay on the bed just as he'd left her. Leg up in the air and eyes screwed closed.

"Damn, baby. Two condos at a price like that? That's hot! It's a good thing I found you because you smart as hell! Beautiful too. I tell you what. How about I cook you some dinner tonight? Just to celebrate?"

Listening as the diva on the line made a few bullshit excuses, Blow broke out in a genuine grin. This sister was amazing. Not only was she the bangingest woman he'd met in years, she was multitalented and tops in all areas.

A few weeks earlier he'd received a card in the mail from a Miss Teesa Blake regarding prime real estate ventures. The woman pictured on the card was stunning, and the card had listed the names of several top professional athletes who had benefited from her services. Since he'd always been interested in amassing property, Blow had given her a call.

They'd met for coffee on a Thursday, and by Sunday Blow was in love. Tee was so hot and fine that it was almost unreal. He couldn't even keep up with her conversation because he was too mesmerized by her stunning brown skin and striking features.

"So," she had said almost as soon as he sat down at their first meeting, "what I do is find lucrative deals for clients who have the capital to invest but just don't have the time to do the market research. Some of my deals are made nationally, but lately I've been finding some pretty amazing property across the borders and overseas too. It all depends on the timing, which is why I typically limit my clientele and only deal with those who can make quick decisions on the move and have enough money to strike while the iron is hot."

Blow was all for that. Her teeth were amazingly white, and her flawless skin looked like light brown sugar. Her black hair was thick and wavy, and the way she had it styled brought out all her great features. Gazing into her brown eyes as she spoke, Blow knew he could go for any damn thing this girl dished out. He was just about tired of all the stupid groupies, tired of the endless, nameless, faceless, emotionless fucking. The girl sitting across from him had a brilliant mind to go along with that angelic face and dick-crushing body, and with all his fame and all his money, a woman like her was something Blow was missing from his life.

And right now, even under the threat of revealing his small dick, and with the dumb broad laying there showing her pink pussy on the edge of his bed, Blow wanted Tee. He wanted her real bad, and he would have said and done anything to have her.

"C'mon, Teesa," he begged into the phone. "Just this once. You said they call you Ice Tee but you ain't gotta be so cold! You can trust me, I swear. I owe you, baby. You've found me a lot of good property over the last few weeks and I appreciate that shit. I know you don't like mixing business with pleasure, but your business is my pleasure. C'mon, sweetie. Let me cook you dinner. I've got my mother's shrimp scampi recipe and it's off the hook. I'm serious. You'll love it."

Blow listened as he walked over to the window and peeled off his wet condom.

"What? Yeah, I know you're a Realtor and a psychologist, too! But that don't mean you know what's in *my* head!" He laughed loudly, stroking his hardening erection and forgetting the dumb trick on the bed behind him who was still holding up her leg.

"Okay, okay, so how about this then . . . let's eat out. You pick the restaurant and the time, and I'll swing by your crib and drive you there, okay?"

Blow crossed his fingers as he listened to her try to talk her way out of it, but he was relentless. Five minutes later she finally gave in, and Blow couldn't believe his luck.

"Yeah!" he shouted, forgetting all about the white chick on his bed. "You just made a damn good decision, baby girl. Thanks, Tee. For giving me a chance. I promise, baby, you won't ever regret it."

Dinner with Tee was off the chart. Blow was bent. Shook to the bone by her beauty and by her spectacular smile. The girl was it. She was tantalizing, intelligent, and built for a man's comfort. She was a Harlem girl and had a quick, shrewd mind for business, but Blow could also see that she had a big heart as well. Tee struck him as the type who would throw down for the underdog, and he found every little thing about her cute and remarkable. The way she held her head to the side when she laughed, the way she sipped her iced tea then dotted her mouth with a napkin. She had shine on her. Sunshine. Blow watched her as they ate, and even though he joked and laughed and kept up with their conversation, in the back of his mind he was busy banging the hell outta sweet Ice Tee.

He knew just how he would handle her, too. Like she was a high-end Mercedes-Benz. Wouldn't be no holding her leg up and tryna get in her belly while gutter shit flew outta her mouth. Nah, he would play nice with that professional punanee first. Get it to the right temperature and then stir some thick cream into that coffee.

Blow envisioned Tee laying on her stomach with her round ass high in the air. He wanted to taste her from the back. Stick his nose all up in her stuff like he was her puppy dog. Under the table, Blow's dick got hard as he envisioned licking her out. He wanted to part her ass mounds and open her wide, then take his time and nibble and suck and lick until she was begging for the dick.

And then he'd slide his hands up her tight waist and play with those big titties while tagging her from behind. Slowly and gently, treating her like a lady as he made sure she was completely satisfied. There wouldn't be no bedroom complaints coming from a lady like Tee. This sister had manners, and she was intelligent enough to know that not every black man was gonna be swinging a long rope. Nobody could control what size dick they got handed in life, and Blow knew Tee would appreciate his efforts to make her feel good without making him feel like less than a man.

"What do you think about building wealth in Mexico?" Tee was asking. Blow coughed and brought himself back. He'd been watching her lips move, but his attention had been completely focused on that other set of lips she possessed.

"I got wind of something off the record," she continued, her voice dropping to a slight whisper, "that could generate a huge return. I'm talking *huge*. I have to do a little more research, but if it pans out are you interested in hearing about it?"

Blow forced himself to pay attention to what was coming from her mouth. Already he respected her mind. He really did. But right now, sitting close enough to feel her heat, his thoughts were firmly wedged between her legs.

"Yeah," he answered softly, his voice thick from wanting her. He needed to touch her. Before he could stop himself, he reached out and laid his big hand on her thigh. He had expected a slap or some kind of rejection and was relieved and encouraged when all Tee did was smile. "Hell, yeah," he continued. "I'd be down with that Mexico shit. I'm down with whatever you're pushing, baby. You get all the details together and I'll follow your lead. Just tell me where to sign."

Chapter 7

Iwas licking barbecue sauce off my fingers the first time I met Blow's latest diversion, Ice Tee. Now, y'all already know my weaknesses. I've owned up to my issues and fessed up about my little problem. But if you thought my man downstairs zoomed north at the sight of Sugar and Honey, well baby I shoulda been arrested on the spot for the way old Oscar acted up at the sight of Ice Tee.

It was ten o'clock at night and the rib joint was packed out with wall-to-wall niggahs. Rainey's had the best damn ribs north of Texas, and I'd grubbed down in enough pork holes from New England to Florida to know what I was talking about. Every seat in the house had an ass in it, and people were lined up at the counter and crowded around the bar, too.

The front door had been swinging all night long. In fact, Rainey shoulda gone and had one of those revolving joints installed because that bad boy didn't stay closed for more than a minute or two at a time.

But this time when the door swung open I could tell something was up. In fact, the whole damn restaurant went mute. All action came to a halt and not a jaw moved as this chick pranced in on Blow's arm looking like she shoulda been bronzed and worshipped. Sauce dripped from my lip and hit the table. She came up in the joint wearing some shiny red pants and sporting a nice fat camel toe. Her sukkey-print was bold and defiant in them hot pants. Her thick pussy lips were sep-arated and spread open east and west. I stared hard at the spot where I imagined her clit would be, and that's when my man Oscar jumped up and started acting a fool.

I nudged my boy Stanley. "*What*—" my voice came out squeaking like a bitch and I swallowed hard and tried to catch my breath. "What the fuck is *that?*"

Like I said, it had gotten real quiet. Nigs had put down those ribs and were breaking their necks turning around to see as much of her as possible. Even the ladies were watching, and I saw a few hard-looking chicks whose eyes were glued so tight on that gushy between Tee's legs that it was obvious that they were getting their boners on too.

Stanley didn't answer. He couldn't. Like everybody else, he couldn't take his eyes off the girl. They had glazed over and he was biting down hard on his right thumb.

"Damn. I ain't never seen anybody so beautiful," I whispered. My entire groin was on boil, and my man Oscar was screaming at me to find some lotion and let him out!

Seconds later Blow stood in front of me looking like the King of New York. He was draped in a five-thousand-dollar suit and flashing his million-dollar smile.

"We look good together, don't we?" he bragged, with a grin.

On any other night Blow woulda been the top piece of eye candy in the joint, but he damn sure wasn't the main attraction tonight. Not by a long shot. I mean, I gave my boy props for his skills and all, but tonight it was all about the sexy caramel-colored *mami* he had on his arm. She was straight luscious. Major breasts and sweet, banging hips. Blow had done real good for himself with this one, I thought with ap-proval. In fact, he had outdone himself and outshined Nap and Tomere, too. Blow was a winner, and if my dick wasn't so big and hard I woulda stood straight up and shook his hand!

"My man, Ribs. Meet my future queen, son. Her name is Teesa. Ice Tee."

Her name mighta been Ice Tee, but with all that fat coochie show-ing between her thighs she looked like a warm hunk of apple pie to me.

I could barely look at her, she was just that fine. I felt unworthy under her gaze. I felt fat, ugly, and oh so damned ashy. I'd lost over fifty pounds by eating right and working out with Sugar, but I still had a ways to go. The only thing I'd ordered tonight was a plate of coleslaw, but I'd cheated a little bit by swiping Stanley's empty plate and dipping my finger in his leftover sauce. Guilt had that barbecue sauce tasting like ten extra pounds in my mouth right now, and I wanted to shove Stanley's plate right back in front of him, but instead I wiped my fingers on a napkin then rose halfway out of my chair, pretending like I was gonna stand up.

"Hey there, Tee." I offered my clean hand and tried to be cool. "I'm Rishawn Rawlings. Good to meet you."

She touched my fingers and my dick shot up two more inches. Her skin was soft like butter, her flesh felt sweet and warm. The girl had it. There wasn't one damned flaw to be seen on her. Something so perfect seemed almost unreal. But when she closed those slender fingers of hers around my hand I nearly lost my boner. The girl had a grip on her that was as good as any man's, and when she clamped that sucker on me I felt something strong in her that told me Blow better not fuck around on this one or he might run up on some trouble.

"Rishawn?" she said and fixed her beautiful cat eyes on me with an air of classy confidence.

"Just call him Pork Ribs," Blow cut in. "If you wanna know why, just look at his plate. This niggah inhales the meat and crunches through the bones."

I glanced down at Stanley's greasy plate that was sitting dead in front of me. A battle had gone on between Stanley and his rib dinner, and the remnants looked like a windswept graveyard with bone fragments as the headstones.

"Ribs, huh?" Tee said. Her stunning face lit up and I couldn't stop myself from glancing down at her camel toe. "I get down on barbecue, too," she admitted. "And don't let my athletic looks fool you. It's all about the cardio kickboxing, baby, because sister can eat, okay?"

I fell in love with her right then and there. Tee had softened the blow and broken the ice, and as we laughed together I gazed at her fineness and once again wished I'd been blessed with the looks and the rock-hard body of a man like Blow.

A couple of seats were opening up a row or two away, and Tee waved good-bye as Blow led her off. I sat there staring at her slim back as she walked away, wondering how all her body weight could be so perfectly proportioned on that phat, beautiful ass of hers.

Stanley laughed beside me.

"What, niggah?" I barked, my eyes still on Tee.

He laughed again. "Nothing, man. Yo, ain't this about the time you should be making that trip to the bathroom?" More laughter, but that shit wasn't even funny.

"Nah," I said, my dick straining and my heart thumping. "I ain't going no damn where."

And I wasn't. Oscar could scream all he wanted. Tee was far too special to take care of with a quick trip to the bathroom. She was beautiful to a fault, classy and elegant. She deserved way more time and attention than that.

"No damn bathrooms," I told him, brushing his laughter right off my shoulders.

I was gonna take care of Tee, all right. But not inside no dirty stall of a men's room. Tee was a lady. The kind of chick you had to take your time with and treat right. *Chill, Oscar,* I told my man, even though I knew he'd be awake and hollering for the next few hours. Tonight I was gonna plan a real nice evening at home for Tee. Fuck the lotion. I'm talking about a long shower, some soft jazz, a little warm scented oil in the center of my quivering palm . . . yeah. I had something for Miss Ice Tee, for real. And as soon as I was locked behind my bedroom door and wrapped in the privacy of my own fantasies, I was damn sure gonna give it to her.

Chapter 8

The preseason was coming to a close and things were beginning to work out for me on all fronts. My diet was clean, the exercise was getting easier, and I was beginning to feel like a new man. But a few days earlier I'd answered a call on the house phone that messed me up. It was Blow's hot new girlfriend Tee, and as soon as I heard her voice I passed my man the telephone and walked away.

"'Sup, baby girl," I heard Blow say. "You just called me a minute ago. You missing a niggah or something?"

I wasn't trying to dip on my man's conversation or nothing, but it was hard not to hear him since I was still right there in the room.

"*Who?*" he said like he'd heard something crazy. "For what?" Long pause. "You ain't never asked *me* to come." Pause. "Yeah, whatever." Short pause. "Hell nah I ain't jealous. Why should I be? Girl, look at him and look at me." Pause. "Damn right, so kill that noise." Pause. "Yeah, cool. Hold on."

Blow shot me a dark look and threw the phone at me like he was making a pass.

"Ribs! Telephone, niggah!"

"For me?"

There had to be some kinda mistake. I mean, I'd holla at Tee a little bit whenever Blow brought her by the crib, and I'd run into her a couple of times when the whole crew was hanging out, but I couldn't see why she'd be calling the crib for me, especially when she knew her man was home.

I gave Blow a look like, 'what the fuck?' and when I spoke into the receiver and realized that Tee actually did wanna speak to me, I almost missed the fact that she was inviting me to join her at her cardio kickboxing class.

"Me?" I said. Either she had me mixed up with somebody else, or the girl was crazy.

"Yep," she said cheerfully. "You're Rishawn, right? I teach a cardio kickboxing class. I want you to come check it out."

Thanks to Sugar, the exercise bug had taken a big chunk out of my ass and kickboxing sounded like fun. I told Tee I accepted her invitation, and when I hung up the phone and looked at Blow, he was grilling me like I'd intercepted his game pass or something.

"What?" I said innocently. Hell, I hadn't called his girl. She'd called me.

"Nothing," Blow said, but I could tell he didn't mean it.

I went to class with Tee that night, and it was so cool that I went back the next week, too.

Blow started acting real ill after that. The Polish dude at work had a heart attack and I'd gotten a promotion to interim senior athletic trainer. Unlike the old-head, I was up on the latest technology and took my job seriously. I liked to keep things running smooth and the atmosphere light. I laughed and joked with everybody, and the administrators really dug me.

"I'm about to get a phat raise," I told Blow one night as he popped in a DVD to watch a movie on our seventy-six-inch plasma screen. It was cardio kickboxing night for me. I was a regular at Tee's class by now, and while I hated to miss a session it was raining like a mahfuckah outside and so windy the trees were damn near bent in half.

Some of the fellas and their girls were over drinking beer and eating popcorn, and I felt like bragging on my temporary raise. "I'm only holding the spot until they can hire somebody else, but the guys upstairs like me so they offered to pay me extra as long as I do a good job."

Blow dissed me in front of everybody.

"Niggah! I'm the one who got you that job in the first place!" he said real loud. "If it wasn't for me old Pork Ribs would be frying bacon in a Country Kitchen somewhere!" He turned to our friends. "This niggah over here thinking them crackers *like* him! Man, Ribs, you so far up them white folks' ass that every time they open their mouths I see your big fuckin' head sticking out."

"Man, fuck you!" I said that shit like I was joking, the way I always did, but this time I really wasn't.

Blow laughed and dapped Tomere. "You probably wish somebody would fuck ya hand-humping ass, Ribs. You probably wish somebody would."

I ate Blow's bullshit right there in front of everybody. I didn't say nothing. But I was beginning to see Blow and all them cats in a whole new light. All of their asses was grimy. They did foul shit to people and never thought about it twice. From his sheisty business dealings to the way he took down the competition, Blow didn't miss no sleep regardless of what he said or did to other people. He didn't give a damn about the next guy. He damn sure didn't give a shit about me.

A couple of days later, I pulled him to the side and told him I was just about fed on all his mouth, but that niggah was still chumping me every chance he got. Especially in front of Ice Tee. I liked it when it was just the two of us hanging out. She'd challenged me to take a second class each week, and I got turned on just watching her sweat.

But Tee was also spending more and more time at the crib with Blow these days, and the joint was starting to feel cramped. I'd told her to let me know if some decent rentals came up because it was time for me to move outta Blow's shadow and do my own thing. And not because of Tee, either. She made me feel comfortable and I really liked being around her, even though it looked like Blow worked real hard to make me look small whenever she was listening.

But Tee was a real lady. She had some gangster about her too, and would unleash loudly on that niggah whenever he tried to shit on me.

"What kind of damn friend are you?" I heard her scream on Blow one night after he took all the toilet paper out of my bathroom and wouldn't bring me a roll when I hollered for some.

Blow cracked up laughing. "Ribs is *always* in the bathroom. You don't know what that boy be doing in there! Son be getting *down*."

I was *not* masturbating, and if Tee wasn't out there I woulda told that niggah that!

"Rishawn," Tee called out. "Would you like me to bring you a roll?"

I panicked. *Hell no!* Sugar had me eating extra vegetables at each meal. I'd just taken a huge green dump and I was scared Tee might fall out from the fumes.

"Uhm, nah, that's okay!" I yelled. "I found a roll under the sink!"

"See?" I heard Blow laugh. "That niggah don't need no damn toilet paper. Go take that boy a bottle of lotion and he'll be straight!"

Tee got on him. "Damn, Byron. You don't have no scruples, baby. Rishawn is your boy, and if you'd leave him stranded like that what would you do to me?"

"I'd do anything for you, baby," I heard Blow say. "Any damn thing."

Don't believe that shit, I wanted to yell, but I didn't. Tee was obviously smart, but I wished she was a little smarter. It killed me to think that Blow was kissing her, fucking her, and getting all in her head. When it came down to Tee, I didn't wanna just be *like* Blow. I wanted to *be* that niggah!

It was torture seeing his hands all over her. So I stayed away from the crib if I thought Tee might be there. I kept up with my workouts and concentrated on getting fit. Sugar had been running the hell out of me and forcing me to push myself harder and harder with my weight training, too. It was crazy to see it, but none of my old clothes fit anymore. Not too long ago looking down on myself naked made me think of a big, fat balloon with a thick string dangling between my leg. Now-a-days, I got out the shower and looked down on myself and the balloon was definitely deflating. My stomach had shrunk like a mahfuckah and I could actually see my dick without bending over. All that exercise didn't fuck with Old Oscar, though. He still looked phat as shit hanging halfway down to my knees!

"Wow, Rishawn!" Sugar exclaimed one evening as we worked out together at her gym. "Look at your arms!"

I straightened my right arm and glanced in the mirror. My bicep popped out nicely and I dug it. I raised both arms and fired my guns, and my triceps looked even better! Where I used to have saggy, fatty meat was now a nice muscular bulge.

"Yeah," I grinned at my reflection. "They're doing a li'l something."

Sugar rolled her eyes. "A little something? Is that all you can say?" She lifted the end of my shirt and peeked at my stomach. "You're developing real tone and definition, you know. You're hiding your results under all those big clothes you wear. Don't be so modest, Rishawn. Go shopping and buy some new clothes that'll show the world how hard you've been working."

I shrugged.

"Seriously. I'm sure you feel good, but you deserve to look good as well. Go buy yourself a few muscle shirts and some nice shorts. Show the world what you're working with! You're changing your body for the better, Rishawn, and now it's time to change your outlook, too."

I smiled at Sugar, then on impulse, I leaned over and kissed her.

On her forehead.

We'd done some real bonding in the gym, me and this girl. There's something pretty damn intimate going on when you're panting and sweating, grunting and farting right next to somebody five nights a week.

Even with sweat rolling down her face Sugar was still one of the most attractive chicks I'd ever seen. Her body was blinding in its curves and proportions, and sometimes when she bent over to pick up a weight, I still caught myself peeking down the front of her shirt, eyeing those knockers and hoping to see a quick wink of brown nipple.

But Sugar didn't fuck my head up anymore. She didn't make Old Oscar get crunk and start causing trouble each time she was near. I really liked Sugar, but I wasn't off the charts sexually attracted to her anymore. The girl was just nice. Nice and friendly, and somebody that I dug talking to and hanging out with. Sugar was becoming like a little sister to me, and when I busted niggahs in the gym peeping her phat ass I didn't get jealous anymore or wish I was them. I got mad and wished I had the balls to knock a nig on his ass for disrespecting her like that.

One thing did bother me though, and that was the fact that Sugar was still hanging with Nap. I had to admit it. My boy had *changed.* At least in some ways. Nap was still the same cheap, scheming, egotistical asshole that he'd always been, but the difference now was the dude had his nose open. It was laughable the way he hounded Sugar, and some of the shit she told me about him was so damn incredible I couldn't believe it.

"Your boy is stupid," Sugar told me in the gym one day. It was raining outside so we were running side by side on the treadmills. My wind and endurance had improved, but Sugar could still outrun my ass. She could talk, laugh, and even sing at the pace we were going at, while the most I could do was nod or gasp a one-word answer every now and then.

"He had me riding around going nowhere in his 750i last night. He wanted to show off those thirty-two-inch rims he just got."

"I seen them. Tight."

"They're all right. You know he likes to show off. New ride, fresh rims, got me sitting next to him in the front seat . . . all he needed was some crazy paparazzi out there snapping his picture and he would have been straight."

She was right and Nap's ego was real funny, but all I gave it was one good chuckle. We were running at top speed and one chuckle was all I could afford.

"Actually," Sugar continued, and I noticed that not only wasn't she sweating, she wasn't even breathing hard. "He looked stupid as fuck driving around wearing that damned football helmet. I don't know why he does that."

I gasped out a real long answer. "He does it all the time. It's his trademark. He gotta be known and noticed."

"Well, he's about to mess around and get noticed by the wrong people. He wants to start a women's clothing line under Nappy Fade, you know. He's been stealing ideas from that hot urban wear collection called Birthday Cake. He bought up samples of their entire line and then hired some guy to sew him some *very* similar designs."

I nodded, legs pumping, arms stroking. Nap was always looking for a way to make illegal money. Everybody knew that. I wasn't surprised that he was biting off somebody else's designs. That cat wasn't gonna spend his money on a good idea if someone else had already spent theirs. That was Nap's life philosophy.

"He wants to use me to launch his ad campaign called Nappy Dugout," Sugar went on, "but I don't like dealing in underhanded shit.

I'm all about conducting business, but stealing other people's ideas smells like some foul-ass monkey business."

"Yeah," I managed to say. "Nap is known for monkey business. He's dirty. I thought you knew that."

I had vowed to match Sugar's speed, but just those few sentences had taken everything out of me. I pushed the panel button to reduce my pace, then held on to the sides of the treadmill so I could catch my breath.

"Oh yeah, I know," Sugar answered as I slowed down to a quick walk. There was an evil look in her eyes and her voice came out cold and deadly. "I know exactly how dirty Nap can be. That's why I chose him."

Chapter 9

A few nights later I had taken Sugar's advice and was out shopping for new clothes when I ran into Honey. Normally, I would have been straight embarrassed to let a fine chick like her catch me buying elastic-in-the-waist pants and XXXL plaid shirts from the Big & Tall man's rack, but I was feeling pretty damn good as I stood in the mirror modeling a size 38 slacks in the regular men's section.

"Rishawn!" she called out.

I had already peeped her in the mirror, but now I spun around to face her.

"What's good, Honey? How's it going?"

She walked toward me with her eyes wide, her mouth opening and closing.

"It's going great! Especially for *you!*"

She reached out to hug me, and I took her in my arms and kept my lower body at a distance as I patted her back. It was a strange feeling because normally, one of two things woulda happened when I was giving a cute chick a friendly hug. Either my big-ass stomach would get in the way, or Old Oscar would jump up and start performing his one-man show. This time, nothing happened at all, and there was a big gap between our lower bodies as we embraced up top.

"You're looking good," Honey said, and I could tell by her smile that she really meant it. "Something good must be happening in your life because almost everything about you has changed for the better."

"Well, you know," I gushed, ducking my head like a shy choirboy. "I been taking care of biz. Doing a little of this and a little of that. You know how it goes."

"Well, whatever you're doing, keep it up because it's working for you."

She dropped her gaze and looked at the pants I was trying on.

"Nice cut. You'll need to find a tailor who can hook that snazzy cuff up again after you get them hemmed, though."

I looked down. I hadn't even thought about that.

"And that shirt looks real nice with the pants. A perfect match. Where'd you find it? I think Tomere would look good in that color, too."

Busted. Now I was embarrassed. The shirt was a knit polo with a flat collar. I usually went for the striped cotton joints because they were loose enough to camouflage my man-breasts. I'd thrown this baby on just to see if anything had changed. Yeah, my stomach was flat and trim, and my pec muscles were hard, but my nipple area still consisted of two muffin-looking lumps. I pointed toward the rack. "They're right over there."

Honey turned in the direction I was indicating, then quickly turned back to me with a strange look on her face.

"Listen, Rishawn," she said quietly. "Can we talk for a moment?"

I shrugged. "Whattup?"

Honey led me over to a mannequin stand. She sat down on one side of his bare feet, and I sat on the other.

"Look," she said and reached for both of my hands. "I hope you won't be offended by what I'm about to say, but I can tell you've been making some positive changes in your life, and I believe I know of something that might help you progress even further."

"Something like what?"

"Like surgery. Breast reduction surgery."

What the fuck? I pulled away.

"No, listen," she said, tightening her grip on my hands. "I work with a top black surgeon and he's got a lot of experience with those types of surgeries. You're a prime candidate for that kind of procedure because you've managed to lose a lot of body fat and gain some great muscle definition at the same time."

"I ain't even done yet. I still got a ways to go."

"That might be true," she insisted, "but you can't lose breast tissue the same way you lose body fat. You can't just burn it off, no matter how much you diet or how hard you exercise. There are a lot of men who have excess tissue in the breasts. It's a hormonal imbalance, but it can be reduced by surgery."

"Sorry, I don't dig hospitals," I told her.

Honey smiled and her whole face glowed.

"We do the procedure right in our office. No hospital stay is necessary. It's so fast and routine that we usually begin at eight and we're done before lunch."

"I don't mess with needles, either. And what about all the people who never wake up after doing stuff like that?"

"There are risks with any surgery, Rishawn. But we take risks every day. You took a risk just by driving to the mall and getting out of your car. Anything could have happened to you on your way here, but it didn't."

I still wasn't going for it.

"Listen," she said and took out her business card. "I graduated high school and started college when I was sixteen. By the time I was twenty-three I had my PhD. I'm a licensed anesthesiologist, and I look at every one of my patients like it's my sister or brother laying there."

"I didn't know you had a sister."

"Well, I'll tell you a little secret. I've got two sisters. And one brother. But that's not the point. The point is, you don't have to walk around feeling self-conscious about something you can overcome. I've been told that you're a really good guy, Rishawn. Somebody who cares about other people." She laughed. "Why you hang around in such shitty company goes right over my head, but I like you, and I think you should at least consider what I'm saying. I could put in a good word and get you a priority consultation if you want me to. And later, if you choose to go ahead with the surgery, you can rest assured that I'll be standing right beside you the whole time."

Okay, I admit that shit. I was vain. I didn't have to do a whole lot of soul-searching to arrive at my decision. All I had to do was take a good look in the mirror. The rest of my body had shaped up way beyond my expectations. It was time for the man-breasts to go!

A week after running into Honey I gave her a call and she got me an appointment. The minute I'd decided to go ahead with the surgery I had become a beast. I'd doubled up on my workouts, especially my runs, and told myself that if I lost another five pounds my chest would look even better after the surgery. The consultation with Honey's surgeon was a blast. He was my fraternity brother, and he made the procedure seem like it was a small thing that he did on the regular.

"Trust, frat," he told me, hitting me with the secret frat shake as I went out the door. "You're gonna get great results, man. You'll definitely see a difference that you like."

I was convinced. I hadn't been naked in front of another man for as long as I could remember. But Honey had been real correct about ol' boy. Dude made me feel comfortable, like seeing a condition like mine was a real small thing.

They had an open appointment near the end of the following week, and I told them to put my name down on the list. I was required to take a quick physical and yeah, I had to get a mammogram, but I wanted that damned surgery so I planned to take a few personal days off work and get all that done.

Later that night I pushed Honey's digits real quick, just to thank her, and she sounded real excited for me. "I'm happy for you, Rishawn," she told me, and I could tell she was smiling on the other end of the phone. "Like I said before, I've heard about you helping people out when they're down, you know. That means a lot to me. So if there's ever anything else I can do for you, just let me know, okay?"

"Yeah, cool," I said, but then a quick thought crossed my mind. Since Honey had been sweet enough to give me the hookup at her office, I felt like I owed her a little solid too. I didn't have no special services I could offer her in return, but I did have something that was valuable as hell.

Information.

"Yo, listen Honey. I know you and my boy Tomere been swinging pretty hard, and if you happy with him then you know I am. But I just wanna pull your leg to a little something, cool? I mean, you been so nice to me that I don't wanna see you walking around blind and in the dark on something that could really, like, effect you, nah'mean?"

"What are you getting at, Rishawn?"

"I'm getting at you, Honey. Or at least I'm trying to. I want you to understand that most of my friends ain't like me. Some of them cats on the team can be kinda devious, and Tomere is one of them."

There was a brief pause and then Honey said, "Is that right?"

"Yeah. That's right. I mean, he's my boy and we go way back, but you're a cool person, Honey. I just don't wanna see you get hurt."

"Oh, I've got Tomere all figured out, Rishawn. I'm all up in his Kool-Aid. Hell, I've got access to almost every area of his life. What do you think could be going on with him that's so bad it could hurt me?"

There was something funny in her voice, and I backed off. "Nothing. I mean, it's really nothing, when I think about it. You're just a lot older than the girls that Tomere usually goes for. That's all."

She laughed. "I just turned twenty-five, Rishawn. That's not old! Especially if you consider the fact that I've either been in college, grad school, or medical school for the past nine years."

Shit. Honey was hot and brilliant and she was way ahead of 99 percent of sisters her age, but she was still about ten years over the hill as far as Tomere went. I didn't wanna say my boy was no pedophile or nothing, but he usually liked them right around the little titty stage, between thirteen and sixteen. If Tomere hooked up with a fish much older than that he usually tossed it back.

"You're right," I agreed. "Twenty-five is very young, especially when you look eighteen." And Honey *could* pass for eighteen, too. Her whole package screamed "hot young *mami*," even though her stacked credentials made it obvious that she was older.

"Just keep your head up and your eyes open," I said, giving my final warning. "I ain't trying to drop no dimes or nothing, but I hang around a lot of crazy dudes, and let's face it, we all have our inner demons."

Honey laughed. "I hear you, Rishawn. And good looking out, too. But really, I'm not the one you should be worrying about. You didn't drop any dimes on your boy. I can see right through his ass. I know all about his grimy little demons and trust me, just like the cream always rises to the top, where I come from the trash always gets taken to the dump."

Chapter 10

If I thought Blow was acting foul before, it was nothing compared to how he nutted up after I had my surgery. He bust up in my bedroom two days after my breast reduction with two lame cats from the team and our boy Tomere, who was swinging a tiny pink bra over his head like a lasso.

"What size you wearing now, niggah?" Tomere laughed.

I was laying in bed, bandaged up and sore as hell.

"Ribs got his titties cut! Ribs got his titties cut!"

Blow was worse than a little kid, and I woulda kicked his ass if I could have.

"Lemme see one of them things, man. You sure you wanted to get rid of those? Ain't like you messing around and squeezing nobody else's. What they do? Suck the fat outta ya nipple, man? Damn! That shit sounds *fucked up!*"

I endured their torment like I always did, but these days I saw that shit for what it was. We weren't kids in college no fuckin' more. This wasn't no frat house bullshitting by cool brothers who just liked to clown. Nah, Blow's shit had risen to a whole new level. Nap's and Tomere's, too. Between the drugs, the young girls, the shady business deals, and the phony front companies, those dudes were set to self-destruct.

* * *

It was a couple of weeks before my swelling started to go down, and I was amazed at what I saw! I had mad muscles! My shit was looking tight! My surgeon had promised that even more results would begin to show over the next few weeks as the swelling completely disappeared, but the results already looked hot to me.

I fucked Blow's head up a few nights later. He was having some renovations done on my end of the crib, so I was forced to use the bathroom on the other side of the kitchen. Nobody was around except me and him, so I walked through the living room naked while he was sitting on the sofa watching an old game tape.

"Damn, niggah!" he shouted as I strolled past him looking like a prizefighter. "I don't wanna see ya fuckin nuts!" But his eyes were buck wild and he was staring at me like a mahfuckah! I'd lost close to seventy pounds of fat and gained about thirty pounds of muscle. The look on Blow's face was priceless! He was fuckin' jealous! Blow had never seen me ass-naked before, but I'd sure seen what he was holding! That niggah couldn't believe how fit I was, or how long my dick was neither!

"Whattup," I nodded, then cupped my big nuts as I strolled on by. Blow's mouth was wide open, and I laughed inside as I stepped into the small bathroom to take a piss. I left the door open on purpose too, 'cause I had something Blow didn't have, and now he knew it. Standing in front of the toilet, I dangled my hose over the bowl and let my water flow, and then in a voice loud enough and deep enough for Blow to catch my fuckin' drift, I hollered, "God*damn* this toilet water is cold!"

It was Saturday morning and Tee and I were going out looking at apartments. She had compiled a list of places that weren't too far from the stadium and were within my price range, and I was looking forward to seeing what was available out there.

It had been a minute since I'd talked to Tee, even though we still did kickboxing together twice a week. She'd been by the crib and had even e-mailed me a few times to ask a few questions about what features I was looking for in a crib and which areas I'd like to live in.

I figured out that I'd been avoiding Tee without even realizing it. Seeing her with Blow wasn't easy. That shit really hurt. That fool didn't deserve to have a winner like Tee, and I couldn't understand what she saw in him, either.

"We've got four appointments," Tee said, crossing her legs under her long black skirt and putting her purse on the floor. I'd held her door open, and when I got in on the driver's side she reached over to give me a friendly hug. "Two in North Jersey and two a little further south. I figured we'd hit the closest two first, then work our way out from there. Okay?"

Whatever Tee said was cool with me. I punched the first address into my GPS system, then pulled into traffic as she chattered away about the features in this crib and the number of rooms in that one.

The first place we looked at just wasn't it. The crib itself was cool, but the neighborhood was almost tapped out. Trap boys were on the corner conducting business in broad daylight, and we had to walk through a group of three or four of them on the way out the building.

"It's cool," I told Tee as we walked through the lobby. I put my arm around her shoulder and pulled her close. Then I nodded at them young thugs like I had a big toolie in my pocket and guided Tee through with no problem.

I was still holding Tee real close when we got to the curb. For once Old Oscar didn't have shit to say. Them thugs had punked him out and he stayed his ass downstairs with his one eye closed. But something was going on between me and Tee, and it didn't seem one sided neither because she walked to the car leaning into me like in my arms was where she wanted to be.

"Thanks," she said, moving away as I unlocked the car and held the car door open for her. "That was nice of you, but I wasn't scared back there, you know."

Shit! I thought. *I* was! Them boys had looked at me with a little bit of respect, but it probably wouldn'ta gone down like that if I was still fat. People treated me real different now that I had a tight physique, and I guess I was carrying myself differently too.

"Oh, so you a G or something? You got some gangsta in you?" I joked. "You got a burner in that little pocketbook or something?"

Tee laughed.

"I might just be strapped. I'm from Harlem, remember? I'm not as innocent as I look. I can handle mine."

It was my turn to laugh. "I'm not crazy enough to underestimate you, baby. You dealing with my man Blow, so you better be able to handle yours. You seem pretty bullshit proof, and that's why I can't figure that shit out."

"Figure what out?"

I shrugged and shut up. I was really digging Tee, but it wasn't for me to tell her nothing about her man.

The next place we looked at had already been rented out. Tee went off on the landlord for not calling her to cancel our appointment, but I told her it was all good because I wasn't crazy about the joint anyway.

"Sorry about that," she apologized when we were back in the car. "I'm a professional, Rishawn, and anything I get into I take very seriously. I called this morning to confirm our appointment and he told me that we were still on. I'm very thorough when I make plans and I hate wasting time."

She wasn't wasting my time. I was hyped just to be near her and I woulda been cool with driving her around in circles all damned day.

I was impressed with the next crib before we even got out the car. It was on the fifth floor of a nice building that had a little doorman standing outside and everything.

"This one is a bit pricey," Tee said as we walked inside the lobby, "but as you can see by the decor, it's a lot nicer than most."

She gave me that gorgeous smile as we waited for the elevator, and I smiled right back. When the elevator came we got on and Tee pressed five.

"Now, I know you said you wanted a two-bedroom," she said as the doors closed and we lifted up, "but I put this one on the list because it has a full bedroom and a loft that's really—"

A sudden jolt threw her against me and the lights flickered out. The elevator jerked to a stop, its momentum tossing us around. We were stuck as fuck. We banged on the doors and stomped our feet and all that, but that baby didn't move.

"Hold up," Tee said. She dug in her purse and got her cell phone, then clicked it on and examined the elevator panel in the dim light. "I'm from the projects, ya know? We know elevators. There's an alarm button on here that'll make all kinds of noise."

Tee leaned on the button and the noise was instantly off the chart.

"Lemme get that," I said, moving her hand. "Stick your fingers in your ears so you don't go deaf."

Pretty soon we heard banging coming from below us, and I raised up off the button.

"They'll be sending somebody in a minute," Tee said in the darkness. "We just have to chill and wait."

And that's exactly what we did. Leaning against the walls, we talked for about twenty minutes, and when nobody came to get us out neither one of us sweated that shit. Tee had some good conversation. I was digging her flow like crazy in the darkness, and something bold jumped up in a brother because I found myself wanting to be closer to her.

"Come over here," I said, even though I was already moving toward her. My hands searched for her on their own, and when they found her I pulled her next to me and held her close. To my surprise, Tee's arms went around my neck and the next thing I knew we were kissing, with Tee taking the lead and me following. Old Oscar was up outta the basement and just a hollering, and I backed off just a little 'cause I didn't want to scare her.

Tee's hands were on my arms, roaming and squeezing, and where she would have found lumps of fat in the past was now all muscle. I slid my hand down her back and cupped her ass through her skirt, balancing the weight of it in my palm.

Squeezing gently, I pulled her close until our groins collided, grinding deeply against her as I moaned and breathed the scent of her hair.

"Rishawn," she whispered, breaking our kiss.

I used the opportunity to move my lips down her body, licking the top of one breast through the open neck of her shirt. Tee put her head back and offered me the whole thing, and my fingers were quick on her buttons. Her nipples were like hot bullets in her bra, and I released one breast and covered the tip with my lips.

We were both moaning as I ran my tongue back and forth over her peak, that warm brown titty in my mouth the best damn thing I had ever tasted. Well, almost the best thing.

Something got into me and I found myself on my knees, lifting her skirt. Her scent was out of this world, and I pushed my face between her legs and inhaled as deep as I could. I pulled her panties aside and parted her pussy lips with my tongue, then lapped at her softness with wet, gentle strokes.

It had been a real long time since I'd had the taste of pussy in my mouth. Far too long. Tee was dripping with juice and I couldn't get enough of it. She hiked her skirt higher and threw one leg over my shoulder, then her hands were on my head, on my cheeks, guiding me to her spot. She talked to me too. Gently, like she appreciated what I was giving her. "Yeah, baby. Just like that. Oh my God . . . my clit . . . lick my clit. Now back inside. Put your tongue inside me. That feels so good. Yes, squeeze my ass. Damn, Rishawn, you make me feel so good, baby."

I felt the storm building up inside her, and when her muscles clenched and she arched her back, I knew what time it was. It was that time for me, too, and for once I wasn't ashamed as Oscar did his thing and filled my drawers with that hot sticky love. Me and Tee came together. Her in my mouth, and me . . . well, y'all know how I usually do it. But it was good for both of us, and even though Tee belonged to someone else, for that moment she was all mine.

Afterward, we laughed quietly in the dark. Tee took some tissues from her purse and I helped her get cleaned up, then took care of Oscar's mess the best I could. I expected things to get kinda awkward, but they didn't. Instead, Tee and I learned some things about each other, we laughed, and we shared some of our hopes and dreams. By the time the firemen arrived to get us out, Tee and I were close. Something between us had really clicked. We'd done some bonding during those ninety hot minutes in the dark, and even though we had missed our appointment, I'd found something with Tee that for me was much more than just for the moment.

Chapter 11

Iwas meeting Sugar for lunch at a salad shop in Manhattan. We'd been hanging out together after our workouts, and I felt like we were starting to get pretty close. So close that it fucked with my head to know the things I did about Nap, and I didn't believe he deserved a girl like Sugar. I knew for sure that she didn't deserve a bonehead like him.

We'd taken a nice long jog the day before, and I was watching her towel off when we'd finished. Some shit just came down on a playa, y'all. I swear. I was used to keeping secrets, but sometimes being down for somebody else's cause meant you really didn't have one of your own. Sugar looked so innocent standing there in her purple and white jogging outfit that it fucked with my heart and I opened my mouth and committed a series of deadly sins.

"You a cool lady," I told Sugar as we headed inside the gym to shower and change clothes. "I don't think I ever really thanked you for butting into my life and making it so much better."

She laughed and leaned against a row of lockers with one foot up behind her. "No thanks necessary. I'm the one who should be thanking you."

"I don't know about that," I said, "but I like you, Sugar. I think you're a winner and you deserve the best. And because of that," I said, pulling the ends of my towel then flicking it at her playfully, "I'm gonna tell you a little secret."

I pulled Sugar over to a little wooden bench and sat her down, then I ran down all the dirty, diabolical, dastardly shit that Nap had participated in, going all the way back to our college days in the frat house. I violated some major fuckin' laws, and I coulda had my playa card torn up on the spot. But I didn't care. I was tired of all the grimy shit I'd seen and heard, and a winner like Sugar deserved to know what kind of shithead she was dealing with.

So I told her. Yeah, I did. I opened my mouth and crossed the line and shit all over Nap with a vengeance. I shit on Blow and Tomere too, just so my other two homeys wouldn't feel left out. Instead of looking stunned and pissed off like I thought she would, Sugar looked fuckin' amused.

"So you mean to tell me that your best friends are bankrolling drugs in the hood, shaving points for bookies, running internet gambling schemes, and cheating the IRS out of thousands of dollars?"

I shrugged and thought about Nap's bullshit business ventures, all the young girls Tomere had turned out, and the dirty, career-ending injuries that Blow had caused over the years. "Yeah," I admitted. "That and a whole lot of other shit too."

Sugar shook her head and got real gutter. "Those dumb motherfuckers just don't know who they fucking with. But they will."

Oh, so she *was* mad.

"Don't let it get to you, baby," I said, waving my hand. "I just wanted you to know what kinda dirt you hanging around with. That way you can keep yourself clean."

Sugar grinned. "Thanks, Rishawn. For looking out for me. I really appreciate you putting me down on Napoleon like that." She reached for my hand. "But since you've shared so many secrets with me today, I've got a few that I'd like to share with you too. Meet me in midtown tomorrow at two, okay? Dress nice. I'll be treating you to a late lunch."

Getting stuck in that elevator with Tee had definitely had its benefits, but it had had a small drawback, too. I didn't get that nice apartment, but she did help me find another that was almost as cool and in a better neighborhood too.

I crashed until noon the next day, then I got up and started packing a few things and then hit the barbershop to get my hair edged and a fresh shave. An hour later I stepped into the Lovely Leaf salad shop as hungry as hell and ready to grub. Eating late had thrown me off my careful regimen but it was better for my new body than eating lunch twice. This was gonna be my first time grubbing in this joint, and I was thinking about a nice big salad and maybe a piece of chicken on the side.

"Over here," Sugar called and waved to me just as I was scanning the crowded tables trying to find her. She was all smiles, but I was struck dumb as I stood there shocked by what I saw.

Sugar wasn't by herself.

There was not one, but three sexy ladies waiting to have lunch with me.

Sugar, Honey, and the amazing girl who had grabbed my heart, Ice Tee.

"Whattup?" I said, walking over to their table. The dumb look was all over my face. I kissed Tee on her cheek and squeezed her a little, then kissed Sugar and Honey too.

They were grinning like shit and I knew the joke was all on me.

I looked from one gorgeous smiling face to the next one and shook my head in disbelief. "What's going on, ladies? Why are the three of y'all together?"

Busting their slick smiles, I shook my big head again and chuckled. "Hold up. Y'all smile a whole lot alike . . ." I glanced at Tee, throwing the question her way. "What's up with that?"

Sugar answered for her. "Well . . . Rishawn . . . like I told you yesterday . . . since you were nice enough to share your secrets with me, here's one that I wanted to share with you. We're sisters. Me, Tee, and Honey are all sisters."

They laughed, so I did too, but somehow that shit wasn't all the way funny.

"I see the resemblance," I said, almost at a loss for words. "Yeah, put y'all side by side like this and I can *really* see the resemblance. So," I said suspiciously, "How'd the three of y'all manage to hook up with my boyz? Did y'all set it up that way, or something? You ladies scheming on my boyz, or what?"

Sugar grinned at me and suddenly all the craziness fell in place. She said, "The secret I promised to tell you is not who my sisters are. It's who our brother is."

And as the sound of Charlie Baker's name rung in my ears, I gazed at the three devastatingly determined beauties sitting across from me and gave each of them mad props.

Sugar. Honey. And Ice Tee.

Devious. Devilish. And diabolical.

Quality traits indeed.

Chapter 12

Sugar tore into the large white envelope and pulled out the paper-work inside.

"Gotcha motherfuckah!" she said under her breath as she read through the information contained in the commercial insurance policy. The signature at the bottom of the page looked damn good, and one of her best friends, who was a handwriting expert, had assured her it would hold up in court. If it ever came down to that. A wicked smirk passed over Sugar's pretty face as she checked the policy enforcement date and the coverage amount. The final play had been set in motion. She was about to kill the sweet act with Nap and hit that bastard right in his balls. No more free pussy for his stank ass, and no more show-boating all around the city with her on his damn arm, neither. Nap was a grimy bastard and Sugar had hated him before she'd ever met him.

She slid the papers back into the envelope, then walked naked into the spare bedroom that Nap used as an office. The cheap bastard ran a multimillion-dollar company from a room no bigger than a closet simply because he was too tight with his money to pay rent on some real office space.

Well his tight ass was about to feel a squeeze, Sugar thought, with a laugh. He'd been complaining about production costs in the United States and bragging to every damn body who would listen about his little move to India. He'd already transferred all his inventory and high-value machinery to an international moving company, and now the asshole was the proud owner of three million dollars' worth of insurance on an empty fuckin' warehouse.

"Let's see." Sugar giggled as she mentally ran down the checklist of charges that Nap was about to get slapped with: insurance fraud, tax evasion, falsified reports, money laundering, employee abuse, arson. Sugar had been real careful with the details of her little scheme. There were gas-soaked rags and a pair of his gym shoes waiting to be found in Nap's garage, and some plastic gloves and matches in the trunk of his car.

The best part of her plan had been the craziest part. Everybody knew how much Nap loved his whip. He drove around town in his lucky fuckin' football helmet looking retarded all the time. Well, Nap's luck had just run out. While Sugar had kept him occupied by sucking his dick and fucking his brains out, her boy from the projects had been driving around in Nap's car, wearing Nap's helmet. He'd driven past the empty warehouse three times, just to make sure he was seen, and not long after he drove away the last time, flames were seen shooting from the windows of the warehouse.

And right about now, Nap's dreams—no fuck that—his whole life was going up in smoke.

Tomere was in the shower washing his nuts, and for the eighth day in a row Honey was logged on to his laptop and hanging out in a chat room. Getting his password had been easy. Tomere kept careful records, and Honey had simply gone into his BlackBerry files and looked it up. She'd given him the screen name 2Mere100 and made sure he was a familiar presence in this particular chat room.

What are u wearing? Honey typed.

She'd been having an ongoing conversation with a girl named Ownlee13 for a week now. The girl supposedly lived outside of Montclair and they'd been laying out all the nasty shit they wanted to do to each other in bed.

Ownlee13: panties. shirt.
2Mere100: Take off ur clothes. Do u have webcam? I want 2 C u.

Ownlee13: Dad won't get webcam. I wanna C u 2. Wanna tio?

2Mere100: Cud b dangerous. cops cud b watching.

Ownlee13: idk. We cud b careful. Dad working. Mom in hosp. Lonely. Cum c me.

2Mere100: ur a virgin right?

Ownlee13: yea lol except my finger lol.

2Mere100: u ever had ur pussy licked?

Ownlee13: no. wanna try it tho.

2Mere100: wdyl?

Ownlee13: 1689 Register. Private road. Brown house.

2Mere100: u sure its safe?

Ownlee13. yea. Cum at 8. dad gone by 7.

2Mere100: I'll bring wine. make u feel gd 4 ur first time.

Ownlee13: I can't wait. POS. ttyl.

Honey logged off the Internet just as Tomere walked into the bedroom.

"Let me do that," she said, taking his towel and rubbing his back dry. "You feeling better now?"

Tomere reached around and patted her on the ass. It was rounder than most of the girls he was used to getting with, but that phat ass had grown on him and he was hopelessly stuck on that shit.

"Yeah. I'll be better when you let me get up in some of that."

"Not yet," Honey said, clutching her belly. There was no way in hell she was ever fuckin this niggah again! "My period is still too heavy. I'll be straight tomorrow, though."

She draped her arms over his back and kissed his neck.

"I'll make it up to you, though. There are plenty of other things I can do to make you feel good, baby. You know that. But I need to ask you a favor first, okay?"

Tomere grunted. He wanted some pussy or some head or something. But he'd do anything for Honey, especially if it meant she'd use one of her unique tongue tricks on him later. "What kinda favor you need?"

"My aunt just called and my cousin Derrick is stranded in Montclair. He's only thirteen, but he snuck in the house with his little girlfriend after school, and her parents came home before he could sneak back out. He stayed in her bedroom closet for hours before he had enough sense to jump out her window. My aunt's car has a boot on the tire from getting too many parking tickets, and Derrick is too embarrassed to face her anyway. Could you go pick him up? He's hiding on the side of the girl's house."

"Way in Montclair?"

"Yeah. I would go myself, but he's already ashamed and embarrassed. I think he'd be more comfortable dealing with a guy right now."

Tomere stood up and pulled on a shirt. "Little nig just oughta be embarrassed. Sneaking up in some thirteen-year-old girl's house. What the fuck is this world coming to? I don't know what the hell that boy was thinking."

Honey nodded and sighed. "Me neither. Feel free to knock him upside his head when you get there because I know my aunt won't mind."

Tomere grabbed his keys. "These fuckin' kids these days," he muttered. "They're even hornier than I was at that age."

Honey grinned. "It's hard to believe that . . . judging by the way you put that thing down nowadays." She thought about her friend Stacie, a police officer who worked in the child protection division of Internet safety and whose screen name was Ownlee13. Honey laughed like crazy inside.

"Here's the address," she told Tomere with a smile. "It's sixteen eighty-nine Register. It's a big brown house down a private drive."

Tomere sped toward Montclair with an old R. Kelly jam blasting from his whip. If he wasn't so fuckin' bent on Honey he would have put his foot in her cousin's young ass for having him out on the streets looking for him instead of being at home getting his brain delivered nice and juicy the way Honey always put it down.

Anticipation had his joint on rock, and he couldn't wait to get back home. Honey was on her period for the second time this month, but her top game was so perfect that whether he banged between her legs or pounded down her throat, it was all good either way.

Tomere was no stranger to Montclair. He'd gotten down with a young thang or two on this side of town on occasion, and he was familiar with the streets. He located Register Street with no problem and followed it straight across town until he found himself on a dark private drive. He flicked his high beams on and took the curved road slowly, wondering why the fuck a kid with no car would let himself get stranded so far away from any kind of transportation. The answer was pretty obvious: pussy. Tomere had made a few dumb decisions in the name of pussy himself, so he really couldn't fault the young buck too hard.

He was at the end of the drive when it opened up into a big clearing that contained a row of about five houses. The big brown house sat at the end, and Tomere hit his lights and pulled up beside it.

He figured the boy would see him and come running out to the car, but no dice. Tomere rolled down his window and scanned the bushes planted along the side of the house as he looked for the li'l asshole. Honey said the boy had jumped outta a bedroom window, and Tomere wondered if he was hurt or just hiding somewhere.

A second later a side door opened on the house and a kid stood silhouetted against the interior light.

"Tomere?" called the voice of a young girl, and he answered.

"Yeah," Tomere said, wondering where in the fuck Sugar's cousin was and whether or not the girl's parents were still home.

"In here," she said quickly, then disappeared leaving the door open.

"Shit!" Tomere cursed, getting out the whip. "Stupid mahfuckah supposed to be out here waiting for me!"

He stomped up the four stairs and into a brightly lit yellow and green kitchen, and to his surprise, instead of finding a teenage boy holding his dick in his hand, he was met by two grown men holding badges and handcuffs in theirs.

"You're under arrest," the man with dark hair said grimly. "Turn around and put your hands in the air."

Tomere laughed. Blow was a real dickhead. "What? My man set up this stupid stunt and my girl helped him?"

Out of nowhere three other men appeared. One snapped mad photos while the other two pointed their expensive video cameras at Tomere and let the tape roll.

Tomere shook his head. Blow had spent a gwap on this stunt. "I swear that niggah play too much. But he got me," he said, turning to leave. "That niggah sick for real, though. He got me this time."

A strong hand clamped down on Tomere's arm and he was jerked around. The man with dark hair slammed his elbow into Tomere's face then mushed a nine millimeter up his nose.

"You're under arrest!" he said again. "For sexual solicitation of a minor child. Now get your fuckin' hands in the air!"

"What?!?" Tomere's hands shot up and a hot bolt of piss soaked his drawers. The dudes with the camera clicked away. This wasn't one of Blow's stupid fuckin jokes! These cats was serious as shit!

"Cuff the sleazy motherfucker," the older detective said to his dark-haired partner, and no matter how much Tomere cursed and protested, that's exactly what the fuck they did.

"You've got your passport, right?" Tee asked.

Blow nodded and touched his jacket pocket. "Right here."

"Good," she said as Blow loaded their two small suitcases into the car.

"This is the sweetest deal I've ever seen," she exclaimed. "I just hope the guy holds it until we get there. You've gotta see it, baby!"

Her excitement was contagious and Blow was grinning from ear to ear. His girl was a genius. Fuck the fact that she had the hottest pussy in the world. Tee had a brain on her that worked like a computer. She was instinctive about making money and could sniff out a good deal thousands of miles away. Already she'd found him so many lucrative properties that his net income had soared. Blow saw the future in his baby's eyes, and it had dollar signs written all over it.

"I got a game tomorrow evening, baby. We'll be back on time, right?" he asked.

Tee nodded. "I booked the earliest flight I could find," she said as he drove toward the airport. "Mexico is still pretty hot this time of year, so I rented a one-day villa on the ocean just in case we have time to catch a quick scuba-diving tour before our flight leaves, okay?"

Blow laughed to himself. Tee wouldn't admit it, but the girl was definitely mixed with something because sisters weren't into scuba diving and they damn sure didn't choose vacation excursions where they were liable to get their hair wet.

"You're sure we can bypass the Mexican taxes, right?" Blow asked.

He could have kissed Tee when she nodded yes. He stood to make a gwap on this transaction and although the money was good in real estate investments, he'd always wanted to be a real estate developer.

"Absolutely," she answered. "So many states have passed anti–illegal immigration laws, it's unreal. Illegal Mexicans are being deported like they're Haitians or something. Whole families are being forced to head south. They need housing when they cross the border, and that's where you come in." Tee put her hand on top of his and smiled. "Good thing you're the kind of man who can get his hands on a lot of cash, Byron. That's gonna be a big plus in our favor because not a lot of investors know about this opportunity, and out of those who do, not many of them can come up with the cash at the drop of a hat."

Blow felt a surge of energy run through him. Every last illegal thing he'd done over the past few years was about to bear fruit. Tee had gotten the phone call only hours earlier, and she'd been waiting at the door with their things packed and ready to go when he came home. He'd never seen her so hyped about a deal before, and he hoped like hell that he was the first investor on the ground.

Blow rubbed her fingers in excitement, then took her hand and placed it in his lap. His baby was good. He didn't have to say a word. He didn't have to worry about the size of his dick, either, because Tee always made him feel like nobody else had ever fucked her so good.

Her hand moved around in his lap, and then cool air hit his crotch.

"Lemme slide back," Blow whispered, keeping his eyes on the road while adjusting his seat and anticipating the dick licking he was about to get.

He sucked his breath in sharply as Tee freed his dick and lowered her head to his lap. Her lips were wet and warm as she sucked his swollen dick into her mouth, and Blow couldn't help moaning out loud.

Tee's top game was fuckin' superb, and Blow fought to maintain control of the car as he humped into her mouth. He smiled as he busted a nice long nut and felt her jaws contracting as she swallowed every drop.

This girl was good, Blow thought. Too damned good. He was gonna have to put a ring on her finger soon or risk somebody else snatching her up. He grinned as she tucked his limp dick away, then sat up and kissed his lips. She opened the overhead mirror and hummed a song as she fixed her make-up and rearranged her hair. Blow adjusted the driver's seat again and concentrated on getting to the airport. He had mad appreciation for the woman who was sitting by his side, and as soon as they got back home he planned to shop for an engagement ring so he could tell her so.

Blow slept through the flight, and it landed without a hitch. Tee nudged him when they pulled up to the terminal, and right away Blow could tell something was wrong.

"What's the matter?" he asked, his voice full of concern.

"We're late," she moaned. Her skin was a funny color and her eyes were watering. "We had to circle around and wait for clearance to land."

"Cool, but what's the matter with you?" Tee looked sick as hell, and when Blow touched her face her skin was cool and clammy.

"I don't know . . ." she whispered. "My stomach . . ."

Blow didn't like the way she looked, and he didn't know what to do about it. "Damn, baby. Should I call the flight attendant or something?"

Tee shook her head and motioned toward the crowd of people who were standing up in the aisles and getting their luggage from the overhead bins. "We'll be off in a second."

Blow stood up and pushed his way into the aisle. He pulled Tee in front of him and waited impatiently as the line of people trickled off the plane. It felt like forever before they were able to get off the aircraft, and by then Tee was so weak she could hardly stand up.

"I'ma have to get you to a doctor, baby," Blow said, his voice shaking. He was scared for her. He'd never seen her sick, and he'd never taken care of anybody who was sick, either. He didn't know what the hell to do.

Tee shook her head vigorously. "No . . . I have to go to the bathroom and we don't have time for all that." She pushed their baggage claim stubs into his hand. "Take these. The realtor won't wait for us. Go to baggage claim and get our suitcases. They're both in your name. Get the bags, then meet the Realtor right outside the terminal."

"Nah, baby. Let that mahfuckah wait! I'll stay with you until you feel better and then we'll go together."

Tee leaned against the wall outside of the women's restroom. She waved her hand and shooed him off. "Baby don't be silly. This is Mexico. Anybody could walk off with our suitcases and this deal is too important for that. The sooner I get in the bathroom, the sooner I'll be fine. Just do this for me, okay? We can't miss out on a deal like this just because I have to take a crap. Go. The Realtor will be right outside of baggage claim, holding up a sign with your name on it. Get down there real quick and I'll be right behind you. I'm straight. I promise."

Tee gave him a quick wave, and before he could protest she fled into the restroom, leaving Blow standing there looking a worried mess and clutching the baggage-claim stubs in his hand.

Tee had never laughed so hard in her entire life. She stood inside a handicap stall and wiped the gray-toned eye shadow from her face and the smeared mascara from around her eyes, then took a piece of gum from her purse and chewed the last taste of Blow's tiny dick from her mouth.

That greedy bastard was about to get everything he had coming to him, and Tee's only regret was that she wouldn't be there to see it. He'd given her his combination, and she'd packed the four hundred thousand she'd found in his wall safe in the suitcases, just like he'd told her to. Then she'd called to make their flight arrangements and she'd made a few other phone calls, too.

Tee had been real busy over the past few weeks. Not everything she had told Blow was a lie. She did know somebody important down in Mexico. He was her uncle on her father's side and the chief of police in a town that was busting at the seams with illegal drug activity.

Her uncle was real sorry about what had happened to Charlie, and together, they'd devised a scheme to kill two birds with one stone. As soon as Blow retrieved their baggage containing almost half a million dollars in cool cash, the wheels would be set in motion to slay his grimy ass!

Tee giggled into her hand as she visualized the takedown. Her uncle had a crooked officer on his staff who was providing protection to a drug cartel. He'd told him about an American football player who was looking to score big and set up some action in New York City, and promised the officer a big cut if he'd send his connect to the airport to meet the *negrito* and make the transaction.

Tee had also done her part from her end. She'd gotten on the telephone with the alphabet boys from the Mexican authorities and explained in perfect Spanish how a major drug dealer from the United States was coming into Mexico to make a large buy. She'd given them Blow's description and their flight information, and they'd promised to have a team of Federales waiting to meet them.

The guy who'd be holding up the sign for Blow was none other than Tee's uncle, and he'd been instructed to let Blow put his bags in the trunk, then have him sit in the car and wait for the connect to arrive and try to complete the transaction. Blow's football days were over! He was set to get caught up in a major international drug bust, and if Tee hadn't hated him so much she would have felt sorry for his wicked ass.

She thought about her baby brother Charlie, and any remorse she might have felt for Blow went straight out the window. Fuck Blow. Charlie was a good man, and he didn't deserve what Blow and his friends had done to him. All three of them were about to go down hard, and they deserved it, too. Now they'd feel what it was like to have your dreams stolen in a heartbeat, and everything you'd worked hard for snatched away. Tears came to Tee's eyes as she remembered getting that call from Charlie. The pain in his voice had cut into her heart, and Tee and her sisters, Sugar and Honey, had sworn on their mother's grave that they'd make all three of those motherfuckers pay for what they'd taken from him.

Tee brightened up. She had another flight to catch in a couple of hours. This one to Puerto Rico, where her sisters were waiting at a luxury resort with a suitcase full of fly new clothes and jewelry just for her, courtesy of the soon-to-be convict and ex-NFL star Byron "Blow" Ford.

She giggled as she pictured Blow spread eagle on the cold dirty floor of a Mexican prison. Shit moved real slow down here. It could take months before he got to see a lawyer, and years before he was actually brought to trial. Tee didn't give a damn how long it took. That grimy bastard was out of money and out of a job, and as far as she was concerned the Mexican authorities could keep his ass locked down eating shit-flavored tortillas for the rest of his life.

* * *

Leaving Tee all alone was the last thing Blow had wanted to do, but this deal had way too much doe riding on it to miss out on. His girl had looked bad as hell. Black circles around her eyes, her pretty skin all clammy and gray. She'd scared the shit outta him when he opened his eyes on that plane and saw her sitting there looking like a shook-up zombie.

"Go ahead, baby," Tee had begged. "We're already late. Hook up with the Realtor, or he'll think we changed our minds!"

Blow strode through the airport like he was covering a football field. He rushed past old people and almost knocked a young mother on her ass. Hustling into the baggage-claim area, he searched for and found the carousel for their flight. A couple of pieces of luggage had already come out the chute, and Blow pushed his way closer and tapped his foot as he waited to spot his bags.

He had worked up a little sweat, but that didn't matter. The only thing he was worried about was getting that doe and getting outside to make the deal. He looked out the glass window and scanned the busy street outside. Cars were steadily pulling up and pulling off. He thought he spotted a green sedan parked a little ways down from the doorway, and sighed with relief when he saw a small man leaning on the car and holding a large white sign up in the air.

Blow couldn't read the sign, but he was almost sure it had his name on it. Minutes later both of his bags appeared at the top of the slide. He snatched them up as soon as they touched the conveyor belt, then made his way over to the exit where an airport official was matching claim tags to their computer-generated luggage tags.

Blow shoved his paperwork toward the official, then breezed through the exit without a hitch. Outside, the man leaning against the green car was indeed holding up a sign with his name on it. Blow practically ran toward him, suitcases in hand.

"I'm Byron Ford," he said in a rush, stepping to the back of the car and throwing his suitcases into the man's open trunk. "I'm the money-man. You're waiting for me."

The olive-skinned little man looked Blow over quickly, and when he recognized him from the photo his niece had attached to an e-mail, he greeted Blow with a big, wide grin.

"Oh yes, senor," the portly man said cheerfully, and held the car door open so Blow could get in. He glanced at the drug connect, who was sitting in a parked car behind him, then signaled the alphabet boys, who were waiting across the street. "You are the one. I've been waiting for you."

Chapter 13

Walking down the street watching chicas, go by watching Tee! Slave had that shit right, and I couldn't get the tune out of my head as I lounged by the poolside sipping a piña colada spiked with Puerto Rican rum. San Juan was crunk this time of year, and there were tons of hot *mamacitas* strutting past with flat stomachs and sexy hips.

I reached over and rubbed my baby's firm brown thigh. She was stretched out on her back with her head in my lap, letting the sun bake her soft skin an even deeper shade of brown. A cute sister with braided hair smiled as she strutted past in a thong and a t-shirt, and I grinned back. She was a tourist, I could tell. She had the style of a New Yorker and she was killing that thong. It seemed like the dopest girls in the world were hanging around our hotel pool, but none of these chicks had shit on my baby, though. Tee was so fine, her body so bad and bodacious, that even the prettiest girls took a sip of haterade as they glanced at her beauty, made a mental comparison, and came up short.

Tee and I had something real going on. She was helping me see all the good in myself. All that shit she'd had with Blow had been a front. An act. I'd flown to meet her in Puerto Rico this morning, and we'd already done the wild thing three times. Ya boy put it down on her too! My shit was tight now, and I wasn't ashamed of my body anymore, but there were still some embarrassing things about me that I wasn't sure Tee would understand.

"I got a problem," I had told her that morning, panting hard and rubbing my fingers across her firm breasts. If I'da known I was gonna get me a shot of pussy in the airport restroom I woulda gotten there early and taken care of Old Oscar with some lotion in my hand!

I was leaning against the stall door and Tee had my shirt up and was licking my hard stomach. My abs clenched and bulged, and I struggled to concentrate on team stats as I tried not to bust a big one right there in my pants.

"I wanna give you all a this," I said, sucking air between my teeth as she slipped her fingers down the front of my pants and skimmed right over Oscar's fat head, "but I don't have a lot of control right now, baby."

Tee nodded. Her kisses trailed wetly up my chest until her lips were on my neck.

"I know all about that," she said, cupping my dick and stroking Oscar the snake through my pants. "Blow told me. But that ain't no problem, baby. I don't mind if you take care of yourself first, sweetie. That just means you'll last longer when it's my turn."

I'll be damned, I thought. All the barriers I'd been hiding behind fell away at that moment and Tee's eyes got big as hell as I unzipped my pants and let Oscar loose. I almost passed out as Tee gave me a big smile and took Oscar in both of her pretty hands, squeezing him tight. Then me and Oscar both almost hollered out loud as Ice Tee stood up and kissed my lips, then bent down again and opened her mouth. With a sexy sigh of anticipation, my baby placed Oscar's swollen head on the tip of her tongue, then opened her throat and sucked real deep as she listened to my black snake moan.

My BlackBerry lit up and I snatched it off the poolside table as Tee opened her eyes.

"Hello?" I said, tapping Tee and whispering, "Your friend," with a big grin.

"Yo, Ribs!" Blow hollered. My boy sounded pressed as fuck, and I almost felt bad as I put him on loudspeaker so my baby could hear the conversation too.

"Whattup, homey?" I said cheerfully. "How's it hanging, my nig?"

"Shut the fuck up and listen," Blow barked on me. "I got a big prob-lem and I ain't got a whole lotta time to explain it all, neither. I need a lawyer, man. Somebody good who can get down to Mexico and get me the fuck outta jail."

"*What?*" I acted like I was shocked.

"I got arrested, mahfuckah! Knocked! It was a set-up. I just got a note saying Nap and Tomere got took down, too."

"What!?!" I repeated again, but this time there was laughter in my voice as Tee dug her fingers in my armpit and tickled the hell outta me.

I knew all about the take-downs. Right about now, slumlord and sweatshop owner Nap was sitting on Rikers Island, booked on charges of intentional arson for personal gain, and 2Mere100, aka Tomere Williams, had woken up to a nightmare this morning after getting caught in an Internet predator sex sting in Montclair the night be-fore. By tomorrow both of their NFL contracts would be cancelled and even more of their grimy capers would be revealed as the author-ities got deeper into their investigation. But I could dig the panic and surprise I was hearing in Blow's voice because cats like those three never, *ever* banked on getting caught.

"It was those *bitches!*" Blow hollered. "Those three bitches! Teesa and Sugar and Honey. They're sisters, man. *Sisters!* Watch your back 'cause they dicked all of us down real good. They prolly gone try to fuck you too, Ribs, so keep your eyes open."

"Oh, they're open," I chuckled, tracing the outline of Tee's erect nipple with one finger. Pellets of cold water suddenly splashed over us and I ducked and flinched like a little bitch.

"Hey, now!" I yelled at Sugar and Honey, who'd been playing around with some teenagers in the swimming pool and were now over near the edge fuckin' with me and Tee. "If I wanted to get wet I'da jumped my ass on in!"

"Who you talking to, man?" Blow practically screamed. "Man did you hear what I just said? I'm in *jail.* In greasy fuckin *Mexico!* Where the *fuck* are you?"

"Oh, I'm on a weekend vacation, dude. In sunny Puerto Rico," I said, then lifted Tee's head and gave her a quick kiss.

"Yo, you gotta get me a fuckin' lawyer, Ribs!" Blow screamed. "Them girls is fuckin' with us! They tryna take us all down. After everything we did for them bitches, they fucked us up like this."

Tee sat straight up and busted him out.

"Yeah, you dumb motherfucker!" she screamed into the phone. "You got fucked by Charlie Baker's sisters, you little-dicked bitch!" Then she snatched the phone from my hand and turned to her sisters.

"Say hello to Senor Blow! I hear Mexican men like their salads tossed with salsa and red hot chili peppers, motherfucker!"

"Hey, *Byron*," Sugar yelled sweetly and Honey laughed and gave him a big shout-out too.

Tee laughed along with her sisters, and when she handed the phone back my boy was straight up whimpering through the line.

"I trusted you, Ribs," Blow sobbed. "You was my niggah, man. All these years. My niggah from way back in the day, and I trusted you. . . ."

I sighed and broke it down for him.

"You ain't got no niggahs, Blow. You got flunkies, man. Cats that you misuse, shit on, and disrespect. You real comfortable dicking everybody else down, right? Well now it's your turn to bend over and take a fat one, homey."

"You was my *boy*," Blow sniffled. "And you turned on me like our friendship wasn't nothing. That's some shit, Ribs. That's some real cold shit."

"Nah, bro," I laughed as I got ready to hang up. "That ain't no *shit*, my nig. But it *is* some Sugar-Honey-Ice-Tee!"

Acknowledgments

Father, thank you.

Big ups to my Harlem fam for keeping my feet on the ground. Much luv to Reem and Black for your music and your tireless grind, and to Nisaa, Missy, Man, Jay, Ty, and our new baby girl Tia for being who you are.

Thanks to Mary B. Morrison and Selena James for embracing me and making this collaboration a whole lot of sexy fun.

Mad affection and crazy thanks to my fans who send me endless luv and continue to ride this urban erotic train with me every single day.

I luv y'all right back!

Ride hard, homeys! We're doing big things!

STAY BLACK

NOIRE

Discussion Questions

1. Rishawn "Pork Ribs" Rawlings is the odd man out in Sugar-Honey-Ice-Tee. In a world full of diesel-body professional football players, his less-than-perfect physique leaves his self-esteem in the gutter even though he is a good man with a big heart and a great job. If you are female, have you ever tossed a good brother off because he wasn't all that in the looks department? Did you come to regret your decision?

2. Professional athletes and ballers often have endless doe and big-time pull with the ladies. In this age of "get-all-you-can-get," can you be swayed by money and star appeal alone, or does a baller have to bring something of substance to the party?

3. Nap, Tomere, and Blow were three star athletes with phat pockets and swollen egos. Do they remind you of anyone on the professional sports scene today?

4. When Charlie Baker got taken out by one of Blow's grimy capers, he knew who to call on to get some retribution. Who would have your back in a similar situation? Would they be able to concoct a clever get-back scheme for you?

5. Blow, Tomere, and Nap were sheisty to the core. If a baller was lining your pockets and lacing you in fine clothing and bright jewels, but you knew the money was coming from illegal activities, would you accept the gifts?

6. The ballers in Sugar-Honey-Ice-Tee were constantly scheming on financial capers. If your man was working a caper that you knew was dirty, would you turn him in? Could you snitch on your boo?

7. Nap was a slumlord and a fraud. Sugar played him to the left by setting him up for insurance fraud and money laundering. Is outsourcing one's company an exploitation of another country's workforce to the detriment of American workers, or is all fair in business just as long as you turn a profit?

8. Honey had Tomere bent on her. If you knew a man had eyes (and hands) for very young girls, could you get loose with him and set him up, even for revenge?

9. Ice Tee pulls a slick move on Blow and gets him sent to a Mexican prison where he will probably get bent over in the shower. If your man went to the joint and admits he was once violated by another inmate, would you take him back once he was released?

10. With Sugar's help, Ribs was able to turn his life around with exercise and a healthy diet. As a result, his confidence and self-esteem improved so much that he was able to feel worthy of a beautiful diva like Ice Tee. What would you have to do to improve your self-esteem? Does your physical appearance have a lot to do with how you see yourself, and how you relate to members of the opposite sex?

He's rich, he's famous, and every woman wants him . . .

Darius Jones

Available August 2010 in hardcover from Dafina Books

Chapter 1

Darius

For once in my life, I was happy. I mean, genuinely happy. My mother, wife and son were my world. My mother was my rock. My wife was my rib. My son kept me focused on what was important in life . . . family.

Some thought me to be arrogant, cocky, a shit-talker, an asshole. Others thought of me as *the shit*. Fans begged for my autograph and photo ops, or lingered near the arena exit to touch my jersey or shake my hand. Groupies stalked me, followed me from city to city. Some even knocked on my hotel door, praying for a chance to suck or ride my dick.

I considered myself the best. I was the best in the professional basketball league. I worked out and practiced every day. Shot around on game day. I lived and breathed basketball. I could easily get into a zone and block out people and the things happening around me.

My wife taught me to make time for her and my son—who, by the way, wasn't her son. I slipped up and got my stepsister pregnant. At first, that was the worst mistake of my life. But having my son in my life was no mistake. Couldn't have created him with any other woman.

My mother showed me that people are more important than things and that things happen. Not beyond our control, but sometimes because we lost control. Letting ourselves go with the flow, we occasionally chased the people and things we felt were good for us, but not important to us. Mom said, "Sometimes we're right. Sometimes we're wrong. Darius, what's more important than making mistakes is learning from your mistakes."

I was happy my wife hadn't given up on me. Fancy was the only woman who could satisfy me. In my heart, my head, and the bedroom, that woman drove me fucking nuts. My nuts were hers and hers alone. I wasn't tripping off of no groupie chick tryna suck or ride my dick. I'd had enough head to know no woman sucked my dick better than my wife. And Lord, no woman had fucked me senseless until I'd met LadyCat.

MaDear, my grandmother, probably rolled over in her grave whenever she heard me say or even think of using the Lord's name in vain. But I was sure the Lord didn't mind my using his name to express how excited my wife made me.

I didn't ask my wife to sign no prenuptial agreement. I came from a self-made millionaire mom. Made my own millions. Although my wife had earned her own millions selling real estate, my money was my wife's money. Money didn't make Darius Jones. Took me awhile to realize that shit.

I looked at my wife and smiled. "Baby, I love you so much, I want to marry you again."

Her hand was at the top of the steering wheel. She slid her hand down and around, turning onto Wilshire Boulevard, then letting the wheel slide between her fingers as the tires realigned with our SUV. Damn, she had the sexiest mannerisms. Her hair flowed over her bare shoulders. Her titties were perched high under her summer dress.

"I'd marry you again in a heartbeat, too," she said, smiling back at me.

"Daddy, I want you to marry my mommy. Can you marry her too?" my son asked.

Kids said the darnest things, but my son was brainwashed by his mother, Ashlee. No telling what would come out his mouth. Ashlee had planted so many seeds in his head about our being a family one day and how he shouldn't call my wife "Mother" or "Mommy" but to call her by her first name, Fancy.

Fancy chuckled at DJ. I turned to my son, who was strapped in his car seat and said, "My man, marrying two women would send your daddy to jail. You don't want me to go to jail, do you?"

"Nope, but Mommy does."

I shook my head, then dialed my mom. She answered, "Hey, baby."

"Ma, what's wrong?" I asked right away. The tone of her voice indicated she was disturbed about something.

Fancy looked at my face. She frowned too. I held up my hand to my wife, letting her know I'd handle whatever was bothering my mom.

"Nothing for you to worry about, sweetheart."

"You still joining us for dinner tonight?" I asked her. "We're almost at Wolfgang's Steakhouse."

"I'll call you back and let you know. I'm not sure," she said somberly.

"Is that Grant Hill guy pressuring you? Is he tripping again? I told you I can make him disappear from your life permanently."

"He wants me to go to a movie premiere with him tonight. I wouldn't mind if his ex wasn't going to be there. Just not sure I'm feeling up to any drama, that's all."

"I'm sending a car for you, Ma. Come have dinner with us. It's not often we're both back in our hometown of LA at the same time."

"I'm okay, sweetheart. I'll call you in a few and let you know what I decide. Give my lil' man a kiss for me."

"That I can do too, Ma. I love you. Thanks for always being there for me. Let me be there for you."

Mom sniffled, then said, "I love you too, sweetheart. Bye."

DJ was too far away for me to kiss his cheek, so I kissed my hand, touched my son's hand, then said, "That's from your grandma."

I had no problem showing my son love and affection. Had no problem keeping him in line either. Didn't want him to become the spoiled brat I was. I'd had so many women, I'd lost count by the time I'd met Fancy. I was glad I hadn't married Maxine, my first fiancée.

She'd contracted HIV. Sometimes I wondered if that was my fault. Wasn't sure Maxine would've cheated on me had I not cheated on her. With my promiscuous ways, one would think I would've contracted the disease, not her. Maxine had two lovers. Me and the dude that infected her. I was the male whore, so to speak, and not ashamed of my past, mind you. My whoring around before settling down made me a better man.

The women I'd fucked, including my son's mother Ashlee, had come to me with their pussies on silver platters. Well, that wasn't exactly true about Ashlee. I pursued her. There was something pure and innocent about her. Ashlee was beautiful, friendly, and naïve. She believed in me, like my mom. And perhaps at one time, I was in love with Ashlee. Until she fucked my brother. I would've cut her off, dismissed her, gotten rid of her, all of that if she'd fucked any man.

But for her to have fucked my scheming, scandalous, trifling, conniving brother Kevin, the only brother I had alive since my brother Darryl died, was too much. I tried to bring Kevin's ass up, and he tried to bury me by stealing over a million dollars of my money and fucking Ashlee. Talk about ashes to ashes, that dude was dirt. Scum. Blood didn't make him worthy of my respect. Kevin deserved to die in that fire he'd set to my office building. He'd thought I was inside. Instead, Ashlee was the one burned. Her face, like her heart, was permanently scarred.

Fancy's hand slid from the top of the steering wheel to the bottom. "Baby, is your mother okay? We can cancel dinner if you'd like."

That was what I loved about my wife. She always considered my feelings. "Nah, I'll call her from the restaurant."

My wife looked at me and smiled. The steering wheel slid between her fingers.

I pointed at the car speeding in our direction. "Baby! Watch—"
Crash!

"Oh my god." In seconds, my airbag inflated, jamming my body against my seat. My face bent sideways against the headrest. My wife's airbag hadn't deployed. Her forehead was split from her hairline to her nose.

"Daddy!" my son screamed.

Fighting my way from underneath the airbag, I reached into the back seat and unbuckled my son. I pulled him into my arms and held his body close to mine, shielding his face from Fancy. My wife wasn't moving. All I saw was blood gushing from her head. I don't know how much time passed before a paramedic opened Fancy's door. All I could do was cry, "Please save my wife."

I got out the SUV with my son and ran to the ambulance to be close to my wife.

"Sir, we've got to go," the paramedic said, slamming the door in my face.

Anger consumed me. I stormed to the driver of the other car. "What the fuck have you done!"

His eyes were bloodred but he wasn't bleeding. His face was distorted. His apology was slurred: "Look, I'm sorry, man. Hope your wife is okay."

I wanted to punch him in his drunken face. "For your sake, you'd better pray she's all right." Another paramedic and a police officer approached me, so I knew I couldn't leave the scene. So I did the best thing—dialed my mom.

My son locked his arms around my neck. "Daddy, I'm scared," he cried.

"Me too, son. Me too."

Chapter 2

Bambi

The way to a man's heart was through his mother.

I had every news article on Darius Jones since he'd played basket-ball in high school. I also had a video of all his games and his wedding. I was at Madison Square Garden when he was drafted, went to all of his home games in Atlanta, traveled to all the away games. I had photos of his son, his son's mother, his wife, his mother, his biological father, and his stepfathers. Some of the pictures I'd printed from the Internet, others I'd taken. I slept in his jersey each night, made life-size six-nine body-length pillows with images of him. I even picked up a dreadlock that fell from his head when he was sitting on the sidelines during a timeout. I was Darius Jones's number one fan. He just didn't know it . . . yet.

Being a private investigator by trade made me a professional groupie. It was no accident that I'd discovered Darius's mom Jada was attending the movie premiere for *Something on the Side*. Savvy groupies befriended celebrities all the time. Velvet Waters, the star of the movie, had become this overnight Hollywood sensation. I added her to my list of people to know because Velvet used to live in Atlanta. She'd stripped as Red Velvet at Stilettos Night Club in Atlanta before landing the lead in *Something on the Side*. She was paid by Trevor to fuck Grant Hill before Grant started dating Darius's mother, Jada.

Anyone attached to Darius, directly or indirectly, was also attached to me.

I'd been sitting at the bar one day inside of LA's most popular five-star hotel, passing time in between games when I met Velvet. While waiting to head to LAX for my flight back to Atlanta to see my Darius play for our home team, I noticed Velvet stroll in. Hair flowing. Makeup immaculate. Money had done her good.

She'd sat next to me, and I overheard Velvet confirm Grant Hill would be at her premiere. There was such a thing as luck in the PI world. I was at the right place, right time.

I hadn't been in pursuit of Velvet at that moment. I'd flown to Atlanta to temporarily distance myself from Darius. I was in Los Angeles to avoid having Darius's paparazzi get a snapshot of me in their photos. I was careful because I didn't want to be identified as a maniac stalker like the chick who was pursuing Fisher.

After Velvet ended her call, I'd said, "Hi, Velvet. Congratulations. You are my she-ro. And you're so beautiful."

She'd answered with a flat, "Thanks."

I'd leaned closer to her and said, "Girl, you went from stripping at Stilettos to Hollywood." Then I lied, "I use to make it rain on you but you're big time now. Probably don't remember little ole me."

Velvet had stared at me as if trying to recall my face. How could she remember me? I hadn't sprinkled her with dollar bills. How could anyone remember me even if they'd seen me? I was a chameleon. I changed my makeup, hair, and wardrobe every other day.

As she continued studying my face, I said, "Carl Weber is my favorite author. Is he going to be at the premiere? I'd love to meet him." I smiled at her. Shook my head. "My apology. Who am I to think I could ever go to a premiere? Good luck, girl."

Velvet eased from her barstool. Took five steps. I'd counted each one before she'd turned around and took five more in my direction.

"Give me your address. I'll mail you a ticket but I can only give you one."

"Are you serious?" I said, handing her my card with my Atlanta post office box.

She glanced at my card, nodded, then walked away. No "goodbye" or "nice meeting you." A few weeks later I was back in LA to attend the premiere.

Preparing to walk the red carpet, I sat at the vanity in my hotel room. I braided my natural jet-black curly hair into eleven cornrows, then covered my hair with a mesh net stocking cap. I applied a small amount of eyebrow glue to the back of my one-hundred-percent human hair eyebrows, then layered each blond-colored brow perfectly over my jet-black brows. Then I glued and attached my light-brown eyelashes. I trailed a thin line of glue along the edge of my hairline, then attached my full lace twenty-two-inch strawberry blond wig. I stood, held my head upside down, brushed, then fluffed my hair. Instantly, I went from being a fair-complexioned African-American woman to looking like a Caucasian woman with the perfect tan.

I applied my concealer, foundation, and brown eyeliner. I stroked on various hues of sparkling blue eyeshadow, toned it down with a hint of magenta, and brushed a soft pink lipstick on my mouth. I inserted my light bluish-grey contacts. After easing into padded butt-booster panties that would make Serena Williams jealous, I stuffed silicone breast pads into the sides of my bra to sandwich my D cups into a facade of DDs that gave me amazing cleavage. I stepped into iridescent stilettos, picked up my purse, and double-checked to make sure I had my ticket. I kissed the plastic covering on my photo of Darius, then placed it back in my purse. His picture was my good luck charm. With Darius by my side, all things were possible.

Slipping my room key into my handbag, I left my suite and made my way to the lobby. The bellman smiled at me. "You are one gorgeous woman. Can I, make that, *may* I assist you?"

"Thanks, but no thanks. My driver is outside," I politely declined, exiting the hotel.

I eased into the backseat of my white stretch limousine and gazed out the window, lost in thought about how I'd befriend Darius's mother tonight. Was my seat even close to hers? I had the advantage, since I knew what she looked like and she had no clue who I was.

A long line of limos led to the theater. My driver opened my door. I swooped my hair to one side, thrust my breasts forward, arched my back, and smiled as though I was Mrs. Darius Jones. The usher escorted me to my seat. I sat one row directly behind my future mother-in-law. By the end of the night, I'd become Jada's newest best friend or her worst enemy.

A very pregnant woman being escorted by a tall, thin man with a long ponytail stepped sideways in front of Grant and Jada. When the pregnant woman sat next to Jada, Jada turned to Grant and stared into his eyes. Squinted. Frowned. I noticed Jada's right jaw tighten.

Halfway through the movie, the pregnant woman moaned and held her stomach, but continued watching the movie. The screening was nice but I was in PI mode. Things moved quickly. After the credits rolled, the director proposed to Velvet, the pregnant lady's water broke, Velvet accepted the marriage proposal, then Grant asked, "Honey, is that my baby?"

My jaw dropped. I thought I was on top of everything but this was new and valuable information. Jada's cell phone rang, temporarily interrupting the flow of things. Honey answered Grant, "It's not your child but these babies are your twin boys."

Jada stopped speaking into her phone long enough to call Honey a liar. Jada walked off, then cried, "Fancy was hit by a drunk driver. We've got to go to the hospital."

Bingo! I said to myself.

Jada yelled, "Grant! Did you hear me? Darius's wife was hit by a drunk driver! Let's go!"

I guess people had the right to be consumed with their issues. Jada was worried about Fancy. Grant was worried about Honey. And I was concerned with Darius and finding out what hospital Fancy was in.

My intention to get Darius was no fly-by-night suck-his-dick groupie trick. Oh, no. I was determined to either marry him or massacre him. If I couldn't have Darius Jones, no woman would, especially Fancy. I'd make sure Fancy's hospital stay was permanent.

I stood in the aisle, waiting to follow Jada to the hospital.

Get more Darius Jones in the Soulmates Dissipate Series—

Soulmates Dissipate

Never Again Once More

He's Just a Friend

Somebody's Gotta Be On Top

Nothing Has Ever Felt Like This

When Somebody Loves You Back

Available now, wherever books are sold

Turn the page for excerpts from the Soulmates Dissipate Series. . . .

From *Soulmates Dissipate*

The eternal bond of your Soulmate gels the existence of your life.

She vividly remembered their first kiss. Welling-ton Jones gently placed his strong caramel-colored hand at the nape of her dark chocolate neck and whispered, "Diamond, I've wanted to kiss you all night. May I?"

Jada Diamond Tanner struggled to maintain her composure, but Wellington was making it increasingly difficult. How was she to respond without seeming anxious to kiss this tall, sexy man she'd known for all of sixty minutes, give or take ten?

She paused, gazed directly into his eyes, and replied, "Only if I choose where you kiss me." The nearby crowd in the noisy garage became silent. Valet attendants dressed in red jackets and black pants hurried to deliver cars. Although the concert was over, *I've wanted to kiss you all night* was music to her ears.

Wellington seductively shrugged his left shoulder, nodded, and winked his left eye. He looked like a pro but not at all like a player. The outline of his black Armani suit highlighted *all* his muscles. The scent of his cologne traveled in the cool fall night breeze, wrapped around all her senses and danced in her hair. The full moon glowed. His bald head glistened. His thick black eyebrows complemented his dreamy midnight eyes.

Ladylike, she extended her left hand, because it was more sensuous and sensitive to touch than her right. Plus, she wanted to see how creative this man was, and whether he possessed qualitative skills that would interest her in taking the relationship to a hotter level. She was cool, calm, and collected, on the outside.

Slowly, he removed his right hand from underneath her dark silky hair, which flowed down to the center of her back. *Beep. Beep.* "Would someone please move this car!" shouted the man in the black Lexus. She focused, as if they were the only two in the garage. Wellington never missed a beat. He placed Jada's left hand into his right. A long steady flow of air quietly entered her nostrils. Their souls gelled. Her spirit danced. Smooth man. Better proceed with caution. Although she wasn't convinced, he was definitely standing in front of the pitcher's mound prepared to bat.

Like watching a video in slow motion, he drew her French-manicured hand closer. He licked his lips and positioned his tongue between her index and ring fingers. His tongue penetrated her crevice while his full caramel lips—with a trace of natural cocoa—warmly encircled her adjoining knuckles. She closed her eyes. Moisture seeped between her fingers and thighs. This man had knocked more than the ball out of the park!

Unexpectedly, her twenty-six-inch waist moved forward. Her shoulders and thirty-six-inch hips jerked backward, in unison. It was Monday morning. Jada sat at her bedroom vanity and gazed out the window. She daydreamed about that kiss. One by one the treetops came into focus. Lots of tall evergreen trees stood behind her penthouse. They swayed back and forth. Fresh air. Serenity. She loved California. So far, Oakland was the only place she'd lived.

Jada looked at the digital clock on her cherrywood nightstand. It was six o'clock. Time to begin her daily transformation from looking like Sleeping Beauty to becoming irresistibly drop-dead gorgeous. Time to get ready for work.

Photo shooting the finest male models from coast to coast was a tough job. She'd had a passion for photography since she was six years old and an infatuation with great-looking men as long as she could remember.

Unable to move, she sat, thinking about her father. Although he'd passed away three years, seven months, and ten days ago, he'd never left her. She could still hear his deep, Southern drawl. "Diamond." He'd always call her by her middle name. "There's nothing like time off from work with a job, with pay. If you don't have no job, honey, you don't need no time off." Daddy was right; he was always right. Jada smiled. Today was definitely designed with Diamond in mind.

Mr. Terrance Murphy was the new owner of Sensations Communications. He'd purchased the company a year ago when the previous owners liquidated their assets.

The phone rang six times without an answer. Jada's finger curved toward the off button. Then faintly she heard:

"Sensations Communications."

"Hi. Karen. I'm glad you answered. I was just about to hang up."

Karen was Jada's loyal assistant, or so she thought.

"Oh, Jada girl. You know I'm here every morning at six-thirty on the dot."

"Yeah, I know. Listen. I won't be in today, so call Marvin Jackson and reschedule him for Thursday at the same time. Reschedule my Thursday trip to Los Angeles to early Saturday morning. I must arrive no later than seven. And Karen, be sure to call my L.A. client, Terrell Morgan. Tell him he's rescheduled for eight o'clock."

"Consider it done. Will you be in tomorrow?" asked Karen.

"I'll see you bright and early. Good-bye."

"Bye."

Jada pressed nine on the speed dial. Before the phone rang, she hit the off button. Never put off until tomorrow what you can do today. She decided to surprise her fiancé. He had recently moved his financial advisory business, Wellington Jones and Associates, into his home.

Jada cherished surprises. All of them had been good, so far. Her parents bought her first camera when she was seven. It wasn't her birthday. She traveled with her best friend on a cruise to Mexico when she was eighteen. In college, she received four marriage proposals. "No. No. No. No," she replied each time. She "crossed her t's and dotted her i's." She refused to be any man's showpiece. Confidence was a major component of her Lady Leo characteristic.

Perfect. Jada loved most things hot and steamy. She stepped into the shower and lathered her purple scrunchie with strawberries and peaches shower cream. Leisurely she stroked each part of her five-foot nine-inch temple. The water pulsated against her breasts. Her chocolate nipples hardened. Unable to resist, she licked each one. She turned up the water just a notch, parted her legs, spread her lips, and rotated her clit to the perfect beat. Her eyes closed. Knees bent. Quickly she suppressed her flow.

The mist suspended in air. Jada stepped onto the purple, green, and gold rug. It was a gift from Wellington while they were at the Mardi Gras in Nawlins. She wrapped the matching towel around her waist and brushed her pearly white teeth. The combined results of Daddy's money, and the three years she'd worn braces.

Jada's hazel-colored almond-shaped eyes reflected from the bathroom mirror. Her slender fingers caressed her radiant skin with chocolate-flavored cocoa butter lite. She glanced at her ben-wa balls and smiled, knowing she would use the real thing today. Jada loved being a woman. She'd do coochie crunches all day long and the men didn't have a clue. If he was boring, she'd nonchalantly squeeze her gold balls. *"Okay,* that's ten sets, ten reps." On the other hand, if he was interesting, she'd grip so hard she could hear the metal balls grind. She'd mask. And enjoy multiple orgasms.

She looked at the clock. It was 8:00 A.M. Keys. Purse. Sunglasses. The scent of Zahra and Eunice lingered. The white cotton ankle-length dress with thigh-high splits gently clung. Her diamond anklet—Daddy bought for Valentine's Day before he died—sparkled. She grabbed her FUBU travel bag with lingerie gear intact. Body and Soul was her favorite "gear" store. They catered to women of contour.

The front and back splits bared her chocolate thighs to the sun while she cruised in her red convertible. Through her dark designer sunglasses, traffic on the Bay Bridge flowed. Traffic along the Peninsula was a breeze. Her ponytail dangled in the air. The projected high was one hundred degrees. Thoughts of making love on Wellington's patio by the pool increased her body heat. *Let's get it on. Oh, baby, let's get it on,* echoed on KBLX-FM 102.9. Jada loved to sing ahead of her favorite songs. She adored Marvin Gaye.

She shifted to a lower gear. The engine roared three-quarters of a mile, until she reached the last house up the hill. An unfamiliar car with D.C. plates sat in the circular driveway between Wellington's indigo Mercedes and black Expedi-tion. Oh well, he had thousands of clients. Prob-ably one of his out-of-state's checking on their portfolio.

Jada looked in the rearview mirror. Hair. Makeup. Flawless. Her peripheral vision detected movement on the balcony above. She glimpsed over the windshield. A beautiful woman disappeared inside Wellington's bedroom. Jada's heart raced faster than the hum of the engine.

She tried to shake it off. She rang the bell. Wellington opened the door. His black silk pajama pants—imported from Italy—hung below his waistline. Thoughts of the mysterious woman in her man's bedroom scrolled Jada's mind like it was Judgment Day. His bare caramel-candied chest looked like he'd hired a professional sculptor. Silky-smooth hairs separated and defined his eight-pack.

"Hi, baby." Wellington kissed Jada's coffee-colored lips. A glossy golden-brown imprint remained. "Why didn't you call first?"

Jada slid her sunglasses to the tip of her nose. She felt the hairs on the back of her neck rise. Who was this woman? Where was this woman? And why in the *hell* was she in Wellington's bedroom? She politely said. "I didn't know I needed to call first."

"It's not that you need to. It's just considerate. You know, like I do."

In one swoop, Jada braced her Ray Bans on top of her head and released her ponytail. "Let's skip the preliminaries. Who's your houseguest?" She was cool. But she really felt like acting a damn fool.

"Oh, that's Melanie, from D.C. She had a break from the studio, so Mom invited her to visit and insisted she stay with me. You know how my mother likes showing me off to her friends. Remember, I told you Mom and Dad are in D.C. They'll be back Friday." Wellington flexed the right side of his chest and smiled. "Just in time to host the Jones family's thirty-fifth annual barbecue Saturday." Jada tasted the scent of his Wintergreen Altoids. She inhaled. Wellington's breath was always fresh.

"Yes, Wellington, you've told me how your parents' annual barbecues started on your first birthday. Now it's not only a family tradition but also a societal affair where prestigious folk gather to let down their hair. And let the good times role." Jada spoke so fast, she could hardly hear the words coming out of her mouth. Wellington clamped his hands behind his back.

"I clearly remember you saying no matter how successful we become, we still know how to throw a great barbecue. I've heard the story time and time again. And you didn't invite me last year because we'd just met and you didn't know what I'd think of your parents' tremendous sociopolitical involvement with numerous affluent organizations. *Now*, let's get back to Melanie." By the time Jada got to her point, she had to take a deep breath to regain her composure.

Wellington never shifted his dreamy eyes away from Jada's. She stood in the foyer. Peeped over his shoulder. He lovingly stroked the left side of her face. Wellington's six-feet four-inch, two hundred and twenty-pound frame obscured her view. Jada's temperature must have been well over the today's projected high but for all the wrong reasons.

"Look, sweetheart. I know this is the first time I've had a female houseguest since we've been together. But you have to trust me. She's just a friend. She's leaving next Sunday. Mom invited her to the barbecue and Melanie volunteered to help prepare the food. She's an excellent cook. Get to know her. You'll like her."

Damn! Jada wondered how *well* Wellington knew Melanie. He hadn't budged since he opened the door. Maybe he was stalling while she freshened up.

"Melanie and my mom have a lot in common. They're affiliated with most of the same *prestigious* organizations. You know how important that is to my mom. It's been a long-standing tradition in Melanie's family. That's why my mother respects her so much. You really should join *at least one.*"

Well, don't we just know her whole life history? Isn't that cute. "Wellington, we've had this discussion before and you know I *refuse* to join any of those organizations. Getting back to the subject at hand. If she's just a *friend*, why was she on your balcony and not the guest balcony?"

"Look, Diamond, I don't have to prove myself. It's too hot and too early for ninety-nine questions. You show up unannounced and now you want to interrogate me. Baby, please come in. Have a seat in the living room. I'll prepare breakfast for both of you."

Wellington's foyer was larger than most. Consuming approximately two hundred square feet, the floor was made of crystal clear marble. His favorite color black was swirled in an abstract pattern. Jada had never seen this type of marble anyplace. London. Paris. Italy. China. Two black pillars—ringed with twenty-four-karat gold accents around the top and bottom—stood twenty-four feet high, twelve feet apart. The custom-designed silk African drapes, spiraled each pillar from ceiling to floor.

Convinced he wouldn't tell her the *real deal,* Jada entered Wellington's spacious sunk-in living room like Inspector Clouseau. The furniture was strategically situated near the sliding glass door leading to his main patio. Step by step. Thump. Thump. Thump. The pulse in her throat kept pace. The tailored winter-white drapes were drawn to prevent glare on the seventy-inch television. Ah ha! Melanie appeared right at home. The world news was on the big screen. An X-rated film featuring Vanessa on the other. Melanie's French pedicure blended with the off-white chaise longue. Jada's heart and feet sank into the tan carpet's thickness. She noticed how Melanie's bright teeth shined through the cherry-red lip gloss. So this was what high-society women did on vacation.

"Oh hi, I'm Melanie." Melanie resumed watching TV. "Wellington has told me so much about you."

Before today, he'd never mentioned Melanie. Jada had the inside scoop on D.C. women. They didn't have a problem sharing a man. In California, if women shared, it was strictly for the moment. Do not get attached. For the moment, Jada ignored the video and lay on the couch parallel to the chaise longue.

"Hi, Melanie, I'm Diamond, Wellington's *fiancée.* "

Eyebrows arched. French manicure. Perfect size ten. Small waist. Bigger breasts. Smaller butt. Shoulder-length hair, brown. Teasing tan. Gorgeous. Five-nine. Five-ten. One forty. One forty-five. High cheekbones. Piercing light-brown eyes. Thick lips. Soft shoulders. Lustrous skin. Melanie was too sexy for comfort.

"So, *Melanie,* what brings you *all* the way to California, *in your car?* "

Melanie's light-brown eyes were fixed on the video.

"I needed a break from the studio. I'm a photographer for *Vibrations Magazine.* "

Jada's body went from horizontal to vertical in three seconds. "Excuse me for a moment. I'll be right back."

Wellington had gone upstairs to his bedroom. The Road Runner couldn't have gotten to him quicker. He stood naked. She stood still. He flexed in front of his wall-length mirror. Needless to say, Ms. Melanie could prepare breakfast her damn self.

She entered his suite-size bedroom. "Hi, baby." Her tongue traveled three hundred and sixty degrees around her lips. Jada lusted for Wellington's six-foot-four, two hundred and twenty pounds of succulent, caramel flesh. She felt her heart beat against her thong.

"Hi, precious, you have perfect timing." Wellington did three quick dick curls. "I was just about to shower. Join me."

"You said you were going to prepare breakfast."

"What's the rush? I'll do it later."

Jada realized she'd just gotten out of the shower, but what's a woman to do! White cotton cloth circled her feet. Wellington never could resist her tasty chocolate mounds with nipples that tasted like Hershey's Kisses. It was her favorite flavored cocoa butter lite.

He did an erotic strip-tease move. Spun around. Glided close behind. "You know I love the way you smell, baby, but I can never figure out exactly what you're wearing." The wetness of his tongue invoked a trail of coolness up her spine. His smooth masculine hands caressed her voluptuous thirty-six Ds. The view in the mirror turned Jada on. The flow she suppressed earlier welled up inside her pulsating walls.

Gently, he turned her around and palmed her firm ass. Wellington's winter-fresh tongue invaded Jada's mouth. She greeted it like it was opening day at Disney World.

A video scene flashed across Jada's mind. Vanessa blew softly and feathered this handsome young guy. Absent her touch, his body trembled. He climaxed. Jada had acquired most of her sexual skills from reading. But one day soon, she'd have to try that on Wellington.

They stepped into his 150-square-foot custom-made shower. It was large enough to accommodate six people standing, or one person lying on the shower bed. The walls were pallid with beautiful African American art originals strategically displayed on every accessible wall. Wellington's fetish for fine art ran deep. Art was exhibited on easels and hung on walls in every single room, including the thirteen-person Jacuzzi room.

Wellington's parents, Mr. and Mrs. Christopher Jones, worked extremely smart to achieve their wealth. They taught Wellington how to track his mutual fund at five years old. Now he maintained his lifestyle on interest from his investments and fees from his clients.

"Baby, I've got an idea. Set up the shower bed."

"Precious, this is why I love you so much. Because you're a freak girl, but only for me, and I love it! You know every man wants a little trash in his woman but no man wants a trashy woman."

"Wellington, set up the shower bed." Jada whispered, *"Now."* Inconspicuously built into the wall for convenience and safety, it unfolded horizontally.

"Lie down. Relax. And allow me to give you the most exotic and erotic massage of your life. Today you'll experience cosmic ecstasy."

The four-by-eight-foot bed was crafted with genuine Italian waterproof leather and tailored to suit Wellington. Traditionally he gave Jada full body massages. Not today.

She inserted the attachable pillow. Jada wanted him to watch. Then she positioned the six showerheads. One each above his chest, abs, feet, thighs, one over his throbbing nine-inch penis, and the last underneath his firm ass. A structurally designed opening exposed Wellington's ass. "Now relax and observe *Mama* at work."

Jada lathered up his black scrunchie. Welling-ton was so clean he almost squeaked. She believed cleanliness was next to Godliness. If it wasn't clean, Jada refused to get close.

The warm water flowed over Wellington's body. She rubbed Karma Sutra oil all over his body. Teased his hardened nipples. Massaged his chest and abs. And stroked his circumcised penis. He moaned in a deep passionate voice.

Jada's vagina snapped. Released. Contracted. Her hot watery tongue raced up and down Wellington's shaft. His muscle slapped her right cheek several times. She kissed, licked, and then sucked him hard— so hard she felt the walls of her mouth cave in and tighten around *The Ruler.* With each deep suck, her nose and lips pressed against his pubic hairs. She never disclosed how she'd learned to deep throat.

"Ow, girl."

"You taste so good, baby." Jada drooled.

Her lips explored his inner thighs. Voyaged to his jewels and slowly continued to his knees, his feet. She embraced his toes with her lips. He shivered and muttered, "Come back up."

"In a minute." Jada slid her slippery breasts against Wellington's smooth feet and fondled them. He wiggled his toes as if to say "Fuck the feet!"

The thought of blue balls convinced her to switch. She started performing her special lemon twist. With oily hands she twisted his dick. Left and right. Up and down. The palm of her hand occasionally covered his head to prolong his ejaculation. Wellington watched *Mama* work.

"Whose is it?" She slipped his hardness into her hungry mouth.

"Da-Da-Diamond ru-rules *The Ruler.*"

Each time his head touched the back of her throat, her juices flowed. This time she held her lips and nose against his pubic hair so hard she could hardly breathe. She didn't care. She had to reach her other G-spot. She knew Wellington's excitement heightened whenever she did this. Jada intentionally limited her oxygen supply to intensify her orgasm.

Jada slid her hand under the table and gently penetrated Wellington. Her oily index finger glided in and out of his rectum. His toes curled. "Damn, girl. You sure know how to make me feel good. Don't stop. Please! Don't stop."

She loved it when he begged. Jada's finger test was pass or fail. If a man became paranoid and rejected the gesture, he was too damn conservative. An experienced man who was secure with his manhood understood that dual sexual stimulation was cosmic.

Steadily, she increased the pace. Not too fast. She wanted her man to enjoy every second. Wel-lington could no longer hold back his powerful explosion. He released the loudest and deepest groan she had ever heard.

As he reached his orgasmic peak, he shivered, epileptic-like. She wasn't finished just yet. Her mouth welcomed the thick creamy fluids that flowed like lava oozing over the top of an erupting volcano. Little by little his sweetness flowed from her mouth while she kissed, licked, and sucked him.

Wellington could barely move. He stumbled to his king-size bed, dripping wet. He fell backward on the brown silk comforter. His arms spread east and west. "Damn, girl."

"Mission accomplished," Jada whispered as she kissed Wellington's forehead. She slipped into her dress and went downstairs.

Melanie was preparing a vegetarian omelet. She held the blue plastic ladle in her hand and asked, "Would you like to have breakfast *again?*"

"That depends on what you're serving."

"Omelet. What else?" Melanie's cherry-red lips curved. The flawless arch in her eyebrows extended upward.

"Sure. Why not?" Jada sat at the breakfast nook near the window and admired the architectural design of the kitchen. Wellington's kitchen was designed as if he were a chef. Pots and pans hung from the ceiling. Most of them had never been used. His double stove with eight burners and customized grill rested in the center like a huge island.

Melanie cracked three eggs. She moved about the kitchen like she was right at home. She knew exactly where everything was located. Melanie held the bowl of diced ham and said, "I'm having a vegetarian omelet. Would you like me to add meat to yours, or have you had your fill today?"

Her sarcasm had grown old. Jada crossed her arms and pivoted in her seat. "Look, Melanie. I really don't know you. But the way you're making little snide remarks leads me to believe you're lacking sexual gratification in your socioeconomic and politically correct environment."

She delicately folded the omelet. "No, Dia-mond."

"Stop right there. Only my father—may he rest in peace—and Wellington use my middle name. *Please,* call me Jada."

Melanie sighed. She quietly placed the ladle in the sink. "I'll call you whatever you prefer. But you shouldn't introduce yourself as Diamond if you don't want anyone other than *your men* calling you that. No, *Jada*—as you prefer—to answer your question, I'm not lacking at all. I was simply trying to break the ice. So let's try this a different way."

Melanie sat perpendicular to Jada, crossed her legs, leaned forward, and said, "My name is Melanie Marie Thompson. I graduated from Howard University in 1987. I'm thirty-two years old. Never married. No kids. My grandmother is a Greek. My mother's a Greek. And I'm a Greek. Are you a Greek, Jada?" Melanie returned to the stove and flipped the omelet with ease.

Jada unfolded her arms. "No, my mother never believed in affiliations and I feel the same."

"Oh, so I see. Well, my family has a long-standing history with many *affluent* organizations. Just like Mrs. Jones."

The omelet was almost ready. The aroma made Jada hungry.

"So I've heard."

"Would you like me to add any spices to your omelet?" asked Melanie.

"No, thanks. I've had enough *spice* this morning." Jada tossed her wet hair over her shoulders.

"See, now you're the one bringing it up so I'll just ignore that statement. Here's your omelet."

"Thanks. Let's sit outside by the pool," suggested Jada.

"Sure."

Wellington's Olympic-size pool resembled the number zero on a football jersey. The elevated oval-shaped hot tub—with four diving boards—could accommodate eight people.

It was close to eleven o'clock and closer to one hundred degrees. Jada swooped up her damp hair, wrapped it in a ball, and tucked the ends for security. She looked directly into Melanie's piercing eyes. "So what's the real reason you're here?"

Melanie proceeded to say grace and picked up her fork. "That depends."

Jada almost choked. *"On?"*

"Are you insecure?" Melanie stayed unruffled. "Don't answer that. I'm just kidding. Loosen up. With a man as fine as Wellington, I *do* understand. Mrs. Jones is my godmother. We hadn't seen one another in several years. She invited. I accepted."

Melanie must have graduated head of her class in charm school. After three bites of her omelet, her cherry-red lipstick hadn't smudged. For Jada, Friday could not come soon enough. Insecure? No. Concerned? Definitely.

Jada's mama taught her how to love and treat a man but she never taught her how to *find* a good man. Jada searched all her life for a man like Wellington. He was hers—*only time would tell*—forever.

"So, when's the wedding?" Melanie dabbed the corner of her mouth with the white cloth napkin.

"Valentine's Day next year. Since it falls on a Saturday, and Wellington is my soulmate, timing couldn't be better."

"One day I want to get married and have two children, maybe three, but living in D.C. makes it a challenge."

"Why?"

"Because most D.C. men want to unwrap the package, use it, and then return it—not for a refund—for an exchange. They move from woman to woman, like it's open season year-round. You open. They season. You can get Classic seasoning, Charley seasoning, and if you really want some old spice, you can get yourself some Channel seasoning."

Jada laughed so hard it hurt. Her hands held her stomach. A cute laugh bellowed from Melanie as she stared directly into Jada's mouth.

"Anyway, girl," Melanie continued. "You've got a good man, and when you guys get married, I want to be in your wedding."

"Really, girl!" Maybe Wellington was right. If she got to know Melanie, maybe she would like her.

"Yes! Really. My mother's friend plans weddings for the rich and famous from D.C. to L.A. So I'll be happy to assist you any way I can."

"Thanks." Jada paused. Looked into Melanie's eyes. "Why do you keep staring at my mouth?"

"Because the way you speak reminds me of this woman I went to college with. We were partying late one night in my apartment, when—" Melanie swiftly responded.

Jada thought she would sunburn before the story ended. "I'd love to stay and chat but I've got errands." She carried her plate inside. Melanie followed. Jada turned and noticed Melanie staring at her ass.

Melanie shifted her eyes. "I'm going to get dressed and go over to my godmommy's house. I promised to water the plants and feed the tropical fish. Maybe we can get together before I leave. I want to shop and party 'til I drop."

"Sure, let's do that, girl. Before you *leave.*"

Jada strolled out the front door. Melanie walked into the kitchen and restored it to its original state of cleanliness. Thoughts of Wellington crept through her mind. Melanie went upstairs to Wellington's bedroom, but she was not prepared for what she saw. Wellington was sound asleep on his back naked. His erection was fully extended.

Melanie boldly walked into Wellington's bedroom and stood over him. She zoomed in closer. Wellington snored. Melanie took his penis into her hand and began to fantasize. Damn, he looked so good she could devour him in one gulp. Melanie wanted to experience Wellington for herself. Melanie concluded she would give Jada all the help she wanted but none of what she needed. Wellington was the man for her. Melanie decided there was no need to make a return visit to San Francisco. She simply wouldn't leave.

Jada Diamond Tanner came across classy and confident. Whenever she became insecure, she masked. Growing up with dark skin hadn't been easy. It wasn't until tenth grade that she became popular. The birthday makeover that Henry Morgan and Ruby Denise Tanner surprised her with increased her self-esteem. Prom queen, college queen, she was exquisite. She could have any man she wanted but she was in search of her soulmate. Jada believed her search had ended the night she met Wellington Jones . . .

Life for Wellington Jones had been predominantly mapped from day one. The private schools he attended. The long-term buddies he had. The career he chose. He believed he was in control but nothing happened in Wellington's life unless his mother, Cynthia, deemed it.

Cynthia Elaine Jones controlled everything and everyone around her. She knew one day she'd have to account for her wrongdoings. Until then, the show must go on. Her dance with the devil would last longer than she'd anticipated. The only person she truly adored was Melanie. Melanie was the one child she'd wanted but couldn't bear.

For Melanie Marie Thompson, life was never a dull moment. Money. Sex. Men. Sex. Women. Sex. There was nothing in her life she wanted to do and didn't. Life was great but she knew her biological clock was ticking. She wanted a family. She wanted Wellington Jones.

From *Never Again Once More*

What did love have to do with anything?

If Jada Diamond Tanner had the answer, she'd be richer. After parting from her soul mate, no relationship was quite the same, including her ten years of marriage to Lawrence Anderson. While her body moved forward pushing her life ahead, Jada's spirit remained with Wellington. Like a child insistent upon staying with his father after a divorce, her spirit said, "Naw, you go ahead. I'll wait right here for you." Although Jada loved Wellington, his infidelity rendered love insufficient to preserve their engagement.

Whosoever said, "If you love something, set it free. If it returns . . ." must have not known Wellington Jones. Not as Jada did. He tasted like a sweet caramel candy square slowly melting in her mouth, trickling down her throat into the depth of her intestines, flowing through her bloodstream into her receptor cells. He was her life-support system. Undeniably, his rib had become a permanent part of her anatomy. Each of her taste buds savored the richness of all his bodily fluids. Whenever their lips merged and their tongues danced to rapid heartbeats, Altoids' wintergreen freshness iced her insides like frozen sickles embracing a snow-covered roof. With magical touches, Wellington's mere presence sent chills up Jada's spine.

If you love something, set it free. Set it free echoed repeatedly. Day after day the words rebounded like a basketball bouncing off the edge of the rim. Less than an inch away from scoring, Jada had desperately wanted to reunite with her soul mate, but couldn't find the emotional fortitude. Year upon year *set it free* resounded.

The best sex they had shared came after their first relationship-threatening argument. The warmth of his nine-inch rod penetrating her moist womanhood was all of a sudden a memory. But near the end, Jada had to credit Wellington for trying to keep her when he asked, "Where do we go from here?"

She had already given their unresolved issues countless considera-tion. The most logical solution remained the same, so Jada stood firm on her final decision and replied, "I'm still in love with you, Welling-ton. You will always have a place in my heart. I don't know where we go from here. But I do know I've renewed my lease on life. I have a business to start and a plane to catch to Los Angeles. Maybe I'll call you. Maybe I won't." Watching Wellington walk out of her Oakland Hills penthouse for the last time was by far the hardest thing she'd ever done.

Jada was adamant, but when she boarded that plane the next day, she could have worn a white straight jacket instead of a black leather blazer. The more she told herself, "Don't call him. Be strong," the weaker she'd become. Both of her Myers-Briggs personality tests—taken five years apart—resulted in an ISTP (Introverted, Sensing, Thinking, Perceiving) rating. Jada was a terrific analyst and business-woman, and great at following up on unresolved issues. Diva should have been highlighted as one of her qualitative traits. Even the "Brain Works" test rated Jada perfectly balanced. Maybe she was too bal-anced. Her left brain discounted the right, and her right conflicted with the left, which explained why she had such difficulty deciding whether or not to stay with Wellington. Professional decisions were much easier than personal choices.

Trying to bamboozle her way out of depression, Jada initiated con-versation with the elderly man seated next to her in first class. The moment the aircraft landed and the captain turned off the fasten seat belt sign, she powered up her cellular phone. The left brain keyed in zero zero one to call Wellington so the right brain could tell him she'd be on the next plane back to Oakland to be with him forever, but she was obsessively thinking and couldn't convince herself to press the talk button. Jada's heart grew so heavy at times she could hardly breathe. Short, quick, and frequent intakes of oxygen accompanied mucus buildup in her nostrils that intensified tears, migraines, and nausea.

Had she ended their relationship to avoid looking foolish? Jada's best friend Candice had warned her Wellington couldn't be trusted. Jada masked a happy face because Candice was meeting her at the gate at LAX, and Candice harbored no sympathy for her breakup with Wellington. Would Candice have accepted the same advice about Terrell? No man had ever slam-dunked Jada, and she wasn't about to let Wellington set a precedent.

Before Jada could yell, "Time out!" the referee—Wellington's evil mother Cynthia Elaine Jones—called a foul on her when it should have been a charge because Melanie Marie Thompson knocked her down, ran her over, and literally scored with her man. And Broom Hilda had twitched her nose to cover up a lie because she wasn't Wellington's biological mother; the lying bitch was his aunt. Allen Iverson stripped his opponents over a hundred times in the playoffs, but this wasn't the frickin' NBA. Stealing was a crime. So why did Jada feel as if she was the one serving the life sentence?

By moving from Oakland to the Los Angeles area—over five hundred miles away from the scene of the crime—hopefully her emotional wounds would mend. As she faced every challenge, Jada had grown secure knowing Wellington was only a phone call away. The distance that existed between them: one hour by plane, five and a half by car, one heartbeat by spirit. Close enough but yet far enough, too.

Jada ignored the voice inside her head that whispered, "Go back. Take that chance on love because life is one huge risk, and each day you screw up, if the Lord allows you to see another, you have at least one more opportunity to get it right. Your entire existence is an audition, and you are forever rehearsing until you take your final bow." A melody interjected, "Don't wanna be a fool never again." Luther Vandross's lyric was emotionally correct. No way was Jada going to bend her backbone and flop into Wellington's arms like a desperate woman afraid she'd never find another man to worship her inner beauty as though she were a true Nubian queen and make love to her sweeter than all the chocolate in Willy Wonka's factory.

Like liquid cement solidifying, Wellington's renewed loyalty gradually reinforced their foundation. Over time they became very best friends. Secrets that should have been shared only with God, Jada also confided in Wellington—except one thing.

From *He's Just a Friend*

"How could you be so stupid?!" Fancy yelled in the mirror at her reflection. *Swish. Swish. Swish!* Her fists chased the July summer night's breeze blowing through the patio screen into her lonely bedroom. How could she have not known that Byron Van Lee was a married man? A man she'd done everything with. A man she was willing to do anything for. What was she going to do? Fancy swiftly turned, landing three blows against her shadow. Mimicking Laila Ali she struck faster. Harder. *Swish! Swish! Swish!* Long strands of black hair whipped around her neck and clung to her sweaty face.

Fancy massaged her heaving breastbone in attempt to give her aching heart relief. Maybe if that were the first time a man had lied to her about his marital status, she'd forgive him. Not this time. Not this one. This kind of shit was supposed to happen to other women.

"Why me? Why? Why? Why? Why? Why me?" Fancy questioned herself repeatedly. Why was it so difficult for her to find an honest man? Byron would definitely regret playing with her emotions.

Perspiration beads gathered on her feverish forehead. The salty streams burned her cheeks. White lines remained where tears once flowed. The angrier she became the more she perspired. The more she cried. New salty lines replaced old ones as Fancy recalled the lies Byron had told on their very first date.

Byron had unmistakably said, *"Actually, I'm happily single. Thirty going on thirty-one. Never married. Would love to have two kids, a boy and a girl, but I hardly have time for myself."*

That night over dinner his roaming brown eyes traveled from her face down to her cleavage and back to her glowing smile. Then he had proclaimed, *"And so far I love what I see, Ms. Taylor."* Following his statement, Byron gradually fed her a large chocolate-dipped strawberry. Setting the green stem aside, Byron eased his manicured nail between her lips.

Fancy shivered at the memory. She felt foolish as she visualized sucking the juices off Byron's finger, pretending it was his dick. "Fuck you, Byron! I hate you! I hate your lying ass!" Fancy hugged herself so tight the only thing missing was a straightjacket.

Maybe if Byron hadn't lavished her with everything she wanted. Maybe if he hadn't spoken all the right words. Maybe if he hadn't spanked her with his colossal dick. Maybe. Just maybe she could think straight and delete his phone numbers from her cell phone book like the rest of her rejects. Tears flowed. The red squiggly veins in her eyes doubled. Tripled. Quadrupled. She hated the thought of letting Byron go, but did she hate Byron enough to let him go?

Rocking back and forth on the gold padded stool, Fancy snatched the red washcloth from her vanity and vigorously dried her tears. Sniffles accompanied short quick breaths that escaped her runny nose. Byron had recently dropped her off after another one of their sizzling dates in the city. Again, he'd taken care of her, showing her off to his rich male friends. And in return—just moments ago—Fancy leaned in Byron's lap while he drove across the San Rafael Bridge, en route to her apartment in Oakland. She sucked his head, because that was all she desired to fit into her mouth. Fancy stroked Byron's shaft long and hard until his cum became hers. With each suck, she'd hoped Byron would change his mind and spend the night at her place, but the screeching sound of his tires as he pulled out of the circular driveway still echoed in her ears.

Removing her tan designer minidress, she tossed it across the foot of her bed. Fancy enjoyed prancing around her apartment in the nude and as soon as she made it home, her clothes made it to the bed. This time all except her neutral-colored thigh-high stockings, a thong, and a garter belt. She forced her fingernails inside the runs she'd created shuffling back and forth on the white carpet and ripped a larger hole.

"Why couldn't he just tell me the truth?"

Even if Byron had told Fancy he had a wife, she still would've fucked him. But she wouldn't have fallen madly in love with him.

Snatching the cordless phone from the charger, Fancy punched in the home number she'd memorized earlier from Byron's cellular ID. After he'd hung up from that call, suddenly their night, which was just getting started, was over. "We've gotta go," was all he said, because Byron never offered an explanation or an excuse. He wasn't slick. He was the one who was stupid! Not her. If he lived alone, who'd call him from home?

Shaking Byron from her thoughts, Fancy dialed the number. A woman's voice muttered, "Hel-lo," as though she'd been awakened.

Faster than a Polaroid snapshot sliding out of a camera, a million thoughts flashed in Fancy's mind. The sun rays peeping through her vertical blinds were fading. Fading right along with her undeveloped hopes and dreams for a future she'd fantasized about for well over six months, with Byron. Friday night happy hour at the Pacific Heights members only club that Byron had taken her to wasn't over until eight and according to her clock it wasn't quite seven. Maybe his conniving ass had returned without her so he could fuck the black Amazon goddess with the London accent all the other men were idiotically hounding and drooling over. Beads of sweat resumed, this time taking turns popping out on her forehead. Fancy watched as a thin liquid necklace formed in the crevices above her collarbone.

"Hello?" the woman's voice repeated.

Sitting quietly at her vanity, Fancy pressed the mute button, then rocked back and forth, staring at her reflection in the oval-shaped mirror. "Why do you keep choosing the wrong man?" She rocked faster. Not adoring herself at the moment, Fancy rolled her eyes so hard her green contacts shifted, revealing her natural brown eyes. Green. Gray. Hazel. Violet. Fancy owned a pair of lenses in every color except blue. She flipped the swivel mirror horizontally so she could no longer see how pitiful she looked.

This was insane. What was she going to do if the woman was his wife? Stalk her? Harass her? Make her divorce Byron? Shoot her? Maybe Fancy could beat the woman with the belt she used to spank Byron with during role-play.

"Hello? Is anybody there?" the woman asked with a tone indicating if someone didn't speak up this time, she would hang up.

Suddenly Fancy stopped rocking, pressed the mute button again, and delightfully said, "Hi! Is this the lady of the house?"

Fancy wondered many things about the woman on the other end of the line. Was she the same woman who was with Byron the night they'd met? Was she Byron's wife? If so, how long had they been married? Did the woman have a nine-to-five job? Maybe they weren't married. Maybe they were separated. And in the process of getting a divorce. That's probably why Byron hadn't mention he had a wife.

"Yes, this is Mrs. Lee." Mrs. Lee's voice was choppy and faint, like she should have cleared her throat but she didn't.

Fancy spoke happily. "I'm calling from the *Chronicle Tribune*. We have an introductory special that your family is guaranteed to enjoy. We're combining the best articles and advertisements, and we have a fabulous sports edition I'm sure the man of the house would love! Instead of ordering two papers or missing out on both, your family can be among the first Bay Area residents to get all the news in one paper! Delivered to your front door! For an unbelievable price of twenty-nine ninety-nine for an entire year."

"Really?" Mrs. Lee spoke slightly louder. "I'm sure my husband would love that. But then again . . ." she hesitated. "We—"

"Your husband is a sports fan, isn't he?" Fancy asked, already knowing Byron sat on the Board of Directors for the Oakland Coliseum. Byron had suite tickets for the Warriors, Raiders, and the A's games. He also had season tickets for the Sacramento Kings. He'd taken Fancy to enough games for her to know if she ever met Chris Webber face-to-face again she'd become Mrs. Webber. What sense did it make for her to be loyal to Byron's lying ass?

"He's the biggest sports fan. Okay, why not. It's only thirty dollars." Mrs. Lee had finally spoken in a normal tone. "We'll sign up."

Nervous, still wondering if Byron would arrive home soon, Fancy said, "Wonderful! All I need is your name, delivery address, phone number, and credit card number with the expiration date. And you'll start receiving the paper in three to five days."

"Can you hold for a moment?" Mrs. Lee asked. "I was trying not to wake the baby but he's crying."

Fancy pressed her ear to the phone and listened carefully.

"Waa. Waa." She heard crying in the background.

Oh, hell no! Fancy jumped up from her vanity stool and began pacing the floor. What baby? How old was this wailing kid that sounded like a lamb? Byron was a father, too! Maybe Mrs. Lee was baby-sitting. Or the bitch had Byron's baby, trying to trap him so he wouldn't divorce her ass.

"Hello. Are you there?" Mrs. Lee questioned.

"Of course I'll hold." Fancy smiled to brighten up her voice, then said, "After all, we are a family oriented newspaper group." Fancy hit the mute button and screamed, "Hurry the fuck up!" then pressed the same button again.

When she reached the patio door, Fancy turned around. This time she was too angry to cry. When she reached the bedroom door she turned back around. Too pissed off to sweat. She turned back around again. Too upset to stop moving. She turned again.

"Thanks for waiting. Here's our information."

Racing to the stool, Fancy grabbed her pen. Her naked shoulder pressed the phone to her ear while she listened carefully. She drew a bold letter X across the front of one of her business cards, then wrote Mrs. Lee's information on the back.

Byron could be replaced, perhaps by her boss, Harry, but definitely not by her friend Desmond. Finding a man of Byron's caliber, great looks, and dick stature would be virtually impossible. Byron's six-foot four-inch, two-hundred-thirty-pound frame appeared to have zero-percent body fat. His dark brown skin was smooth. Each time Byron came to her apartment he drove a Benz, a BMW, a Cadillac, or he was escorted by a driver. Whenever he opened his wallet, all Fancy saw were Benjamins and platinum credit cards.

Begrudging Mrs. Lee, Fancy said, "Thanks for your subscription." Fancy gazed at the address so long that her vision blurred. Byron's address in Oakland Hills—the house he'd given her keys to, the house where they had spent many nights and almost every weekend together, the house she'd partially decorated—was different from the one she'd written down. Mrs. Lee lived in one of the most prestigious areas in Northern California. Cupertino.

"Excuse me, but isn't a supervisor supposed to call me back to—"

Fancy's inner voice yelled inside her head, *Fuck you!* right before she hung up the phone. If Fancy had had an ounce of religion, between Byron and Mrs. Lee, she would have truly lost it instead of losing her mind. Fancy ruled out killing Mrs. Lee because of the baby. *The Nanny Diaries* would read completely different if Fancy Taylor had to care for another woman's kid. Fancy loved Byron too much to just let him go. But another woman was living under her future roof, married to her future husband. One way or another that bitch had to go!

From *Somebody's Gotta Be On Top*

Monogamy wasn't natural. Monogamy was a learned behavior that Darius couldn't be taught. When would women realize, sex wasn't a bed partner of love? Besides, who could teach Darius how to be faithful? Jesse Jackson? Bill Cosby? Willie Brown? Bill Clinton? His dad, the ménage à trois king? All the men he respected, all the men he knew, were men. Fornicators. Adulterers. Players. The distinction of a real man was that a real man kept his family in the foreground and his females in the background. Like backup singers. Once the song was over, their job was done. Thanks for having made him cum. Now go. With Darius, not many of his lovers deserved an encore.

"Ha!" Darius laughed, then said aloud to himself, "You a fool boy." His office was quiet all morning. No constant phone calls or welcomed interruptions by his sexy secretary, Angel.

Any woman who wanted Darius Jones had to commit to him and only him. His woman had to have a job. Not any job. A high-paying job. Preferably her own business. So what if he had enough money to take care of her. Her mama. And her grandmamma. A woman without a steady income was venomous. A woman with too much idle time was lethal. No piece of ass was worth his millions of dollars. He was the only heir to his mother's empire and one day would split his father's fortune with one of his stepbrothers who was barely four years old.

Darius flipped through the Los Angeles *Times*, pulled out the sports section, then slid the rest of the newspaper to the edge of his desk. He'd read the business section next. Darius bit his bottom lip in disgust. On the front page, another brother handcuffed, this time a football player, charged with allegedly raping a groupie. "Stupid-ass athletes. That fool was so busy trying to get laid he couldn't see that trick was tryna get paid. Now his ignant ass might end up broke and in jail. Trick was probably smiling the whole time she was fucking dude." Darius learned observing his mother how a woman could be a man's best advocate and his worst enemy at the same time.

Scanning the other twelve pages, Darius thought, *that would've never happened to me if I had gone to the NBA.* Those broke leeches in thongs, jiggling their asses on beaches or benches, at the bus stop, were the ones who were constantly plotting and planning—pregnancy, rape, battery—on how to become rich off of a man. For sex. For real. Any wealthy man would suffice. Mike. Kobe. Deon. Including him. Bullshit conniving tricks. They weren't privy to suck his dick.

Fed up with the media favoring the woman's side, Darius traded the sports section for business. While he'd slept, the value of his stocks increased. Money made Darius think about how rich pussy like the Vivica As, and Mary Js, Halles, and Janets of the world needed stroking too. But they also had reputations worth protecting. To them, lawsuits translated into bad publicity. Lost revenue. They'd end the relationship before bringing forth charges. That's the type of women Darius wanted. And if Darius ever caught one of his women cheating, she didn't need to waste his time explaining because he'd personally dismiss her. Immediately!

Thinking about women brought his number-one lady to mind. Darius smiled, picked up the phone, and pressed sixty-nine on his speed dial. His lungs expanded. The warm air escaped his nostrils, grazing his smooth upper lip. Darius removed the elastic band holding his ponytail. Three-hundred sixty-two black pencil-width dreadlocks fell slightly below his shoulders. Darius mastered and measured everything about his body. Dick: nine and three-quarters of an inch long, and four inches thick. Body fat: six point seven percent. Pimples: none. Birthmarks: two. One faded abstract image on the right side of his ass. The other was a black spot on the back of his left earlobe beneath his princess-cut two-carat diamond earring.

"Hey, you," she happily answered.

Her voice penetrated his soul. Chill bumps invaded his skin. The hairs on his arms stood tall. Darius wasn't cold. He swallowed the lump of air clogging his vocal cords then said, "You packed yet? I can't wait to see you tonight. Make sure you arrive two hours early at the airport." Darius deepened his voice then emphasized, "You'd better not miss your flight this time."

Unbuttoning his collar, Darius rolled his burgundy leather highback chair until his abdomen pressed against the edge of his glass-top desk, creating a crease in his brown Versace jacket. Slowly he placed his finger over the photographic image of her naturally pink-colored lips. Thin and seemingly oh-so-very soft. She looked righteous—not as in holy, as in fine as hell—in the family picture they'd taken a month ago at Thanksgiving dinner with his parents.

"Are you still in the office?" she asked.

Darius's hand traveled from her temple and traced the outline along her straight black hair, which cast a strikingly beautiful contrast against her nearly white complexion. His eyes fixated on hers. She was always nice and polite with a caring-Cancer demeanor other women despised. She was perfect marriage material. She was the ideal woman to rear his kids.

Loving someone more than himself, more than life, more than making money, was absurd and not what Darius had planned. But this special woman—naw, she was more than a woman, she was a lady— had stolen his heart. First she'd become his platonic childhood playmate. Now she was his best friend. With the exception of his boy Keenan whom everyone called K'Nine, she was Darius's only other friend.

The honeysuckle scent of her hair, the subtle movement of her hips when she walked, the provocative melody of her voice each time she innocently laughed while calling his name, the gentleness of her touch whenever she groomed his dreadlocks, the taste of her words lingering on his palate as he gasped into the receiver consumed his thoughts. Nervous energy rumbled in the pit of his stomach. Consciously he erased his boyish grin. She evoked feelings Darius swore he'd never possess for another woman after having been betrayed by his ex-fiancée.

"Of course I'm still in the office, woman. And my staff too. Just because it's the week between Christmas and New Year's doesn't mean the entire week is a holiday. They're not entitled to leave early but I might let 'em go at three. Maybe. Now answer my question." Darius began rearranging the few items on his desk.

"Don't worry. I packed last night. And my dad is dropping me off in a few. I'll call you when my plane gets into LAX." She paused, then whispered, "I miss you, brother."

Why did she keep calling him brother? He was more like a play-brother. Everybody in California claimed relatives that weren't blood related. Play cousins. Sisters. Aunts. Uncles. Mothers and fathers too. His birth parents weren't hers so technically they weren't related. And since Darius's mom was remarried to Wellington Jones, the man his mother should've married instead of marrying Lawrence, Darius felt Ashlee and he were two consenting adults capable of making their own decisions.

Darius remained silent. He rearranged his gold-and-crystal triangular clock to the left side of his nameplate then moved his in-and-out baskets to the opposite end. The shuffled newspaper, cordless phone, notepad, and gold-framed photo were neatly positioned on his spotless desk.

Although Darius spoke with Ashlee every day, three-to-five times each day, he'd practically forgotten about the incident with her dad. Darius hadn't seen Ashlee's father since the day, almost two years ago, when he'd beaten her father for abusing his mother. In retrospect Darius understood Lawrence's frustrations with his mom. After Lawrence's black eye and bruises healed, Darius's mother gave him the shock of his life. Since that day, Darius's feelings for his mother numbed his compassion toward women even more. If his mother were a liar, then every other woman was too. Except his lady on the opposite end of the phone. But the feasibility existed so he couldn't completely trust her either. *What a fucked-up world to live in,* Darius thought, when the only person he could trust one-hundred percent of the time was himself.

Forgetting about her dad and his mom, Darius massaged his erection through his pleated slacks, hoping she'd continue talking but hopefully not about her dad. Anticipating the sound of her voice made his dick harder. She had him so turned on he wanted to make love. To her. For years. *Say something. Anything. Please.* His dick urged repeating her tone in his mind. *I miss you.* He'd missed her too.

She finally broke the silence. "Did you hear me?" Lightly she articulated, "I said, I miss you."

Ashlee's delayed response made Darius believe she was also thinking about him. The cordless phone slipped from between his ear and shoulder so Darius quickly activated the speaker. "Of course I heard you. I just wanted you to repeat it. That's all." He placed his fingers against his thick chocolate lips then laid the same two fingers atop the glass frame over her mouth.

She inhaled then softly said, "I miss you. I miss you. I miss you. I miss you. I miss you. How's that? Turn on your cam so I can see you."

No way, Darius thought, staring at the flat-screen monitor on the glass-top L-unit connected to his desk. Kimberly's nude layout changed from covering her tits with sand on Venice beach to clenching a lollipop between her vaginal lips with a caption that read, "Sweeter than candy." Darius unzipped his pants and squeezed his head, suppressing the pre-cum trying to escape his hard-on. He imagined what Ashlee looked like in the nude. Although they'd visited one another for more than ten years, he still had no idea if her nipples were lighter or darker than her breasts. If her pubic hairs were curly or straight. If her clitoris was small or large. Would Darius care for Ashlee the same if they lived together? Would he love her if he married her?

"Hey, lady. I've gotta run. I'll see you later." Darius stood. He secured his relaxed muscle into his black silk boxers, then watched the tiny metal clamps overlap until the last one reached the top.

His lungs suctioned in the much-needed oxygen for his brain when she exhaled an intoxicating, "Bye."

Darius waited until Ashlee hung up, then removed his coat and tossed it onto his chair. He entered the private rest room connected to his office and vigorously rinsed his face with cold water. While staring at his reflection in the mirror, Darius wondered why his mother had lied to him about his biological father. Why she'd waited twenty years to reveal the truth. Why didn't his biological father, Darryl Williams, Sr. display the same love for him as he did for Darius's two half-brothers, Kevin and Darryl, Jr.? The relationship Darius's father had with Darius's half-sister didn't count because daughters were naturally closer to their fathers than sons.

Darryl was a former NBA all-star whom Darius idolized most of his childhood, including the four years Darius started on the varsity basketball team in high school. Darryl was his college basketball coach at Georgetown, which explained why Darius's mother never came to any of his college games. His mother apparently had had an epiphany when her mother died and decided it was time for a damn confession. A truth that mentally scared Darius. Possibly for life.

"Fuck Darryl Williams!" Darius's fists swung fast. Hard. Hitting nothing but air. "Darius Jones don't need anybody but Darius Jones." Darius's anger resurfaced each time he relived the day his mother told him the truth. Tears swelled his eyes. Darius squinted and sighed. His beloved grandmother, Ma Dear, the only woman that never lied to him would've said, "Don't waste time disliking people who don't like you when you can appreciate the many people who do love you." Regaining his composure, Darius knew Ma Dear was right but after his grandmother died, disappointment and resentment befriended him.

Although sometimes Darius drowned in waterless tears, real men, when their hearts ached with sadness and their souls suffocated from failure, didn't show signs of weakness. Darius remembered because Ma Dear's husband Grandpa Robert, whom she'd joined in heaven, told Darius when Darius was four years old, "Boy, looks like you been crying. Crying is for girls and sissies. Remember that." Darius never forgot. Tears. Confessions. There was no way Darius would ever let down Grandpa Robert by displaying a wimpish attitude. Sensitivity belonged to losers like Rodney, the undercover bisexual brother who infected Darius's ex-fiancée with HIV. Darius thought again, *what a fucked-up world to live in.*

Buying his three-story office building and loaning him a million dollars was just another one of his mother's ways to compensate for her guilt. And Darius had every intention of making his mother suffer for the next twenty years or at least until he felt she'd repaid her debt. Everyone was indebted to something or someone. But if his mother hadn't married Lawrence, Darius wouldn't have met his number-one lady. So perhaps he should've been grateful, but gratitude required expressing feelings.

Shifting his thoughts back to his lady, Darius smiled in the mirror, running his fingers over his locks. He gathered each strand back into a ponytail then admired the sweet brown succulent flesh that hundreds of women had enjoyed feasting upon. Ashlee's flight would arrive at ten o'clock tonight. What would she wear to his parents' New Year's Eve ball? Hell, it didn't matter. Possessing the same qualities as his mother, his stepsister always looked great. Just like his ex-fiancée, Maxine. Ladylike. Feminine.

Darius returned to his desk wondering why was his childhood so gullibly innocent and his adult life so cynical? As a child, if Darius had done wrong, he was easily forgiven. Women adored him. Fantasies of having his own family. A loving wife who'd only love him and he'd exclusively love her. At one time Darius believed that was possible. Until those two fifth-graders told him he could have both of them or his boring girlfriend. She wasn't boring. She was quiet. There was a difference. But two were definitely better than one. Darius had once believed marriage was sacred. Until he witnessed his mother divorcing Lawrence for no apparent reason other than she wanted to marry Wellington.

Why did grown-ups simply lie about shit? Santa. Where babies came from. The Easter bunny. Who was this dude Cupid? Someone who was supposed to make Darius believe he was in love? Most people weren't. Most people were lonely or afraid of being alone so, good or bad, they clung to the familiar. Not Darius.